LESSER EVIL

LESSER
BOOK 1

PENELOPE SKY

HARTWICK PUBLISHING

Hartwick Publishing

Lesser Evil

CONTENTS

ONE
CAMILLE

It was the perfect night.

Million-euro Bugattis, bright-yellow Ferraris, and a few Lamborghinis pulled up to the Parisian estate. Rich people in tuxedos and gowns stepped out, and they let the valets take their cars away. The three-story palace was lit with a golden glow, the fountain in the center splashing with a gentle backdrop of water.

When my driver pulled up to the front, I felt my heart tighten like a fist.

Would the black wig disguise me?

The bright-red lipstick?

The green contacts?

Would he see right through the charade?

The door opened, and Raymond helped me out of the car.

I recognized him.

But he didn't seem to recognize me.

Hidden in the crowd of aristocrats, I emerged into the downstairs parlor, immediately swallowed by waiters with trays of bubbly champagne and triangles of bruschetta. I had business to take care of, but that didn't stop me from grabbing a flute and a slice of bread. I enjoyed both, my eyes scanning for the man of the hour.

It didn't take me long to find him.

As if he had the focus of a spotlight, he was surrounded in that golden glow, a shine to his eyes. A woman was at his side, a petite brunette who had her arm tucked in his, looking up at him like every word he said was utterly fascinating.

His dark hair was slicked back, and his dark eyes looked like fresh espresso first thing in the morning. Instead of holding a flute of champagne, he held a glass of scotch. It was a power move—like everything else he did.

Rich. Powerful. Handsome.

Every man wanted to be him. Every woman wanted him to be her husband.

But he wasn't quite what he seemed.

I knew the mansion like the back of my hand, so I snuck away from the crowd, keeping my eyes on the butlers to make sure they were distracted, and then made my way upstairs. My heels tapped against the hardwood, but the sound of violins seemed to muffle it. The brightness of the chandeliers disappeared as I arrived on the second floor. The music and conversation were lower, like someone turned the dial on a stereo.

The second floor seemed vacant.

I left my empty flute on the nearest surface then continued up to the third floor.

The anxiety worsened, because now that I was so close to my goal, I was more terrified of losing it. I put my life on the line for this, but it was worth it. I crept to the third floor, careful to remain quiet even though no one was around. My breaths grew louder and labored because my lungs weren't getting the air they needed. I turned down a couple hallways until I found the spot.

I tried the door.

Locked.

I'd anticipated this scenario, so I pulled out the pins hidden in my hair and tried to open the lock. I picked at it exactly as Bones had told me, hitting the mechanism just right to get the lock disabled. I'd practiced on several doors, but in the heat of the moment, it was hard not to tremble and fumble.

Click.

Thank gawd.

I pushed the door open and found his most prized possessions behind glass, as if it was a jewelry store.

There it sat, right in the center, the pearls iridescent and flawless.

I crept forward and tried to find a door to slide open, a lid to lift, but there was nothing. Then I saw the gentle flash of red light, the alarm that protected all the irreplaceable gems inside.

Motherfucker.

I'd have to break the glass with my elbow, grab the necklace, and hightail it out of there as quickly as possible. The servants had an elevator so they could bring their food cart to the different floors and serve His Grace… or whatever the fuck they called him. I would use that to make my escape, take the elevator to the basement. It was the fastest way to get down there, so they wouldn't be able to follow me immediately.

"Jet-black isn't your color, darling." The deep voice was playful on the surface, making the threat underneath indistinguishable. But it was there, masked by his charm, subtle as it left his handsome mouth.

I released the breath I'd just taken.

"But that dress…was made for you." His eyes drifted down my body as he spoke. It was obvious in his tone that his gaze ravished my body, that his hands would grab my hips once they came near enough.

I'd come all the way here for this necklace—and I wasn't leaving without it.

I slammed my elbow against the glass. It shattered into pieces, cutting my arm in the process and setting off the alarm.

I snatched the pearl necklace and ran for it.

He blocked my path, a slight smile on his lips, threat in his eyes. "You think I didn't recognize you? You think an ugly wig and cheap lipstick are enough to hide all the details my hands could recognize in the dark?"

I faked to my right then ran to my left, my heels wobbling around my ankles.

He grabbed me by the elbow, but his hand slipped on the blood.

I tripped and fell to my knees, the necklace still in my hand.

His heavy body dropped on top of mine, forcing me onto my back, his fingers squeezing my throat so tight I could barely breathe. His handsome face hovered over mine, an indulgent sneer spreading over it. "I knew you'd come back."

I kicked out my knee but missed my target.

He squeezed me harder. "What is it about that stupid necklace?"

The rage burned me alive, gave me a surge of strength I wouldn't have had otherwise. I jerked my head up and smacked him as hard as I could.

It hurt like hell, but it was enough to give me time to crawl away.

He grabbed me by the ankle and dragged me back.

We locked into a battle, his hands trying to pin mine down, my legs flailing and kicking whatever I could reach. I bit into flesh, scratched his skin, did whatever was necessary to break free. I got a fist to the face for it, a scar to my neck from the tightness of his choke hold. He wouldn't kill me—but everything else was on the table.

"Darling." He pinned me hard to the floor.

"Don't fucking call me that!" I threw both arms down on his head and found my opening.

I ran for it, but then I halted after only making it a few feet.

The necklace. I'd dropped it.

From his knees on the floor, blood smeared across his teeth, he held up the pearl necklace. "You aren't going anywhere." He slowly rose to his feet, ready to pursue me once again.

I had to make a choice. Leave it behind—or become a prisoner once again.

I ran for it, his footsteps loud behind me. I knocked down everything in my path to create obstacles, kicking off my heels because they were only slowing me down, and took the stairs instead of the elevator.

I heard a loud thud behind me, as if he'd slipped on one of my heels.

Good. That'd buy me some time.

I made it to the main floor, and everyone turned to see me sprint down the stairs and push through the crowd.

Surely, he wouldn't let himself be seen chasing me right in the middle of a dinner party, would he?

When I got to the front door, I turned around and realized how wrong I was.

He had just made it to the bottom of the stairs, his maniacal eyes locked on me with blood lust.

Shit, shit, shit.

I bolted outside and saw a Ferrari parked in the roundabout. The owners had just exited the car and tossed the keys to the valet.

I ran like the wind, snatched the keys out of the valet's hand, and apologized the whole way. "I swear, I'm not stealing your car!" I jumped in the door, slammed it shut, and hit the lock button.

Through the passenger window, I could see him sprinting down the steps, yelling at his men to stop me.

"Bitch, you can't stop me now!" I slammed my bare foot to the pedal and gave a lurch when it accelerated faster than I'd anticipated. I nearly crashed the car before I regained control. "Damn, this thing is fast." I turned the wheel and sped down the drive, and once I made it to the open road, I really pushed it.

I looked in the rearview mirror and didn't see a line of cars behind me, but I wasn't foolish. I knew that wasn't the end. It would never be the end—not until he was dead.

I should be grateful I made it out of there with nothing but a black eye, but it was hard not to be disappointed about leaving empty-handed.

Leaving the necklace behind.

TWO
CAMILLE

I continued to wear my sunglasses inside the café, doing my best to hide the bruise that had only gotten worse with time. Now my eye was so dark it looked like I'd had too much fun with a new shade of eye shadow.

He paid for his coffee and took a seat, elbows on the table, so bored he looked tired, despite the fact that it was the middle of the afternoon. A black wedding ring was tattooed on his left hand, and his muscular arms stretched the sleeves of his t-shirt.

I sat across from him, not bothering with the coffee.

He took a drink, his eyes looking over the rim as he stared at me. "Janice, I'm a busy man—"

"Camille."

"Whatever," he snapped. "I told you I'm out of the game."

"Everyone has a price, right?" I asked hopefully.

He continued to stare at me with that bored look.

"I have a couple million—"

"I told you I'm out of the game. I've never made an exception, and I'm not going to start now."

"Come on. There's got to be something you want."

He took another drink before he set down the paper cup. "No. I've got a wife who's a fine piece of ass and two beautiful children. No amount of money would ever tempt me to put them in jeopardy, even if I wanted to kill the person you're asking me to kill."

"Fine piece of ass? That's how you talk about your wife?"

He gave me a cold stare. "Damn right." For a man who had fallen into a life of retirement, he still had a body primed for battle. No dad bod for this guy. "She likes it. Trust me."

I was a bit jealous because I would never have a husband at all, let alone one who wore his heart on his sleeve like this guy. "Bones—"

"It's Griffin now."

"You've got to help me out."

"*I* don't have to do anything. You aren't my problem."

I grabbed the sunglasses and pulled them off my face, showing my hideous bruise.

Griffin didn't blink an eye.

"I'm in deep shit and was told you could be helpful."

All he did was stare.

"I hope to be a man's fine piece of ass someday, but that's not going to happen if I'm dead in three weeks." My arms folded on the table, and the blender at the counter went off as it mixed a drink. "There's gotta be something you can do."

The only soft feature he possessed other than his wedding ring was his eyes, startling blue. Far too pretty for a man so rough around the edges. "Who's the guy?"

"Grave Toussaint. He's in Paris—"

"I know who he is. Even if I were still in the game and in my prime, that contract would cost a fortune. More money than you've ever seen in your life, I assure you."

I released a sigh, my disappointment heavy. "Then maybe I can get some free advice?"

"Move every year. Start in St. Petersburg. It'll take him a long time to trace you there. Then a small village in the Hungarian countryside. Marrakech—"

"I'm not doing that." I shook my head. "I'm not going to spend my life looking over my shoulder every fifteen seconds."

Griffin grabbed his coffee and took another drink, slouched down in his chair, his expression still a bit bored. "Then his enemies are now your allies. I would start there."

"And do you know who those people are?"

He considered the question for a long time, his arms folded over his chest, his tattooed wedding ring clearly visible under the fluorescent lights. "Only one name comes to mind. Cauldron Beaufort."

"So you think he'd help me kill him?"

"I don't know. Never met the guy. But word on the street is Cauldron is the only man Grave has ever feared."

I couldn't picture Grave fearing anyone. "Why?"

Griffin gave a shrug.

"Do you have his number?"

"You think your proposal should happen over the phone?" he asked incredulously. "And I just told you, I've never met the guy."

"Well, I need to find him."

"He lives in Saint-Jean-Cap-Ferrat. That's all I know."

"That's the French Riviera, right?"

"You must have gotten an A in geography."

"You talk to your wife this way?" I snapped.

He grinned. "She'd slap me if I did."

"I have a feeling she and I would get along pretty well. Unless she walked in here right now and saw us together…"

"Why would that matter?"

"Because you're having coffee with a woman she doesn't know."

"My wife knows her ass is the only one I'm interested in."

THREE
CAULDRON

The girls sunbathed on the loungers toward the front of the yacht as I sat in the shade, a drink in my hand, an untouched charcuterie board on the center table with cured prosciutto, Tuscan olives, chocolate-covered almonds, and fine French cheeses from Beaulieu-sur-Mer. My linen shirt was open down the front, the sea breeze running over my bare chest, licking away the sunscreen I'd applied for the fifth time that day. The ocean was a fair blue, Cap-Ferrat still in sight in the far distance. Other yachts were visible, keeping their distance, their helicopters parked on every top deck for a quick getaway.

One of the staff approached. "Hugo says they're ready for you, sir."

I gave a slight nod in acknowledgment and downed the last of my drink. Wiping my mouth with the back of my forearm, I headed inside the parlor then into the private study where I conducted my business.

I sat on a white couch that faced the enormous screen, another charcuterie board waiting for me, this time with smoked salmon and crystallized oranges. My drink was already on a coaster alongside it.

The screen changed, showing my appearance on the couch, my shirt still unbuttoned, my skin kissed by the warmth of the French sun. Then Hugo appeared, in his study at my estate in Cap-Ferrat. "Jeremiah is ready for you. Shall I patch him through?"

"Yes."

"When the meeting has concluded, there's something I wish to discuss with you, sir. If that's alright."

"Yes."

Hugo connected the meeting, and that was when I saw Jeremiah, my lead analyst in Botswana. "Mr. Beaufort, how are you?"

I hated small talk, so I didn't answer. "Give me an update."

"Of course, sir." Jeremiah seemed unaffected by my callousness. He was used to it by now. "The new mines have been fruitful, yielding some of the largest stones we've secured. Transport will begin soon."

"Good."

"But we do have an issue."

"Always do." I drank from the glass sitting in front of me.

"The competition has found our location. They've begun their dig from the opposite end of the mountain. It is my belief that they're trying to reach our mine as covertly as possible."

"Dunglar?"

"Not sure, but most likely."

"You'd think he'd learned his lesson."

"In my experience, you cut off the head of the snake, it grows two more."

I gave a slight smirk. "Well said, Jeremiah." We finished our meeting, and then I was returned to the screen where Hugo waited for me.

"Hope all is well."

"It wouldn't be well if I didn't have to kill someone." I took a bite of the smoked salmon with the brie then grabbed a few berries. "What did you want to discuss?"

"I hate to trouble you while you're on vacation—"

"I'm always on vacation, Hugo."

"On the contrary, you're the hardest working person I know, sir."

I ignored what he said. "What is it, Hugo?"

"A woman has visited the residence more than once looking for you."

That wasn't that unusual. "Name?"

"Camille."

"I don't know a woman by that name."

"I assumed so. I've tried to dissuade her, but she says it's urgent that she speak with you."

"About what?" I asked, growing impatient. "She's just desperate for my attention, like all the others."

"I thought so too, until she mentioned Grave."

I was about to reach for my drink, but the name shattered my thoughts. My arms returned to my knees, and

I stared at Hugo, eyes narrowed, my temper primed. "What about him?"

"She wouldn't say more. The only reason she confessed that much is because she was being escorted from the property."

"She made it on to the property?"

"She's determined, sir."

I stared at the screen, feeling my annoyance in my clenched jaw.

"How would you like me to handle this?"

I rubbed my palms together, frustrated that the past was knocking on my front door. "If you see her again, threaten to kill her. If that doesn't dissuade her, then shoot her in the fucking head."

FOUR
CAMILLE

The property was surrounded by French limestone, and the golden gates were far too high and precarious for me to climb. The grooves in the stone were deep enough for my fingers, so I climbed to the top and dropped to the other side of the property. Lush landscape gave it complete privacy. A fountain was in the center of the roundabout, large lily pads and fallen flowers floating on the surface.

I'd never seen Cauldron in the flesh, and as far as I could tell, he never came and went from his property.

It made me wonder if his butler was telling the truth— that he really wasn't home.

I walked to the front doors, rang the doorbell several times to announce my presence, and waited for the butler to answer.

He opened the door, his expression far more irritated than it'd ever been before. "Mademoiselle——"

"Just let me talk to him. I'll take a phone call at this point, alright?"

With one hand on the door, he stared me down. "Your entitlement is very obnoxious, to say the least. Mr. Beaufort's time is extremely valuable, and it's not for you to claim just because you say so. Consider this your final warning. Trespass on Mr. Beaufort's property again, and you'll be shot."

"*Shot?*" I asked incredulously. "Come on, you're really going to shoot me even though I clearly pose no threat to you?"

"Your disturbance is enough reason," he said. "And it wouldn't be the first time."

Wow, okay. "Your threat would be a lot more terrifying if I weren't running from threats far worse than yours. Could you tell him that I wish to speak to him about Grave? Just pass on the message."

"I have," he said in a bored voice. "I wish I could convey how little he cares, but that's just not possible."

The disappointment hit me like another punch to the face. "If I could just talk to him—"

"Everyone wishes they could talk to him. But peasants don't make the rules, royalty does."

"Wow, I'm a peasant now?"

"Lower than that." He started to shut the door.

I shoved my foot inside. "I'm not going to stop until he speaks to me. My life depends on it."

He tried to shut the door. Shut it hard. Even slammed it.

I didn't move my foot out of principle, even when my eyes watered.

"Mademoiselle, if you don't leave this property, I will call the police."

"Good. I'll tell them you threatened to shoot me when they arrive."

"They would be unsurprised." This time, he lifted my foot by the pantleg and dropped it on the other side of the door. "I sincerely hope we never see each other again. Not just for your sake, but for my own sanity."

I sat in a café near the coast, watching all the yachts and sailboats in the beautiful blue sea. When I looked up Cauldron online, I saw lots of pictures of him, and most of them were of him standing on a yacht, shirtless, with tanned girls in bikinis around him. As if the guy didn't already have everything, he was sexy as sin. Tall, dark, and handsome. His unbuttoned shirt revealed a hard body defined by a religious dedication to his workouts.

I literally rolled my eyes as I swiped through his pictures, seeing a man on top of the world.

I knew I was just jealous…but still.

The odds of him helping me just got slimmer.

As I looked through the pictures, I realized he was always on the same yacht, meaning he didn't rent it.

He owned it.

"I bet that's where he is…" I paid for my coffee and headed straight for the docks.

Day after day, I waited for his yacht to dock with all the other yachts.

They were basically luxury hotels that floated on water. Some of them had helicopters parked on top. Actual helicopters. It was common to see a car full of pretty girls pull up to the yacht first and break out the champagne, the billionaire showing up a couple hours later, ready to party on the open ocean.

It was a life I would never know.

Finally, I recognized his yacht. It approached the dock, pure white and beautiful, looking like a cruise ship more than a personal boat. It was midday when it arrived, and it took a bit of time for the captain to position the boat so the men below could secure it in place.

They dropped the ramp from the yacht to the dock, so the girls could walk off, pulling their luggage behind them, their wraps covering bikinis underneath. In their sun hats and sunglasses, they looked as if they weren't quite ready for the vacation to end.

Couldn't blame them.

I took the opportunity to walk up the ramp and step foot on the yacht. There were several sitting areas, the furniture pristine white like no one had spilled a drink during the voyage or no one had ever sat there. The thing had to be three full floors, at least.

Cauldron finally emerged, only the top button of his shirt undone, his sunglasses hanging in the opening. He was in dark trousers and boots, like the vacation had ended the second the yacht pulled into the harbor. He didn't notice me right away, probably dismissing me as a member of the staff because I wasn't wearing a thong bikini and top that barely contained my boobage.

"Cauldron."

He turned at the sound of his name, and once his eyes were on me, everything changed.

I couldn't feel the sea air against my skin, couldn't feel the heat pressed up against me, didn't notice the gentle waves smacking against the hull over the edge. His stare was so powerful that it stole my entire focus.

He halted as those dark eyes stared into mine, brimming with both intelligence and annoyance. It took less than a few seconds for him to figure out exactly who I was, to deduce that I was the same woman who wouldn't stop trespassing on his property. He drew closer, taking his time, utterly calm despite the provocation.

"I'm sorry to show up like this—"

His movements were so fast that I couldn't anticipate them. His hand grabbed me by the throat and squeezed me so hard I choked. Cold metal from a barrel suddenly pressed through my hair and into my scalp, digging into the flesh. Then I heard the cock of the gun. "Was my butler unclear?"

I gripped his wrist and struggled to breathe, my feet almost off the floor because he'd lifted me with that powerful arm.

"You think I won't shoot you because you're a woman?" His nose was close to mine, his handsome face stern with ferocity. "I will blow your fucking brains out and toss your body overboard, you understand me?" He squeezed harder, officially choking me. "My staff will spray the bits of your brain off my deck, and your former idiocy will be chum in the water." He finally released my throat so I could take a breath, but the barrel was moved to my cheek, digging deep into the flesh. "Understand?"

I heaved for air, my lungs screaming from the lack of oxygen.

"Answer me." He kept his hold on my neck but allowed me to breathe.

It was a stupid thing to say, but I said it anyway. "You aren't going to shoot me in public."

"You don't think so?" Out of nowhere, he backhanded me. Hit me so hard I stumbled backward across the deck.

I got to my feet quickly, ignoring the sting in my cheek. When I rounded on him, I was the one who was furious. "Asshole, I just want to talk to you—"

He aimed the gun right between my eyes. "This is your final warning. Show your face again, I'll pull the trigger." His security team stepped onto the deck, carrying machine guns and rifles. "Put this woman on a train to Paris. I want her out of my town for good."

"*Your* town?" I asked incredulously. "Bitch, you don't own Cap-Ferrat."

The look he gave me said otherwise. "*Bitch*, I own everything."

Paris was the last place I wanted to be, but his security detail literally forced me onto the train and blocked the doors until the train pulled out. I ended up back in the place I'd just fled, and I had to keep a low profile until I returned to Cap-Ferrat.

You didn't think I'd given up, did you?

I had an ass that didn't quit.

A week later, I made it back to the coastal village, but I didn't bother jumping over the wall of his residence again.

I knew how that would end.

I had a much better idea.

A private security detail watched over the yachts parked at the dock, but they didn't have enough manpower to keep watch of everything at once, so when they weren't looking, I climbed on to his yacht with a small suitcase and slipped inside.

He was either arrogant or careless because most of the doors were left unlocked. It was easy to find the keys to the palace, and soon, I had access to the entire yacht. There was food in the chef's kitchen, fresh linens on all the beds, more booze than I could ever drink by myself.

Basically, fucking paradise.

Now all I had to do was wait for him to come back.

Grave would never find me there, so I was happy to wait a lifetime for that asshole to return for his next vacation.

I was asleep on the bottom level when I heard voices.

"Mr. Beaufort will be here this afternoon," someone said from above. "Prepare the ship for departure."

My vacation was over.

I wasn't sure if I was sleeping in a bed that would be occupied, so I remade it as well as I could before I changed into a bikini that made my tits look like deviled eggs on a serving platter. I grabbed a sun hat as well, looking the part. Then I hid away in one of the closets and waited.

When high-pitched voices and laughter came from the top of the ship, I knew the girls had arrived. Fuck buddies for Cauldron. I remained in my hiding place. Several hours later, the engine roared, and the ship finally pulled away from the dock. I came out of my hiding place, strutting around the ship in heels and my bikini, and not a single member of the staff gave me a second look.

Too easy.

When I made it to the top deck, I looked over the edge, seeing Cap-Ferrat in the distance, the turquoise water as beautiful as it was in pictures. Other yachts were in sight, other billionaires enjoying their summer vacations. My time with Grave had taught me that most rich men were evil, and you had to be evil to be that rich.

I looked to the seating area, seeing Cauldron shirtless in his shorts, his back to me. One arm was sprawled out over the cushions, while the other held a phone to his ear. He spoke quickly to someone, but I couldn't make out the exact details of what he said.

I walked right behind him and entered the hallway where the rooms were tucked away.

There was an expansive room with a desk and a seating area, as well as a formal living room with a large screen in front, probably where he held his virtual meetings. It was exactly what I was looking for, so I took a seat, crossed my legs, and waited.

The door opened, and one of his staff walked inside. His eyes immediately widened at the sight of me. "No one is allowed in Mr. Beaufort's office."

"Then why are you here?" I asked, still seated on the couch.

"I—I have to set up his meeting."

"Tell him Ambrosia wants him to fuck her across his desk first."

Stunned by what I said, he stood there for another moment before he departed.

It only took a moment for Cauldron to take the bait. He locked the door behind him then strode into the office shirtless and barefoot. His hard body was covered with tanned skin, a beautiful color that complemented that dark hair and those even darker eyes. He might be one of the richest men, but he was also the most foolish, because he didn't recognize me whatsoever. He clearly didn't know the name Ambrosia either, but he probably didn't know any of the girls' names, so he didn't bat an eye over it. I was just another woman in heels and a bikini, there to service him on the seas.

He sat beside me, his arm moving over the back of the couch, while his other hand reached for the string of my bottoms at my hip. It all happened so fast, without a kiss or a touch, straight down to business.

"Whoa, buddy." I pushed his thick arm away before he could pull my panties free.

This man had never been told no, clearly, because his expression turned volcanic.

"I want to talk—and that's what we're going to do."

His coffee-colored eyes shifted back and forth between mine, his mind processing all the details that his hard dick had previously ignored. When the hardness of his jaw set in and the spite in his eyes settled, I knew he realized exactly who I was.

He left the couch and headed straight for his desk. His hand reached in and withdrew a pistol that was tucked underneath. He cocked it and aimed it right at my face, slowly drawing near, keeping the barrel trained between my eyes. "You seem to have a death wish."

"And you seem to have a poor memory."

He dropped the aim to my heart and pulled the trigger.

Nothing happened. The chamber was empty.

"Wow. You really are an asshole."

He opened the chamber and saw with his own eyes that it really was empty. Furious, he walked back to his desk to retrieve the bullets from his top drawer.

"Don't bother. Got those too."

He slammed the drawer shut. "Then I'll just kill you with my bare hands." The moment he looked up, he steadied—because a shotgun was aimed right at his chest.

I smiled, holding the butt of the gun against my shoulder as my mother had taught me. Her father had been a hunter, so I grew up around all kinds of guns. Which was definitely coming in handy right now.

The anger on his face was still present, but his eyes were eerily calm. He hadn't thought twice about trying to shoot me, so he'd gambled away any mercy he would have received otherwise. He didn't raise his hands in surrender, just stood there as the long barrel pressed against his bare flesh. His breaths weren't even deep. I'd be able to feel them if they were.

"Sit."

The intensity of his eyes deepened, his stare locked on my face.

"Don't test me. I don't have a lot of patience for a man who wouldn't hesitate to murder me." I shoved the barrel into his chest to get him moving.

He took his time walking to the couch, his muscled back rippling with strength. He must have a gym somewhere on board and didn't let his little friends distract him from hitting the weights.

He relaxed against the back of the couch, hands resting comfortably on his thighs, his eyes defiant.

I took the seat beside him, the gun still trained on his chest.

A long stretch of silence ensued, his eyes glued to mine, watching me with a mix of pure loathing and displeasure, along with a splash of respect. A shotgun was aimed right at his chest, but he breathed normally, not the least bit unnerved by the situation.

"I've been living on your yacht for the past week. Found all the guns and tossed the ammo overboard. Except this one, of course."

He continued to stare, hardly blinking. "You wanted my attention, and now you have it. Let's get this over with." He sat forward slightly, his arms moving to his knees.

I tightened my grip on the gun, unsure if it was a ploy to steal the weapon.

He smirked, aware that he'd spooked me. "I could take that gun at any time."

"Then why don't you?"

The stare lasted an eternity, sandpaper against my skin, intrusive as it penetrated well past the surface. "Because you're the first to best me—so you've earned a few moments of my time."

My grip didn't loosen on the gun, but the stitch in my chest released.

"Tell me what you want. My patience is limited."

I finally had the undivided attention of the only man who could save my ass. I didn't say anything for a moment, treasuring the victory after so many weeks of climbing over walls and dealing with a bitchy butler on a power trip.

"I was told that we have a common enemy. Thought we could work together to take him down."

His eyebrows furrowed at first, his handsome face even more focused than before. Then the smirk came, subtle and hardly noticeable. "You think breaking in to my yacht and finding my guns makes you an assassin?"

"You even admitted I bested you."

"Because you're half naked," he said coldly. "Bravo."

I glared at him. "I could blow out your brains right now, so I deserve more credit than that—"

He snatched the gun out of my hand so fast I couldn't keep a hold of it. Then he disassembled it in less than five seconds, taking it apart piece by piece, breaking it down until it was in three separate parts on the coffee table. His arms returned to his knees, and he stared at me, his eyes ice-cold. "Whoever your enemy is, I'm not interested. Are we done?"

"Bones told me you're the only person he's afraid of."

"That applies to a lot of people." He reached forward and grabbed the decanter sitting on the coffee table. Judging by the amber color, it must be scotch. He filled a short glass then threw his head back as he downed it in a single swallow. But he wasn't done because he refilled the glass.

"Is that apple juice?"

He smirked then poured another glass—one for me. "See for yourself."

I left the glass untouched. "It's Grave Toussaint."

He stared at the glass in his hand and didn't take a drink. His reaction was subtle, a quick tightening of his jawline, a whiteness to his knuckles. But then it was gone in a flash, as if it was never there in the first place.

"You've got to help me—"

"I don't have to do anything." He turned back to me, his eyes angry. "Let's not forget the circumstances here. You're a peasant asking a king for his army when you have literally nothing to offer in return."

"I have money."

He suppressed a laugh by taking a drink.

"A million euros—"

"You know how much I pay my staff on a daily basis to run this ship? Thirty thousand euros. Your money is worthless to me." He brought the glass to his lips and took a drink. "I'm officially bored with this conversation. I'll tell the captain to return to the dock so you can get the fuck off my property."

"Wait—"

"I don't care about your miserable life." Now he raised his voice. "How can I make that clearer?"

I'd worked so hard to gain an audience with this man. I couldn't let it all be a waste. "Whether you help me or not, I've got to kill this guy. So, is there any advice you could give me?"

He looked away and rubbed the back of his neck, clearly annoyed. "You want my advice? Run."

"I'm not going to live my life like that—"

"Then die." He held my gaze as he said it, just to prove how indifferent he truly was. "Because you aren't going to kill Grave, and you sure as hell aren't going to recruit me to kill him either."

"How can you be enemies if you don't want to kill each other?"

His answer was a stare. "Stop questioning me as if you have the right to my answers."

"Look, if you don't want to kill him…could I at least stay with you?"

Now his eyebrows furrowed deeper than ever before.

"I can be part of the staff. One of the maids. I could help in the kitchen. You don't have to pay me—just let me stay on your property. I know he won't touch me here."

His stare continued, like he didn't know what to make of the offer. "I have plenty of maids. I have several chefs. I have valets, gardeners, personal assistants. My staff is fully booked."

I'd feared that was what he would say.

"Why do you run from him?"

It was too personal to share with a stranger, but he was the one who held the cards. "It's a long story... He basically became obsessed with me, and that obsession turned manic. I couldn't live that way anymore, so I ran for it. He has something really important to me because he knew I'd come back for it. I tried to steal it back, but I barely escaped with my freedom. I know he'll never stop hunting me."

His stare was exactly as it was before, stiffly locked into place. "He loves you."

His version of love, at least. "Yes."

"Do you love him?"

"Would I be running from him if I did?"

"Did you ever love him?"

"No." My answer was immediate, without hesitation, because I could never love a man like that.

"How long did this relationship last?"

"Three years."

"And in all that time, you never loved him?" he asked, slightly incredulous.

I looked away, embarrassed. "It was a job…"

The silence was deafening.

It seemed to go on forever.

I didn't look at him, not wanting his judgment, his ridicule, his harshness.

But it never came.

When the curiosity became too much, I looked at him again.

His eyes were on me, free of callousness. The intensity remained, studying me like I was the prized horse projected to win at the races. Like I was a business he was about to acquire. A piece of art he was about to add to his collection. "You're hired."

"You just said you didn't have any room on your staff."

"That's not where you'll be working."

A flash of heat erupted through my body, stinging my nerves.

"You'll work for me—personally. Understand?"

How could I not understand when he looked at me like that.

"Answer me."

"Yes…I understand."

FIVE

CAMILLE

The ship returned to the harbor, the girls left in the private car that picked them up, and then it was just the two of us in the back seat of the SUV. Two guys were in the front; one was the driver, and the other seemed to be a bodyguard.

Cauldron was on his phone the entire time, reading emails and typing back with quick fingers. His responses were always direct orders. There was never an introduction of any kind, a polite greeting at the beginning of his emails. Just as he was in real life, it was straight to business.

We drove down the scenic roads and farther up the hill, the blue water growing more distant as we headed to his private residence. The village with the shops and restaurants was closer to the water, and that was probably why he chose to live farther away, where he could have the pristine view and the privacy.

When I'd propositioned Cauldron, I'd never expected it to take the turn that it did. I thought we'd come up with a plan, that I would get Grave to meet me somewhere, and then Cauldron would pull in and blow him to hell.

But instead, I was back to where I started.

The gates opened, and we pulled into the roundabout. The front of his property was cloaked in shade from all the trees. I noticed white lights were wrapped around the trunks and branches, like he lit it up for the parties he threw.

It was a three-story house, a large awning in the front with statues, windows with white shutters. It was a mansion far too big for a single man, and most of the other rooms were probably occupied by the staff that lived and worked there.

The top floor probably belonged to him exclusively. That's undoubtedly where I would end up.

The men unloaded the car and grabbed all the luggage.

The butler opened the enormous double doors to greet his master, aware of his imminent arrival as soon as one of the guys in the car radioed in Cauldron's approach. With his hands behind his back and a welcoming smile on his face, he looked thrilled to see his master return home.

That smile disappeared when he saw me.

I smiled back, giving him a playful wave to top it off.

Cauldron walked inside, gave a slight nod in acknowledgment to his butler, then continued on his way like he didn't notice his horror-struck face.

I almost laughed.

"Uh, sir." He abandoned his post and went after his master. "I apologize, but I'm just a bit confused—"

"She'll occupy a bedroom on my floor. She can choose whichever one she likes." Cauldron kept walking, typing on his phone. "What's your name?" He turned back around and looked at me, only realizing then he had no idea who I was.

"Camille."

Cauldron continued forward.

The men carried the luggage to the stairs and began the long journey to the top of the house.

The butler kept at it. "Mr. Beaufort, this is the very woman who trespassed on your property several times, the very one you had me threaten to shoot if she ever returned to the premises, and now——"

"And now she'll live at the residence, Hugo. She's a guest in this house—treat her as such." Cauldron disappeared around the corner, his voice carrying back to us because he took a phone call.

Hugo stood there for a while, completely beside himself.

"I can be very persuasive, you know."

He slowly turned back around and looked at me, his eyes like knives aimed at my throat. "I will do as Mr. Beaufort asks, but make no mistake, as long as you're under this roof, I will watch your every move."

"If that's how you want to spend your time…" I headed upstairs to the top floor, walking along the hardwood floor, admiring the crown molding on the ceilings, the golden sconces that matched the floral wallpaper. Fresh flowers were on display on various surfaces, making the house smell like an outdoor garden rather than an enclosed space. We passed several doors, leading to bedchambers with rosy-pink duvets, crystal chandeliers, threadbare hearthrugs in front of wood-burning fireplaces.

We passed closed double doors, and I assumed they led to Cauldron's bedchambers. There was another closed door, and I assumed that was his office. When we reached the end of the hallway, I decided to take the corner bedroom.

My luggage from the yacht was carried inside, a bedroom that had its own bathroom and sitting room that faced a large fireplace with a flat-screen hanging above. It had its own patio too, overlooking the back-yard that I hadn't seen before.

The men left my suitcase on one of the couches and departed.

Now I was alone, in a place I would call home.

I opened the door and stepped onto the patio, seeing the breathtaking view. He had an infinity pool at the edge of his property, which was what appeared to be the cliffside. The vista of Cap-Ferrat was unbelievable, the ocean as well as the village which held the bakeries and cafés. The estate was large enough to hold a wedding, with grounds that stretched far on either side of the home.

It was much different from Paris.

I grabbed a seat and finally took a breath, feeling untouchable for the first time since I'd fled. I didn't know why Grave feared Cauldron, not when he'd never shown any sign of fear of anyone else since I'd known him, but the fact that he did was reason enough for me to stay, to call this place home.

At least until I found a way to kill him.

SIX

CAULDRON

The fireplace had been empty since spring arrived. There'd been a day or two of rain, but nothing cool enough to warrant a blaze in the hearth. Now I sat at my desk in the study on the bottom floor, in a black linen shirt and jeans, my eyes directed out the window for most of the afternoon.

Hugo gave a quiet knock before he entered my study. In his hands was a tray that contained my lunch. A salad with organic chicken, avocado, and grapefruit, along with tarragon dressing. There was an iced tea as well. He put it on the edge of my desk, and set the silverware wrapped in linen beside me. "Is this to your liking, sir?"

"Yes."

He continued to stand there as if he hadn't heard me.

I looked at him directly. "What is it, Hugo?"

"I don't understand why you've allowed Camille to become the lady of the house."

"She's not the lady of the house, Hugo."

"Then what is she—"

"My whore." I stared him down, telling him not to tread any further.

Hugo stilled, jolted by my tone. "Your companions have never stayed at the house before—"

"First time for everything."

He folded his hands behind his back and refused to depart. "I don't like her, sir."

"You don't like me either. That's never interfered with your work."

"That's untrue, Mr. Beaufort. I have immense respect for you."

Now I'd grown tired of the conversation. "This is my home, Hugo. I can open it to whomever I wish. Is that clear?"

He hesitated. "Yes. I just don't understand why——"

"It's not your place to know why. Understand?"

He hesitated again. "Yes."

"You're dismissed."

Hugo headed back to the door, but he stopped to address me once more. "Laurent informed me he's stopping by."

I had a few missed calls from him.

"Shall I tell him you're busy?"

"No. I'll see him."

"I thought you were on vacation." Laurent lounged in the armchair in front of my desk, switching between his cigar and his glass of scotch.

"Cut it short."

"Trouble in the mines?"

"There's always trouble. But no, that wasn't why."

"Need a new set of girls?" He drew on the tip of the cigar and let the smoke waft to the ceiling. "We could swap."

"I can get my own women, thank you."

"You mean you can pay for your own women." He gave me a wink before he puffed on the cigar again. He tilted his head back and let the smoke release as a cloud. Hugo disapproved of cigars. He never said it, but he couldn't disguise the disgusted look on his face.

"How's business?"

"Fucking fantastic—like always."

"Then what brings you to Cap-Ferrat?"

"Can't I stop by to see my dear cousin?" He smirked at me before he took another puff of the cigar. "How about you ditch the laptop, and we take the yacht out? We can find some girls along the way. You know, the old-fashioned way."

"What's wrong with your yacht?"

"It's in Positano. That's what's wrong with it."

"I've got too much on my plate, Laurent. Maybe another time."

He let the cigar sit between his fingers, a steady trail of smoke slowly rising to the ceiling. He cocked his head slightly, studying me the way Hugo did at times. "You're so full of shit. What's really going on?"

I ignored the question and continued my email.

"You've never been a homebody."

"Like I said, I have shit to do."

Hugo came in through the double doors, an envelope in his hand. He set it at the corner of my desk. "You asked me to bring this to you as soon as it came in." He excused himself again, seeing that we didn't need additional food and drink.

I ripped open the envelope, glanced through all the results, and then tossed it in the wastebin.

Laurent leaned to the side to get a look. "Ah, now I understand."

"Mind your business, asshole."

"Who's the girl?"

I didn't answer.

"Ooh, she must be special."

I still didn't answer.

"How much did she cost?"

"She didn't cost anything—at least not in terms of money."

He cocked an eyebrow.

"Revenge—that's her currency."

SEVEN
CAMILLE

For the first week, I felt like the only person there.

I spent a lot of time in my bedroom, but when I got bored with that, I took a walk across the grounds, lounged by the pool and took a swim, lived like the house was mine. Hugo didn't hide his dislike for me, but he still waited on me as Cauldron had asked.

I hardly saw the man of the house.

He was either in his bedroom or one of his studies. Or he wasn't at the estate at all; I couldn't be sure.

Dinner was usually brought to my door on a tray, but that evening, I received an invitation instead.

"Mr. Beaufort would like you to join him for dinner." Hugo could barely contain his disdain as he relayed the message to me. "Follow me, and I'll escort you to the dining room." He headed down the hallway before I said a word, expecting me to follow him obediently.

I was in high-waisted jeans and a collared white shirt that tied in the middle, probably too casual for a formal dinner, but there wasn't time to change, so I just went with it. I followed Hugo downstairs, through the parlor, and then into a large dining room that could easily accommodate thirty people.

Cauldron wasn't there, but his place setting was at the head of the table.

Hugo pulled out the chair for me then pushed it in.

"Uh, where is he?"

"Mr. Beaufort doesn't wait." He departed the room, leaving me alone with the glowing white candles, the basket of freshly baked bread on the surface, and the bottle of wine. I helped myself, the bread still warm to the touch, and poured myself a glass of the Bordeaux. I wasn't a wine connoisseur, but I could tell it was an expensive bottle the second the aromatic flavor touched my tongue.

Footsteps sounded behind me.

Then there was a quiet scream.

I almost slopped my wine all over my white shirt. "What?"

Cauldron sat at the head of the table as if there was no interruption, but Hugo came around the table and faced me, thoroughly appalled. "Mr. Beaufort is the master of this house, and he samples the wine first, you mannerless swine."

"Jesus...didn't realize it was still 1742." I took another drink, just to be spiteful.

Hugo looked as if he might faint. "And you touched the bread... How dare you?"

"Oh, I dare." I grabbed another piece and tore off a chunk with my teeth.

Hugo clutched his chest and gave a loud gasp.

I rolled my eyes and kept chewing.

Cauldron held up his hand to stop Hugo before the next tirade began. "Hugo, bring out the first course."

"But, sir—"

"It's fine."

Hugo's face got red and scrunched up as if he'd imploded inside but had to keep all the pieces contained. He expressed his frustration by smoothing out his collared shirt with rigid fingers. With his head held high, his anger suppressed, he walked out.

Cauldron picked up the bottle and served his own wine.

"Is he always like that?"

"Yes." He swirled the wine in his glass before he took a drink.

"Then why do you keep him around?"

He looked down the long table, as if there were other dinner guests who had joined us. "You can pay someone to work, but not someone to care. He cares."

"I think he cares too much." I grabbed another piece of bread from the basket.

His eyes flicked to me.

"Oh, I'm so sorry, Your Grace." I bowed my head as I extended the slice to him.

He didn't crack a smile, but his eyes looked slightly amused.

I ripped it into pieces then dabbed it in my olive oil and balsamic.

With his arms on the wooden armrests of his chair, he sat there, comfortable in the silence, not the least bit interested in speaking with me…even though he'd invited me to join him.

Hugo returned and placed two salads in front of us, leafy greens in a light dressing with radicchio and pistachios and a couple grape tomatoes. Hugo unrolled the linen and dropped it into Cauldron's lap before placing the silverware on the table.

Before he could move to me, I did it myself. "Got it."

Hugo couldn't conceal his rage that time. He glared at me before he returned to the kitchen.

Cauldron grabbed his fork and began to eat.

"So…"

His eyes shifted to me, but he didn't speak.

"When you invited me to dinner, I assumed there would be conversation."

He grabbed his glass and took a drink.

As annoying as Hugo was, the food was delicious, so that made him infinitely more tolerable. I focused on my salad because it seemed like Cauldron had nothing to say. He was like a monk.

He broke his silence. "How long have you been in your line of work?"

I hesitated at the question, disappointed but unsurprised that was what he wanted to discuss. "About five years."

Now, he stared at me hard, his entire face focused on the effort, as if he was imagining me servicing strangers in dark alleyways and empty hotel rooms. "And how did you get into that?"

"The same way as everyone else—I needed money."

Half of his salad was untouched, but now he seemed more interested in me than his dinner.

My eyes shifted back and forth between his. "Judge me all you want. I've heard it all."

"Does it look like I'm judging you?"

"It's hard to tell."

"What do you think those girls on my ship are?"

Supermodels?

"That's the only kind of woman I bed."

"Why?"

A long stare ensued. It was obvious I wouldn't get an answer to my question. "How did Grave become a long-term client?"

"It's a long story…"

He extended his hand, as if to say we had all night.

"Why am I supposed to answer your questions, but you don't answer mine?"

"Because I own you." The words were quick, like a knife through the air. "And don't forget it." He held my stare as he said it, as if he dared me to push back.

Hugo entered the room that instant, so I held my silence…not that I knew what to say anyway. He cleared our salad plates then brought us cups of soup. It was classic French onion with croutons on top.

"I don't stand on street corners or linger in clubs looking for clients. I charge a premium for my services, a premium that most men can't afford. I know what I'm worth, and I won't settle for a coin less."

He didn't reach for his spoon. His eyes were glued to my face like cement.

"Grave didn't blink an eye over my nightly fee. One night turned into two. Days added up to a week. Then he said he wanted a permanent buyout. A monthly salary in addition to the luxurious life he could offer me. It seemed like a good deal at the time, so I took it."

His eyes didn't stray from my face, not even slightly. He didn't blink either. With the utmost focus, he stared, treating my face like a masterpiece of sculpture in the foyer. It reminded me of Grave, the way he made me undress as he watched from his armchair. "What changed?"

"He asked me to marry him."

His stare didn't waver.

"I mean, *told* me to marry him. Didn't really get a say in the matter. He already had a wedding dress for me. Didn't even get to pick it out…"

The soup was getting cold, but neither one of us reached for our spoons.

"That was when I left."

"Why?"

"Because…" My eyes broke contact with his face, letting him win the contest we'd never agreed to have. "It made me realize how much I'd fucked up my life. I sold my body because I didn't have a choice, and I'm not ashamed of that. But then I realized the other sacrifices that I was making…like never falling in love."

His stare was still hot on my face. I could feel it.

"I told him I couldn't marry him. Told him our arrangement was over. He didn't like that." I turned back to face him.

He looked exactly the same.

"So here I am."

Hugo entered the room and gave a quiet gasp. "Is there something wrong with the soup—"

"Leave us." Cauldron raised his voice only slightly. His eyes never left my face.

Hugo immediately departed.

It was back to silence.

"He'll never stop chasing me. Nowhere to hide. Nowhere he won't go to find me."

His stare was absorbent, taking in all my emotions like a sponge. But there was no sympathy on his face, barely calm understanding. He was interested in my tale, but not necessarily moved by it. "There is one place he won't go." He reached for his wine and took a drink. "Where you are now."

The sun had finally set, disappearing behind the trees and then the world. When darkness arrived, new noises entered the soundtrack. Crickets sang their songs in the tall stalks of grass, frogs croaked from a nearby pond. It took a moment for the stars to emerge over the edge of the cliff, but slowly, they began to twinkle.

I sat on the couch in front of the TV, looking out the window instead of at the screen. When I had been with Grave, I'd accompanied him wherever he went, shared his four-poster bed in his master bedroom. The only time we were apart was when he was working in his study. In Cap-Ferrat, I was in constant solitude, surrounded by quiet tranquility, the beauty of the small village.

The knob on my bedroom door turned, and then he appeared, his silhouette a distinct triangle, broad shoulders leading to narrow hips. The shadows hid his features for a moment, but as he walked farther into the room, I could see that he was shirtless, his gray sweatpants low on his hips. He stopped at the edge of the couch, looking down at me, his muscular arms at rest at his sides.

"Could you knock next time?"

"I don't knock in my own home."

I was in nothing but a white, long-sleeved nightshirt, a blanket over my bare thighs. After dinner was over, I'd done my nighttime routine by washing my face clean of all makeup and letting my skin breathe before bed. Definitely wasn't ready for company.

Even in the darkness, I could see the deep tan of his skin, the aftermath of days and weeks on his yacht in the Mediterranean. His chest was free of hair, smooth with the outline of the muscles of his pecs and tight stomach.

The TV flashed the room with changes in color. The sound played in the background, but I didn't even notice it, too aware of him standing just feet away. I grabbed the remote and turned off the TV. "Did you need something or...?"

He stared down at me, as if he'd made his intentions perfectly clear.

Now I knew exactly why he was there.

It was heavy in the air between us, like a fog on a winter morning, causing an ache in the lungs with every breath. Now I was even more aware that I was pants-less, sitting on the couch in nothing but a white thong.

The stare continued, endless, no reprieve in sight.

Then he moved around the couch and took the seat beside me, leaving several inches between us. He leaned back against the couch, knees apart, his face turned toward me. "You know why I'm here." His dark eyes shifted back and forth between mine, his voice powerful regardless of how quietly he spoke. "Show me why you're worth the price you command."

My heart quickened. My palms immediately turned cold and clammy. I was nervous…and I never got nervous.

He continued to stare, as if he'd just moved his pawn across the chessboard and now it was time to make my move.

"I…I'm not ready."

His dark eyebrows furrowed.

"I don't really know you—"

"Do you get to know all your clients before you fuck them?" His voice rose slightly, not just in volume, but intensity. "My protection isn't free, sweetheart." The endearment wasn't remotely affectionate, just deeply sarcastic. "Earn your keep, or I'll throw you out on your ass."

"Look—"

"Don't call my bluff."

I'd already learned not to do that. "I thought we could work together to bring him down—"

"How? You have no skills or resources."

"I wouldn't say that…"

"And did I ever say I wanted to kill him?"

"No. But I assumed—"

"Don't assume anything when you don't know me."

"He's your nemesis. Why wouldn't you want to kill him?"

A heavy stare ensued. "Stop asking questions as if you're entitled to answers."

"I don't want to live here forever—"

"And you won't live here by morning if you keep this up."

I was getting nowhere with him, just pissing him off.

"You're in the red, Camille. Better fix that. Before it's too late."

I remained paralyzed, far more intimidated by him than I ever was by Grave.

"Don't pretend you aren't attracted to me."

My eyes flicked back to his face, a bit irked by his arrogance. "Watching a man shoot me in the face isn't exactly a turn-on."

"Really?" His eyes narrowed slightly. "Because watching you hold a shotgun to my chest was."

I felt the heat flush my face and burn my stomach at the same time. His stare made me feel like I was on display, like I couldn't hide anything. Not my thoughts. Not my emotions. Not anything.

"Right there." His eyes shifted back and forth between mine.

My heart gave another lurch.

"I see it written all over your face."

It didn't matter that he was right. It still pissed me off to hear him tell me how I felt.

"The conditions for your asylum were clear. I'm not a man to be trifled with, so don't let yourself believe there was any chance to manipulate me into having your cake and eating it too. You want my protection? You're going to fuck me for it."

I swallowed since my mouth had gone dry.

"Camille." His voice deepened, issuing an order.

I had to obey—or be thrown out onto the street.

He reached for my blanket and slowly pulled it down, the soft fabric leaving my skin and exposing it to the air. The covering was removed completely, revealing my thighs and everything below. My shirt was a little long, so my panties were hidden from view.

He drew near, his face coming closer to mine, his body soap mixing with the scent of the scotch he'd drunk before he walked into my bedroom. His arm moved over the back of the couch, boxing me in there so there was nowhere to go. But he didn't kiss me. He didn't grab me. Just unnerved me with his proximity.

I'd left my life of servitude, but my reincarnation led me to the exact same position. I was still a servant, but now I had a new master. There would come a time when I would be free, when I could fall in love with someone, have a family. But that wasn't possible until Grave was dead—and my new client was the only one who could kill him.

So I did my job.

My hand reached out for his sweatpants, and I immediately came into contact with unmistakable hardness. It was the source of his arrogance, that cocky smirk he sometimes wore. It stretched across the front of his sweatpants all the way to his thigh, traveling down the pant leg because it had nowhere else to go.

As my fingers dragged over the outline, I got to my feet. The shirt fell a little farther down my thighs. I faced the dark TV as I gripped the silky-soft material in my hands and pulled it over my head. The chilled air immediately hit my skin, making my nipples pebble and my breasts tighten.

I could feel his hot stare on my ass.

I turned around and faced him, running my fingers through my hair until I grabbed the elastic that bound my strands together. I pulled it free, letting the waves fall around my shoulders. I was self-conscious about the way I looked because the makeup was gone and my hair wasn't styled, but he looked at me the same way he had when he'd seen me in a bikini on his yacht—like he wanted to fuck me, regardless.

His arms relaxed over the back of the couch as he studied my body, his eyes taking in the sight of my tits the longest. Unlike other women in my profession, I didn't artificially enhance anything. My tits were small, but they were real. He seemed to like them.

I kept my thong on as I drew closer, standing between his open knees.

He didn't move to touch me, as if he wanted to see what I could do first.

I lowered myself to my knees, hitting the softness of the rug that cushioned my body. My tits were between his knees now, and his eyes were staring down. My hands started at his knees and slowly moved up, inching to the waistband against his rock-hard abs. A subtle line of hair trailed beneath his belly button and disappeared under his waistband. There was a thick vein too, his skin and muscles so tight that it popped like a cord. I grabbed the material and tugged, getting the pants down to the base of his hips.

With his eyes still on my tits, he lifted himself slightly, letting me get the material over his thighs.

That was when his stone-cold demeanor disappeared.

His breaths deepened, just slightly. His face became flushed with arousal. Those angry eyes melted like chocolate chips in freshly baked cookies. There was a subtle clench of his jaw, a quick bite at his lower lip, his excitement growing so quickly that he couldn't contain it.

That did turn me on a bit.

With his dick free, it lay against his stomach, thick, long, with a nice vein that ran all the way up the shaft to his head. He was obviously proud of it, knew he was well-endowed. It gave a twitch as I stared at it, as if beckoning me to get to work.

I leaned in close, let my warm tits smother the base of his dick and his balls. The tip rested against my lips, and I gave it a kiss as my small breasts hugged as much of his shaft as they could. One kiss turned to two. Then three…and four.

His breathing deepened as he watched me. He liked to be teased.

My tongue flattened, and I licked the head like an ice cream cone on a hot day.

His body tightened when he felt my tongue. His balls clenched close to his body. The breath he released was audible. His nerves were on fire, and every little touch excited him more. With my eyes locked on his face, I licked him again and again, getting his dick wet without actually putting him in my mouth.

When he was done with the foreplay, he grabbed me by the neck and grabbed his base. "Take it—all the way." He pointed his dick at my mouth and pushed my head down, letting out a satisfied moan as I slid my tongue over his length. He made me keep going even though I would have stopped, getting my face right against his stomach.

It activated my gag reflex, but he wouldn't let me pull away. Tears sprang into my eyes, and I tried to breathe while I had a huge dick in my mouth. He kept me there for another second before he finally let me go and fully catch my breath.

The tears were so heavy they left my eyes and streaked down my face.

"Now you know what to expect." He guided me back to his dick as if the break he'd allowed me had been generous enough. His cock was back in my mouth, but he let me go, his arm moving back to the couch.

I held his dick by the base and pushed my throat over his length, letting my tongue cushion his entrance over and over. It was hard work, sucking a dick this big, and now that my eyes were watery, they continued to water more. My vision blurred, but I didn't dare wipe my face to ruin the moment.

"Eyes."

I obeyed the command instantly, lifting my eyes to see his face through the tears. My nails dug into his muscular thighs as I pushed him down over and over, holding my breath when he was in deep.

It was like running a marathon—difficult and exhausting. I lost all feeling in my legs as I sat on my folded knees, and saliva dripped out of the corner of my mouth because his girth left my lips gaping open.

He lounged there, arms over the back of the couch, wearing that hard expression as he watched the show.

When my jaw started to ache, I grabbed his base and jerked him with my tight fingers, giving me a second to inhale full breaths. My eyes dropped to his base, seeing the way it thickened in my hand like he enjoyed my touch.

"Eyes."

My eyes flicked back to his, my face a mess with the smeared saliva and tearstained cheeks.

"Don't make me ask again." He was the only man in the world who could lose his temper during a blow job. He grabbed me by the neck again and forced me down, ending my break and getting me back to work. Like last time, he shoved me down all the way.

I expected it this time, so I didn't gag.

"Good." He let me go.

With an aching jaw and a flat tongue, I went back to work, pushing him deep in my throat as I held him by the base. I quickly learned that he preferred my mouth to my hand, that he enjoyed watching me gasp for breath around his ridiculously big dick. He got off on the struggle because it didn't just feel good, but it inflated his already enormous ego.

Minutes later, his breathing changed. His calm breaths shortened and became irregular. His tanned skin darkened slightly, a redness entering the skin at his neck and shoulders. He clenched his jaw before he released a quiet moan, his hips starting to move with me so he could fuck me in the mouth.

I knew he was close. I could feel it in the way his dick hardened.

He took a raspy breath before his fingers wrapped around my neck again, this time to steady me.

I knew he was edging himself because he had other plans.

I kept going, this time taking his length at a faster pace.

He didn't fight me at first, giving a moan as I ate his dick. His breaths were deep and loud, his climax so close. His fingers gripped my throat, and he steadied me.

I pushed his arm off and kept going.

"I know what you're doing."

I took his length as deep as I could, almost hitting my gag reflex every time.

His hand gripped my shoulder, but he didn't stop me. It felt too good. He was too close to the edge. He didn't stop it in time. He sank back into the couch and thrust his hips, his eyes locked on mine, his stare deepening into one of ownership. "You like sucking my dick, don't you?"

I kept going, eyes still on his.

"Answer me."

With a mouth full of dick, I forced out the word best I could. "Yes."

When he heard my answer, he released with a loud groan, pushing my face down to his base.

It was so much, I had to swallow twice, and even then, I could still taste it. My nails scratched the tops of his thighs, but he didn't seem to notice the damage. Eyes focused on me, he held me down until he was fully satisfied.

I finally got his dick out of my mouth, a stretch of saliva still attaching us. I licked the corner of my mouth to break it, but it was so thick it was almost indestructible. I severed it with my finger.

He got to his feet even though I was still on the floor in front of him. His dick was semi-hard, still impressive at half-mast. It was right in my face until he pulled up his sweats and hid it away. "You'll pay for that later."

EIGHT
CAULDRON

I sat in my study downstairs, looking over the reports Jeremiah just sent over. My home was protected by my private security, but I avoided all paper trails. Never printed a single document. Everything was done electronically, my information protected by a private server and a solid firewall.

The door opened, but I didn't look up, assuming it was Hugo bringing me something.

It was Camille.

In jeans that stopped just below her belly button and a white collared shirt tied below her tits, she looked like she was ready to go shopping in the village. Her long blond hair was around her shoulders, looking shiny under the light of the chandelier.

I was angry that she had disobeyed me, but it was hard to hold that grudge when the outcome was just as satisfying, nonetheless. Whores were paid to pretend to enjoy you, even through the most uncomfortable acts. That was what I expected from her—but I got something much better.

Authenticity.

She gagged. She couldn't breathe. Tears burned her eyes then stained her cheeks. Her nails dug into my thighs because it was the only way to vent her discomfort. But she also enjoyed it…just a bit.

I liked that.

It was real.

She took her time making her way into my office, like my stare was the barrel of a loaded rifle. Her arms started at her sides, but she crossed them when she drew near. She glanced at the contents of my desk then at the paintings hanging over the wallpaper.

I locked my device and set it on the desk.

She stood, avoiding eye contact as if it would make her relive last night.

My patience grew thin. "Yes?"

"You could try hi." Now she looked at me, her low-burning embers slowly turning into a fire.

I propped my elbow on the armrest, my closed knuckles underneath my chin.

She helped herself to one of the armchairs facing my desk, sitting at the very edge like she intended to stay only briefly.

Good.

A bit of her stomach was visible, along with the piercing I had noticed last night.

Her hands came together on her knees, but her shoulders were back and her spine was straight. She seemed to be nervous as her baseline, but whenever I provoked her, she could quickly turn into an inferno. "After what happened last night, I think we should set some boundaries."

My eyebrow immediately cocked because she had no right to set boundaries. "What part of I own you don't you understand?"

There it was—the fire. Flames were visible right on the surface of her eyes. "Let's get something straight. You don't *own* me. I could walk out of here anytime I want—"

"As long as you're under my roof, I do. So let's get that straight. You don't set boundaries. I do. You knock on doors—I don't. I tell you what to do—and you listen. So don't walk into my office and talk about boundaries as if you have any say in what kind of boundaries we have."

She looked pissed. If she had that shotgun, she might actually shoot me. "You're an asshole."

"And you're a whore."

Her expression immediately changed. There was a flinch in her eyes, like a bullet had struck her in the chest and made her jerk back. It was clear that I'd said something deeply offensive just by the look on her face. "Don't call me that ever again." Her voice was different, still strong, but with a hint of quiet vulnerability.

For whatever reason, she silenced me.

Nothing was said for a long time. Just a lot of staring.

She clearly expected me to insult her again, judging by the guard in her eyes.

I didn't.

"Look, I've been careful not to catch anything. Never have up to this point." She leaned forward and rapped her knuckles on the wood of my desk. "I don't want to trip at the finish line. So, we need to talk about how we're going to keep me safe. You're sleeping with all these other women—"

"If you're as good as you say you are, then you're the only woman I'll be fucking."

As if that was the last thing she'd expected me to say, she turned quiet.

"Are we done here?"

"Is that normal for you?"

"What?"

"Monogamy."

I had several women on my yacht at once for a reason. "No."

"Then why—"

"Because I'm paying a premium price, and I expect premium services. Fuck me how I want, when I want, how hard I want—and you'll get what you want."

It was a long day.

I worked out first thing in the morning, because if I didn't get it done then, I would be too busy to do it later. Then I worked in my study through the afternoon and evening, let my dinner get cold on the coffee table, to Hugo's horror, and then finally retired for the night after a big glass of scotch.

On the third floor, I walked past the double doors that led to my bedroom, the only room in the house that was off-limits to the staff other than Hugo. When the maids cleaned and changed my sheets, Hugo was there to supervise.

I headed to the corner bedroom, the light noticeable in the crack under the door. Like last time, I went inside without knocking, finding her on the couch as before. But now, she was fully dressed, hair and makeup still done, as if she'd expected me.

She didn't look at me.

I took a seat on the edge of the bed and stared at the back of her head.

She didn't move, the glow from the TV highlighting her silhouette.

I gave her a moment, but that moment was wasted because she never came. "Get your ass over here."

She ignored me.

"I don't wait."

"Well, I don't obey." She turned to me, her eyes iridescent.

I raised my hand and gestured to the door.

She gave a quiet sigh of irritation then walked over. Her eyes dropped, like she hated herself for succumbing to my authority.

It only made me want her more. "I assume you were more submissive with your other clients." I got to my feet, towering over her small frame, ready to do things that would make her cry in both pleasure and pain.

"I was a different person then." She turned away, looking out the window.

"Eyes."

She hesitated, like she wanted to defy that command with every fiber of her being. But she obeyed...eventually. Those bright eyes locked on mine, filled with loathing for both me and herself.

It was such a turn-on. "Face down. Ass up."

She didn't blink at my orders, but her face hardened. "I can't do this…"

"Then pack your shit and go." My sweatpants felt tight, my dick so hard because I knew she wouldn't go anywhere.

"I just need more time—"

"I don't owe you a damn thing," I snapped. "Did the others pay a premium just to be told to wait?"

"I told you I'm not that person anymore—"

"Then you'd better be that person again or leave."

She looked away, stepping back slightly like the distance between us didn't grant her enough space. She withdrew, her body becoming smaller, her fire more distant.

The frustration was making me boil, but I kept it bottled deep inside under lock and key. I watched her suffer in silence, watched her abandon all her beliefs just to survive. The self-loathing. The disrespect. The hatred.

"Eyes."

She wouldn't look at me.

"I'm only doing this once."

She turned to look at me, her eyes slightly confused.

I came close, bringing my face just inches from hers.

She inhaled a quick breath when I drew near, but she didn't step away. Her eyes locked on mine, her angry fire extinguished. Her eyes glanced down to my lips, like she knew what was coming and had no protest.

My arm circled her waist, and I pulled her close to me, my lips resting on her forehead. My hand slipped into her hair past her ear, and I tilted her chin up, my thumb sliding down her soft neck.

Our eyes remained locked for a long moment. Hers shifted back and forth. So did mine.

Now there was no objection.

She didn't want to sleep with me out of obligation.

Only because she wanted to.

With my hand on her cheek, I brought her lips to mine.

They came together in a soft landing, a sharp breath escaping her nose when she felt my mouth. Her lips were warm, tasted like blush wine, and they were eager. My hand slid deeper into her hair as I turned my head slightly and kissed her. Kissed her again and again. It'd been so long since I'd kissed a woman. So many years ago I couldn't even remember the woman who had the honor.

Her mouth was hesitant at first, but she met my hunger with her own. Soon, her hands were on me, feeling my arms and my chest, clinging to my back when we came even closer together. Her breaths deepened and her muscles relaxed. She lost herself in me, getting swept up in the fire ignited by our lips.

My fingers pulled on the front of her collared shirt, loosening the knot secured below her tits. My palm flattened against her small stomach then pushed up, gathering the material until I pulled it over her head.

She unclasped her own bra and let the straps fall until the entire thing slipped to the floor. Everything else came off quickly, her jeans and panties ending up on the floor.

This was not how I'd wanted my night to go, but if I had to ease her into it, so be it.

I got her on the bed, her beautiful naked body ready for me to take. Her small tits had pebbled nipples, her pierced belly button reflected the light from the bedside lamp, and the area between her legs was groomed like she expected me to see it.

I dropped to my knees at the edge of the bed, her legs over my shoulders, and kissed her.

She immediately arched her back and drew in a heavy breath when she felt my lips. My tongue tasted her sweetness as I circled the source of all her pleasure. I could have taken it slow and eased her into it, but my dick had been hard for a solid fifteen minutes, and I wasn't going to wait a moment longer.

Her nails dug into the bedding beside her as she gave an unexpected moan. Her body remained tight as I kissed her, but she eventually loosened, rocking her hips as she pushed herself into my lips, wanting more.

If I were a decent guy, I'd let her come first.

But I wasn't.

I got her wet, got her ready, got her to stop thinking about her obligations.

Then I finally rose to my feet, positioned her at the edge of the bed, and pushed my fat dick inside her. It took three thrusts, the first two gentle, and then a third, hard one to get past her tightness.

Then I slid inside her softness, her wetness, her tightness, and I gave a moan of victory.

Finally.

My hands hooked around the tops of her thighs as I anchored her against me, and I thrust, hitting her deep until she winced before I pulled out again. When my dick reemerged, I saw it completely coated in her sticky arousal, so thick it was audible when I shoved myself back inside.

Her hands held on to my hips so she could pull her body back into mine. Her small frame was folded underneath me, her legs wide apart to give my length the room it needed to penetrate her entrance.

I tried to take it slow, but fuck, she felt good, and she looked so damn good.

It was impossible to control myself, and I fucked her so hard. My fingers kneaded her flesh, and my back formed a thin coating of sweat. I didn't realize how hard I was working until I felt the cool air of the room evaporate the sweat off my skin.

Her eyes watered, and she winced here and there, like my big dick was a little too much for her, but she didn't ask me to stop. She continued to tug on me, to pull her body back into mine to take my length.

I stared down at her perfect body, keeping my focus so I wouldn't come too soon. I wanted to enjoy it a while longer, enjoy the high of my victory as long as I could. I was fucking the woman Grave loved—and it felt so fucking good.

If only he could watch.

I wanted to direct my dick just an inch south, to fuck her in the ass for a while before moving back up again, but this wasn't the night. Maybe tomorrow.

I leaned farther over her, pushed my dick as deep as I could without making her cry, and rubbed my pelvic bone right against her clit.

She moaned louder, opened her legs wider, and clawed at my stomach. Color rushed into her neck and cheeks, and the gleam in her eyes was from a new round of tears. Her breathing suddenly became shallow and labored, and her nails sank deep into my skin. Her body tightened around mine, and then it hit her.

She writhed underneath me, tears streaking down her cheeks, her hips bucking against me uncontrollably, her eyes closed.

I leaned over her completely and watched her come. "Eyes."

Her eyes opened and locked on mine as she finished.

I gave a loud moan as I finished, my thrusts deep and hard, pounding into her as I filled her completely. "Fuck…" My thrusts slowed, and then I remained there, my dick gradually softening inside her.

After a few deep breaths, I pulled out of her and released her thighs. "It's down to business from now on."

NINE
CAMILLE

I was sore.

It'd been a long time since I'd felt that way.

Cauldron had a really big dick and wasn't afraid to use it. I hadn't noticed the discomfort during the sex. It was masked by all the good things going on. The second he kissed me, I forgot the reason I was there in the first place.

That was his intention—and it worked.

When there was a knock on my door, I knew it was Hugo instead of the man of the house. "Yeah?"

"*Yeah?*" Hugo mocked through the door. "What does that mean?"

I rolled my eyes. "Come in."

Hugo stepped inside, holding a wardrobe of clothing on hangers. "Gather all your things. I'll pack these for you, but bring other essentials you might need."

"Essentials for what?" I asked, having no idea what was going on. "And what are those?"

"Mr. Beaufort asked me to grab appropriate attire."

"Appropriate attire for what?"

He set them over the back of the couch then looked at me head on. "For not looking like a peasant." He looked me up and down, like I looked like trash at that very moment. "And not embarrassing Mr. Beaufort." He headed back out the door.

"Seriously, where are we going?"

"Paris," he said as he continued walking.

"Why Paris?" I followed.

"Mr. Beaufort has business in the city. He's requested you accompany him."

Paris was the last place I wanted to go. "Uh…can I stay here?"

Hugo stopped in the doorway and turned back around. "If he wanted you to stay here, he would have been clear about that. You leave in an hour, so hurry up and shower."

"I already showered."

"Oh." He looked me up and down again. "My mistake."

"Wow…" After Hugo was gone, I headed to the double doors of Cauldron's bedroom and stepped inside. "Your butler is a catty bitch, you know that—"

"Get out." The first room was a large sitting room with a TV on the wall. He had a suitcase on one of the couches, and he stood there as he buttoned his collared linen shirt. "Don't come in here again."

I stood in the doorway, speechless he would be so cold to me after last night. "You've got no problem having me suck your dick, but coming into your bedroom is a big no-no?" My eyebrows shot up to the top of my forehead.

He finished buttoning his shirt, his angry eyes on me. "Nobody comes into my bedroom."

"Why?"

"I said, get out." His arms dropped to his sides, and he stepped toward the doorway, his stance defensive, like he would throw me out on my ass if I didn't walk away.

"You're serious? You really want to have a conversation in the hallway?"

He adjusted the sleeves of his shirt, rolling them up to his elbows.

"I was about to tell you that your butler is a bitch, but looks like you're one too." I stormed off, annoyed that he would speak to me like that after last night. I wasn't foolish enough to believe it meant anything to him, but I expected at least some kind of affection…just a morsel.

"Camille." His voice followed me.

I stopped down the hallway toward my bedroom. "Hugo told me to pack for Paris, but I'm not going."

He was in tan shorts and a white shirt, the top button undone. I normally didn't care for guys in shorts, but his legs were so toned and his hips so narrow that it looked good on him. His sunglasses hung at the V in the fabric. "No one is permitted in my bedroom. It's not just you."

"Then how does it get cleaned?"

"Hugo supervises the maids."

"So, the entire staff is permitted in your bedroom."

"Like I said, Hugo supervises."

"So, Hugo is allowed. I'm the woman you're fucking, but your servant gets priority over me?"

He slid his hand into the pocket of his shorts. "You're joining me in Paris."

"No, I'm not."

His patience had clearly been tried because his jaw clenched, and his eyes looked furious. "When will you understand that you do as I tell you? That you go where I tell you to go? Never had this issue with another woman."

"Well, I'm not like other women." I crossed my arms over my chest. "And I'm not going to change."

"Where I go, you go. Understand?"

"I'll go anywhere but there."

His eyes narrowed. "Is this about Grave?"

"Obviously."

"We could be living on the floor above his, and it wouldn't change anything."

"Don't be arrogant—"

"You're untouchable with me, Camille. That's not arrogance—that's fact."

"Look, I don't want to go—"

"If he tries to take you from me, I'll kill him. Isn't that exactly what you want?"

I kept my arms crossed over my chest, my interest piqued. "But you said you didn't want to kill him."

"I said I have no interest in going out of my way to kill him. But if anyone tried to steal from me, then yes, I would destroy them, regardless of who they were." He came closer to me, one hand still in his pocket, his dark eyes shifting back and forth as he regarded me. "Pack your things, and let's go."

"Why do you even want me to come with you?"

His eyes roamed over my body. That was his answer. "We're leaving in fifteen minutes."

We sat together in the back seat of the car. It pulled away from the French estate and headed to Nice. Once we were there, we didn't board a commercial flight. We went straight to the runway and boarded a small private plane.

It was a short flight to Paris. We touched down less than an hour later. Now I was back in the city I'd just fled. The driver arrived and escorted us through the jam-packed streets.

Cauldron was on his phone most of the time, typing emails. "Fucking tourists…" He said it under his breath, barely audible, and he didn't even look outside to see them pass on the sidewalks like a herd of cows.

We pulled through the gates of a private Parisian apartment. It was in the heart of the city but kept private by the large gates that surrounded the property and kept the civilians on the street.

The men carried all our things inside, and we entered a three-story apartment with gold sconces, old oil paintings, and cream-colored curtains that had already been pulled back in anticipation of his arrival. There was staff here, as if they were stationed full time whether he was in residence or not.

The butler approached me and gave a short bow. "Mademoiselle Camille, I'm Pius. I'm the head butler at Mr. Beaufort's Parisian estate. Please let me know if you need anything." When he stood upright again, he wore a nice smile.

"I really like you," I blurted.

He gave an awkward chuckle. "Good to know. I'll grab the champagne."

Cauldron moved through the apartment, talking on the phone so quickly it was hard to understand what he was saying. It was probably for work. I noticed he spent most of his time in his study, although I wasn't sure what he did for a living. That answer could be found in a simple online search, but all I'd cared about previously was what he looked like.

I explored the apartment, seeing that the front of the building had a nice view of the Eiffel Tower. Like his other home, the entire place was put together by a designer. Fresh flowers were everywhere, put in place by the staff that continued to work in his absence. I walked onto the patio with my flute of champagne in hand and admired the bustle of the city. I took a seat, thinking about the last time I was there.

I wondered if Grave had figured out where I'd gone yet.

Cauldron joined me on the patio, and before his ass hit the chair, Pius placed a fruit and cheese platter on the table between us, with French cheeses, fresh strawberries, and candied oranges. A fresh basket of bread was placed beside it, along with jellies and jams.

Cauldron sat there, knees spread apart, his eyes on the city in front of him.

I'd already eaten on the plane, but I couldn't resist the spread placed right in front of me. I grabbed a couple things and dug in.

Cauldron didn't seem interested. He was the same way on the yacht. There was food everywhere, but he never desired it. His elbow was propped on the armrest, and his knuckles rested underneath his stubbled chin.

"What business do you have here?"

"A meeting."

"That couldn't be done online?"

He turned his head to regard me. "Not in my line of work."

"And what line of work is that?" I bit into the slice of bread, tasting the brie and fig spread.

His stare hardened. "I don't have time for bullshit, so don't feed me bullshit."

"I really don't know."

His stare remained cold.

"I just looked up what you looked like and your address. I didn't need your life story."

He seemed to believe me because his gaze turned less hostile. "Diamonds."

"You have a jewelry store?"

"It's more than that." He grabbed his champagne and took a drink. "I mine diamonds in Botswana. I only sell the most precious ones. Yes, I sell them in stores around the world, but I take private bids on the largest and most beautiful diamonds that I find. I showcase them to my clients, and that's what I'm doing tomorrow night."

"Wow. How did you get into that line of work? Family business?"

He stiffened at the question, and his eyes grew hostile once more.

I quickly realized I'd said the wrong thing.

"To incentivize the miners, I offer them large bonuses. The size of the bonus depends on the size of the diamond. The bigger stones they find, the more money they make. Competitors choose to pay the workers poorly and exploit their labor in poor working conditions. That works out in my favor because their workers leave their employ and join mine instead. The sites also have a serious security detail."

"As interesting as that is, that didn't answer my question."

"I knew there was money in diamonds, so I walked in there and grabbed all the business." He took another drink of his champagne. "There's always bloodshed, always attacks on the mines, but they're minor setbacks. We always get up and running again."

"How long have you been doing that?"

"About eight years."

"Do you ever visit the sites yourself?"

"Rarely. Botswana is near South Africa—"

"Yes, I know where it is. I know my geography."

He stared at me for a moment before he continued. "There's a lot of civil unrest there. Warfare. Gangs isn't the right term, but it's the best way to describe it. The security team is supposed to repel them as much as competitors. Our weapons are far better equipped, so they usually don't mess with us."

"That sounds scary."

He gave a shrug before he took another drink. "I've seen worse shit on the streets of Paris."

Grave came to mind—along with the pearl necklace he still had.

Cauldron tilted his head back and downed the rest of the champagne. "I'll be out tonight. When I get home, I expect you to be ready."

"Ready for what?"

He gave me his hard stare. "Me."

When I stepped into my bedroom, I found the lingerie on the bed. A black teddy with garters. The fabric was more than just lace and cotton. It looked as expensive as a ball gown. When I looked at the tag, I recognized the label.

Barsetti Lingerie.

Their lingerie was as good as their wine.

I knew exactly what to expect when he walked in the door. He would be the master, and I would be the whore. My heart picked up in speed, but it didn't thud like a drum like it did before. Last night, he'd made me feel like a lover rather than a whore, like it was my choice rather than my obligation, and that did help.

But now, my stomach was in knots again.

He didn't tell me when he'd be home, so I didn't know when I should be ready. I wasn't going to lie around in skintight lingerie all night when I'd rather be in my sweatpants and t-shirt.

But then there was a knock on the door.

"Yeah?"

Pius entered the room, carrying a sleek phone in his hand. "Mr. Beaufort wanted me to give this to you."

It was a brand-new phone, straight out of the packaging. I clicked the button and watched the screen light up. There was a message in the inbox, so I opened it. *I'll let you know when I'm on the way.* It was Cauldron.

"Thanks."

Pius gave a quick bow before he departed my bedroom.

The bedchambers were similar to the other one I had, a room large enough that it had its own sitting room, a master bath with a tub that was the size of a small pool. The windows showed the building across the street, the abundant life of the city I once loved.

At some point, I fell asleep on top of the comforter, the bedside lamp still on.

The vibration of the phone stirred me.

With squinting eyes, I reached for the phone.

On my way.

I looked at the time. It was 3:30 in the morning.

What the hell was he doing until three in the morning?

I wanted to fall right back to sleep, but I knew what the consequences would be if I refused. I was on my third strike, and I would be ejected from his protection if I didn't comply with his demands.

I was still a whore, but now I'd changed hands.

I started to worry if that was all I'd ever be.

Maybe I didn't deserve more anyway.

I put on the lingerie he'd left for me and did my makeup in the bathroom. I went for the midnight colors, the smoky darkness around my eyes, the fake lashes, the deep lipstick. I made my hair thick with hair spray and my teasing comb, and by the time I was done, I hardly recognized myself.

I pulled on the black pantyhose and slipped on the heels then waited.

A couple minutes later, I heard his footsteps outside my bedroom door. He stepped inside without knocking, the only light in the room coming from the lamp on the bedside table. The curtains were pulled over the windows to hide the world outside.

He was in black jeans and a button-down shirt with his sleeves shoved up to his elbows. A shiny watch caught the light. The top few buttons of his shirt were already undone. The cords in his tight forearms were visible even in the dim light. He walked inside with an air of dominance, like he didn't just own the room, but me. Dark eyes locked on my face as he drew near, sweeping over my appearance with powerful intensity.

I left the edge of the bed and felt my heels hit the rug beneath me. Even with me in high-heeled shoes, he was still a foot taller than me. He got closer, the smell of his cologne hitting my nose. My heart was in my throat, and I was nervous even though I'd done this so many times before. I'd submitted to men for money, fulfilled their fantasies, but it felt different with him.

His stare seemed to last forever before his hand reached for me. He didn't brush the soft strands of hair from my face. He didn't graze my cheek with the backs of his fingers. His hand went for my neck, and he squeezed slightly.

I closed my eyes and braced for the hit.

Nothing happened.

When I opened my eyes, he was staring at me, but his intensity had waned.

"I'm not into that." His grip remained tight as he guided me to the floor.

I slowly lowered myself, my knees hitting the thick rug around the bed.

He stared down at me, eyes turning hard as steel. He finally released my neck and undid his belt then his trousers. He pushed everything down, his thick cock popping out and pointing right at my face. His fingers wrapped around the base of his length, and he gripped me by the neck again. "Eat my cock."

My mouth immediately opened, my tongue flattened as a landing strip, and then my throat was stuffed with his enormous dick. I could feel the groove of his vein along the shaft, taste his arousal on my tongue, feel the saliva pool in my mouth until there was nowhere for it to go besides spill out the sides.

He kept his hold on my neck and thrust his hips, doing most of the work while I just took it. He fucked my mouth just as hard as he fucked my pussy, barely giving me the chance to breathe. His eyes were glued to mine, his skin tinted from his desire.

I didn't drop my gaze, knowing what would happen if I did.

I expected him to edge himself before release, but he pounded into my mouth without reprieve until he came. His fingers dug hard into my flesh as he finished, a quiet moan coming from his strong mouth.

It was over in less than two minutes.

He fucked me like it was nothing but a transaction.

He pulled out of my mouth and stepped back.

I swallowed and wiped the mess from my mouth. With wobbly legs, I made it back to my feet, still in the high heels.

He came up behind me, grabbed me by the back of the neck, and slammed my face into the bed. Bent over with my ass in the air, I tried to push against his hold, but he weighed as much as a load of bricks. "I'm not done, sweetheart."

I gasped when I felt him, his enormous dick pushing past my entrance and penetrating deep inside me.

His hand fisted my hair like a leash, and he kept me pinned down, his other hand pressed into my lower back to make my ass stick out more. Like he wasn't the least bit satisfied after releasing into my mouth, he pounded into me as if he was desperate for a reprieve, as if he'd never fucked me before.

Hard and fast, the headboard tapped against the wall like the beat of a song.

My hair was all over the place, obscuring my vision, making the air hot against my face. My hands flattened against the bed with my elbows bent, but he snatched both of my wrists and pinned them against the small of my back.

My body jerked with his thrusts, and the weight of his body pressed me so deep into the mattress that my clit rubbed against it. I rarely felt pleasure in my line of work, and I had to imagine my own fantasies to keep my body wet, but this was the second time he'd commanded my body to do the impossible. He forced me into a climax, made my hips buck against the mattress, made my incoherent moans muffle against the duvet.

He came immediately afterward. If he were a lover, I'd assume it was intentional, but Cauldron didn't strike me as the kind of man that cared about anyone's pleasure but his own. He owned me—so my feelings were irrelevant.

His cock twitched inside me after he was finished, and with a sigh of satisfaction, he let me go. His weight lifted off me, he pulled up his trousers, and then he walked out as if nothing had happened.

As if I was nothing.

TEN
CAMILLE

My job as a courtesan was simple.

I fulfilled their fantasies, and every guy's fantasy was to be good in bed.

I was so good at faking it that nobody could tell the difference.

But with Cauldron...I didn't have to.

Another unusual thing about Cauldron? He did all the work. I was the one who was supposed to tease him with a strip show, to give him a lap dance that made him hard as steel, to instigate every rendezvous, to fulfill his fantasies without asking what they were. But Cauldron was the one in charge, was the one who issued the orders, and all I had to do was obey. I didn't have to think about anything at all.

That was a nice change.

I woke up late the following morning since he'd woken me up in the middle of the night. I couldn't go back to sleep for hours, so by the time I made it downstairs to the parlor, it was already lunchtime.

And Cauldron had company.

Three guys joined him on the balcony, having lunch while they smoked cigars. They were all dressed business casual. Cauldron was in a sports coat with a white shirt underneath, his ankle resting on the opposite knee, his handsome face furrowed in concentration as he listened to one of the guys speak.

He must have felt my stare because his eyes shifted to me through the window.

A surge of flashbacks hit me. My hands clasped behind my back. My moans muffled against the duvet. His hand tight on my neck as he slammed his big cock inside me. It all happened in an instant, an instant I wondered if he felt too.

He brought the cigar to his lips and took a puff before he released the smoke from his mouth. Espresso eyes were locked on mine as he ignored his company. His eyes always looked displeased, always looked irritated, but his features remained handsome, regardless of his mood. The other guys seemed to notice Cauldron's distraction and turned to look at me through the window.

They all stared.

I broke eye contact and walked away from the window. It wasn't until I was in a different hallway that I felt Cauldron's stare truly disappear. I walked down a different hallway and found Pius along the way.

"Mademoiselle, I've fixed you some breakfast if you're hungry."

"What's on the menu?"

"Savory crepes and French toast."

Damn, that sounded good. "Let's do it."

He led me to the dining room. "Unless you would like some lunch items? I realize it's past noon." He pulled back the chair for me and helped me sit down.

"No, that sounds perfect. Thanks."

"Of course." He returned a moment later and filled the table with my meal. There was a glass carafe of coffee and freshly squeezed orange juice. The food was sizzling hot, so I wasn't sure how he pulled that off. "Enjoy your breakfast." He set the newspaper beside me then left the room.

Pius treated me like I was no different from Cauldron, whereas Hugo took shots at me every chance he could, even insulting my appearance. I was in the loungewear provided for me, dark blue pajama bottoms and a white sweater that hung off one shoulder. I wasn't the kind of woman who put on makeup the second I opened my eyes, so my face was all-natural. Hugo wouldn't hesitate to give me a judgmental look.

Voices carried down the hallway. "I'll try to make it." Cauldron's voice was easy to recognize, deep like the bass in a symphony. "Have a lot of business that requires my attention."

"Bring her if you do," a man said. "I'll make it worth your while."

What did that mean?

Pleasantries were exchanged then they departed.

My food didn't taste as good as it had a moment ago.

Cauldron entered the room a few seconds later, reeking of cigars and booze even though it was barely noon.

He helped himself to the chair across from me, one ankle shifting to the opposite knee, his shoulders filling out his jacket and forming the top line of a triangle. He settled into his typical stare, packed with so much intensity and mystery.

"What the fuck was that?"

He had no reaction to my harshness, as if he expected it.

"*I'll make it worth your while?* You're telling all your buddies that I'm your whore and loaning me out now?"

"I didn't tell them anything. They assumed."

"They took one look at me and just assumed I could be bought?" I asked incredulously.

While my voice continued to rise in hysteria, his remained calm like a gentle river. "They're aware of my tastes."

My eyebrow cocked.

"That I prefer to pay for sex."

I was still angry.

His stare hadn't changed during the interaction. "Why are you ashamed?"

"I'm not ashamed—"

"Yes, I remember you said that, but you're offended every time it comes up." His voice rose a little bit, like he was irritated with me. "In case you've forgotten, it's still your profession, so their assumption was correct."

"It's not… It's different."

He stared me down like he disagreed, like he was thinking about the way he'd fucked me last night.

His stare was so penetrating that I had to look away. "If you think you're going to loan me out to your buddies—"

"I'm not."

My eyes shifted back to him.

"I don't like to share."

"It sounds like you've shared before."

"Whores are a dime a dozen. But you're a diamond in the rough."

I let my food and coffee grow cold, let my orange juice warm to room temperature because his stare was so all-encompassing. He managed to control every moment we were together, just by his sheer will alone. He was the thermostat, setting the temperature for everyone else.

"I'll be gone for the day. I'll return tonight to retrieve you for the evening."

"I thought you said you had a meeting."

"I do." He rose to his feet. "You're coming with me."

"Why?"

He stared down at me like that was a stupid question to ask.

"What am I supposed to wear—"

"It's been taken care of." The conversation ended when he walked off, his powerful back stretching the fabric of his clothing, wide shoulders leading to narrow hips. He turned the corner and disappeared, but his presence was still in the room, in every room.

Pius delivered a tight black dress with a sweetheart top. There were heels as well, with just a bit of diamond dust in the black material. Jewelry was included, diamond earrings along with a diamond necklace.

I wasn't a jeweler, but I could tell the diamonds were of the highest quality.

When I was ready, I walked into the main parlor, where Cauldron was sitting on the couch, typing on his phone like he was writing a long text message or email. He was dressed in all black, a t-shirt that showed his muscular arms with boots. Compared to me, he was vastly underdressed.

When he was finished, he got to his feet and looked at me.

Really looked at me. All over. Like he'd spotted me across the room and couldn't stop staring.

I was used to the way men looked at me, but none of them could capture Cauldron's intensity. He was utterly consumed, his body so stiff that it stretched his clothing just a little bit more, made the front of his jeans just a little bit tighter. He was a man of few words, but he could convey everything with just that powerful stare.

Wordlessly, he gestured to the hallway, asking me to go first.

I took the lead, feeling his dark eyes right on my ass.

We took the elevator down to the bottom floor, got into the back seat of the blacked-out SUV, and then drove through the busy streets of Paris. When I looked out the window, I could tell it was bulletproof. I recognized the distinct opaqueness.

Cauldron kept his gaze out his window. His hand didn't move to my thigh. His arm didn't hook around my waist as he directed me to the car. In fact, he never showed affection with me whatsoever. All he did was fuck me. Nothing more, nothing less.

The car stopped at the curb.

We were in front of a building with no windows. There were double black doors and a single word in gray letters above them. Beaufort.

When we approached the doors, they were opened for us by two men holding rifles.

Cauldron stepped inside with me beside him, entering into a darkly lit room. It wasn't the typical jewelry store with glass cases on display. The diamonds were in cases along the perimeter, protected by thick glass and bullet-proof walls. In the center of the room were two couches and two armchairs around a large circular coffee table. A bottle of champagne and glasses were already sitting there.

Cauldron took a seat on the couch. He got comfortable, leaned back against the cushions and watched his men pour two glasses of champagne. His look shifted to me, silently telling me to join him.

I took the seat beside him. "What do you want me to do?"

"Sit there."

"I don't know anything about diamonds—"

"You are a diamond." He looked ahead, his elbow propped on the armrest.

My hands gathered in my lap, and I waited for whatever came next.

Minutes later, the doors opened again, revealing a couple. The man was older, probably in his late forties, and the woman he was with looked like she was my age. She was dressed similarly, in a tight dress and heels that could break your ankles. It was clear she was his trophy, as I was Cauldron's.

The men greeted each other with a handshake.

"Thank you for taking the time, Mr. Beaufort."

"Pleasure is mine, Prince Kline."

Prince?

Prince Kline introduced the woman. "My wife, Ana."

Cauldron shook her hand then introduced me. "Camille."

Once the pleasantries were exchanged, we took a seat and the men got down to business. Cauldron's men brought each diamond one by one to the coffee table, to allow the prince to examine them up close. There was never an inquiry about price. The couple discussed each one quietly, deciding which one they'd like to purchase.

"Ana needs something to wear to our annual lunar celebration," Prince Kline explained, as if there was a justification for purchasing diamonds that cost…I couldn't even guess how much. Prince Kline glanced up often, not looking at Cauldron, but at me.

It made me uncomfortable because his wife was sitting right there. But I got the impression he didn't care.

Half an hour passed until they decided what they wanted, a diamond necklace. It had a simple chain, but in the very center was a diamond bigger than any other I'd ever seen, even on TV. It looked heavy, something that could only be worn on the grandest occasions.

Prince Kline stared at Cauldron.

"Forty million."

Did he just say forty million?

Prince Kline continued his stare. "The Archduke diamond was sold for twenty-one million. This price is steep, Mr. Beaufort."

"It's not steep when you account for the higher clarity of this diamond, as well as the cut and the size." Cauldron leaned forward, his arms on his knees. "Prince Kline, I'll be frank with you. I took this meeting as a courtesy to our mutual friend. I have several buyers interested in this diamond, but I put you on the top of this list only because Sean did me an enormous favor years ago. If you aren't interested, don't waste my time."

It was obvious by the offense in his eyes that Prince Kline was never spoken to this way, but he was power-less to retaliate—not if he wanted the diamond. "I agree to your price—if she's included in the deal." His eyes shifted to me.

Ana immediately dropped her gaze, visibly uncom-fortable.

I couldn't keep my mouth shut. "Excuse me?"

Cauldron's hand went to my thigh to silence me. "Camille isn't for sale."

"Damn right I'm not—"

He squeezed my thigh hard.

Now Prince Kline looked affronted. "You want me to pay this price? I want her."

I was gonna knock this guy out.

Cauldron didn't move or speak, but his face said it all. "If you think this diamond is expensive, then you couldn't afford her. I'll give you one final opportunity to make this purchase. Say anything I don't like, the deal's off."

A silent standoff ensued.

The men stared at each other like guns were drawn.

I wished I'd had a gun because I'd shoot this fucker right in the face.

His wife still kept her eyes down, either hurt or embarrassed, probably both.

Prince Kline was the first to speak. "We have a deal."

Cauldron immediately motioned to his men.

A laptop in a hard case was presented to the table. Cauldron unlocked the screen and typed in a few passwords. The screen was gray with green writing, not like a regular internet page. He finished what he was doing then turned the laptop to face Prince Kline.

The prince seemed to know what to do because he typed in a couple things before the computer was turned back around.

Cauldron looked at the number at the bottom. "Funds have been received. The diamond is yours, Prince Kline." Men came forward and took away the laptop and boxed up the diamond, putting it in a special suitcase with a combination lock code. They handed it to the prince, and then they walked out.

When they were gone, Cauldron grabbed the flute on the table and downed it.

"That guy was a fucking asshole."

He licked his lips before he set the empty glass on the table. "All rich men are assholes—in case you haven't noticed."

I noticed more than I ever had before. "I can't believe he said that in front of his wife."

"Don't feel too bad for her. She knew what she signed up for."

"What's that supposed to mean?"

"A twentysomething doesn't marry a fortysomething for love."

"Maybe she didn't have a choice," I snapped. "Did you think of that?"

He turned to me, his eyes annoyed. "Why are we arguing about this?"

"Because you're being an asshole."

He gave a quiet chuckle and looked forward again. "If *that* comment makes me an asshole…"

I stared at the side of his handsome face, his stubble thicker than it'd been the day before. It outlined his hard jaw, cast a shadow on his monstrous presence. "Why did you bring me here?"

He got to his feet as if I hadn't spoken.

"I asked you a question."

He stepped away from the sitting area, men moving to the door in anticipation. "And I don't have to answer. A perk of being an asshole."

ELEVEN
CAULDRON

Camille didn't speak to me after I put her in her place.

She still had that fire that burned a little hotter in offense, and I didn't care about being the booze poured on top. I didn't care if she was angry. I didn't care about her feelings whatsoever.

I think that realization had finally sunk in.

We entered the apartment and were greeted by Pius.

"Good evening, Mr. Beaufort—"

"I don't need anything. You're dismissed."

The butler gave a quick bow and disappeared.

"Don't talk to him like that." She rounded on me, her long blond hair in soft curls, her eyes smoky and dark.

She was stunning on the outside but a thorn on the inside. "He's so good to you——"

"Don't tell me how to speak to my servants."

"*Staff*. They aren't your servants. They're people. News flash, asshole."

I didn't understand Grave's fascination with a woman who could never shut her mouth. "You're quick to forget your place. You're a servant just as much as they are. Remember that."

Her eyebrows scrunched high up her face, and a volcano exploded in her eyes. "I could walk right out of here——"

"Then do it."

Furious, she stared at me, her breaths deep and labored.

I walked up to her, not sure if I wanted to fuck her or strangle her.

Face-to-face, she shifted her eyes back and forth between mine, a small piece of hair close to one of her eyes.

"On your knees."

Her eyes immediately blazed in defiance.

"Shoving my cock in your mouth is the only way I'm going to shut you up." I grabbed her by the neck and started to force her down, but she elbowed my arm with unsuspecting strength then slapped me.

Fucking slapped me.

I turned slightly with the hit, felt the instant heat from her palm. It was a shock because no one in their goddamn right mind would fuck with me.

Her breathing deepened, as if she realized her predicament after her temper had been satiated.

I turned my head slowly until our eyes were locked on each other.

My expression must have been terrifying—because she looked a little scared.

Damn right she should be fucking scared.

I grabbed her by the neck so quickly she jumped. I pinned her against the wall, my fingers tight on her throat but merciful enough to allow her some air. Her hands instinctively went to my wrist, but she couldn't pull it free, and every time she tried, I gripped her harder in retribution.

Now she looked even more scared.

I pressed my face into her cheek, my lips right beside her ear. "Do that again and see what happens."

She gasped in my hold, drawing in deep breaths just to get enough air to remain conscious.

"See. What. Fucking. Happens." My face moved back to hers, seeing that fire come back to the surface, hardly noticeable under the thick layer of fear. I tugged on her neck, pulled her toward the floor until she hit her knees. I stared down at her, telling her exactly what to do without saying it.

Her hands released my wrist, and she worked my jeans open.

The victory made my cock that much harder. It wanted to explode from my trousers and choke her.

She pulled everything down to my thighs, letting me come free, rock hard.

"Open your fucking mouth." My hand hadn't left her throat, holding her tight like a leash.

She obeyed, the back of her head against the wall.

I grabbed myself by the base and shoved myself deep inside, going so deep that she started to choke. She could hardly breathe as it was, and now she gagged all over my dick. Tears sprang to her eyes, her cheeks turned red. My dick did far more damage than my hand had ever done.

I gave her only a second to recover before I thrust into her mouth, her body pinned in place against the wall. I gave it to her deep and hard, punished her for the bullshit she'd just pulled. More tears. More coughs. Her hands gripped my thighs to hold on because her body was being jerked by my thrusts. "Eyes."

She resisted at first. Didn't want to give up her last shred of dignity.

"*Eyes.*"

Her eyes flicked up, locked on mine with self-loathing, and she took my dick like the servant she was.

Camille avoided me for the next few days.

She never left her room. Took all her meals in private.

I let her sulk in her humiliation. Maybe she could run her mouth like that to Grave and her other clients, but not to me.

Not her master.

On the third day, she finally emerged in the morning, in dark-blue silk shorts that were small enough to be underwear and a loose-fitting white top that fell down one shoulder. Her hair was in soft waves, scattered across her shoulders. First thing in the morning, her face was free of makeup, her smoky look absent and a natural one left behind.

I liked the natural look. She was so beautiful she could pull it off.

I sat at the dining table and read the newspaper as she dropped into the chair across from me. I ignored the news and looked at her straight on, remembering how good it felt to skull-fuck her right against the wall in the parlor. I choked her with my fingers and my dick at the same time.

As if the same memory came to her, she grabbed the cream and poured it into her coffee, her eyes focused on her movements. "When are we returning to Cap-Ferrat?"

I turned back to my newspaper. "Tomorrow."

"Thank god."

"Our accommodations have been more than luxurious."

"It's not the accommodations." She grabbed the spoon and stirred the contents of her coffee cup slowly.

I lifted my gaze from my newspaper and watched her lean over the table, elbows on the surface, looking down into her coffee as she continued to stir it like she had no intention of drinking it. "I don't waste my time thinking about my enemies. You shouldn't either."

Her eyes flicked up, and she set her spoon down. "Easy for you to say."

I closed my newspaper and set it on the table. "How so?"

"I'm not a billionaire with a security team everywhere I go."

"You don't need those things."

"Ha." She released a sarcastic laugh. "It's always the rich people who say you don't need money."

"What you need are balls."

"Excuse me?" she asked, her eyebrows hiked up her face.

"You said you lived with him for years. In all that time, you couldn't steal a knife from the kitchen and slit his throat in the middle of the night?"

"I didn't want to kill him until he asked me to marry him. And by then, everything was different. I didn't have a chance."

I still felt no pity for her. "Let me tell you the difference between people on top and people on the bottom. Things happen to those at the bottom. And people at the top happen *to* things."

Her fire was bigger than ever before. "You have no idea what you're talking about, you privileged motherfucker."

I held her stare, tempted to choke her again. "You don't know anything about me."

"You can be self-made and still be privileged."

"And you can end up a powerful man but start as a traumatized boy."

Her hostility waned just a bit.

"You don't know me," I repeated. "And you'll never know me."

TWELVE

CAMILLE

I put on the teal dress, mermaid style with a sweetheart top with straps that hung off the shoulders. Every dress that was given to me felt like it had been altered to fit my proportions perfectly. There was also jewelry—more diamonds.

I didn't want to go wherever we were going, but at least tomorrow we would return to his private estate in the South of France. Paris would be behind us, and I would be hundreds of miles away from that asshole.

Cauldron was an asshole too, but he was still preferable to Grave.

I stepped into the parlor, finding Cauldron looking at the city through the windows. His hands were in the pockets of his slacks, and his weight was shifted to one leg. He withdrew his hand from his pocket and checked his watch before he slipped it back inside.

"Another business meeting?"

He took a second before he turned around and faced me, handsome in his tux. If he weren't an asshole, he would be the most desirable man in France, if not the world. His dark eyes looked me over like I couldn't see what he was doing. His deep dislike had no effect on his desire for me. He wanted me just the same, whether he loved me or hated me. "That dress looks nice on you." He said the words as he stared at my tits, which were pushed together in plumpness.

"Who are you talking to, exactly?"

Like a rainbow after a storm, a rare smirk moved on to his lips. He adjusted his cuff links as he headed for the door. "I'm going to tit-fuck you when we get home."

"Well, there's my answer."

We got into the back seat of the car and were driven through Paris. We left the city and entered the country-side, past the open landscapes and the aristocratic mansions that sat on top of them.

Knees apart, elbow propped on the armrest, he looked out the window.

"You never answered me. Where are we going?"

His fingers rubbed over his stubble. "A party."

"What kind of party?"

"Does it matter?" he asked. "They're all the same anyway."

My heart gave a lurch at his answer. Grave had parties all the time. I'd thought those fancy events were for diplomats and rich people, but they were for criminals too. "You think that's a good idea—"

"What are you afraid of?" He turned to look at me.

"Uh, that the man I despise will be there?"

"So what if he is? I told you you're untouchable now."

"That might actually make me feel better if you told me why."

He looked out the window.

"Why is Grave afraid of you?"

No answer.

"Why won't you tell me?"

"Because my business is my own."

I'd been with Cauldron for a couple of weeks, and I'd made no progress toward my goal. It was just existing, not living. I had no chance to convince Cauldron to do my dirty work if he wouldn't even tell me why they were enemies in the first place. If nothing changed, I'd have to leave and make my own plan. He'd probably give me a gun if I asked, so I could just take one and wait for the perfect moment.

Minutes later, we pulled up to the estate, a three-story mansion like the one Cauldron had in Cap-Ferrat. A line of cars was ahead of us, fancy sports cars and blacked-out SUVs. A pond was in the center, and the expansive grounds were all bright with uplighting. We inched closer until we reached the front, where the driver opened my door and helped me out first before Cauldron emerged.

Every woman had her arm circled through her date's, but Cauldron never offered his. He walked beside me up the steps and through the double doors from where the sound of violins originated. All these fancy parties were the same, crystal chandeliers, grand pianos, Cristal in glass flutes, appetizers being presented by waiters in tuxedos. Each rich person took a turn showing off their wealth, and in the end, it was just a pissing contest no one ever won. What was the difference between twenty billion and ten? Not much, if you asked me.

A couple men struck up a conversation with Cauldron, discussing his diamonds. "How are the mines, Mr. Beaufort?"

"Bottomless," he answered, wearing a handsome smile. "I just sold my largest diamond to Prince Kline."

"Yes, I heard his wife wore it at their annual lunar celebration in Dubai."

The men talked shop while I was ignored. I stood there with my arms by my sides, seeing people glance my way as they passed.

Cauldron had one hand in his pocket while the other held his drink. He remained close to my side but gave no indication that I was his date, that we were romantically involved whatsoever. It made me wonder why he'd brought me there in the first place. He couldn't show me off as his trophy if he was indifferent to me the entire time.

Cauldron eventually gestured to the necklace around my neck. "These diamonds were found together. I think they were once part of the same stone, but a mudslide in the mine broke it apart." His fingers lifted the heaviest diamond in the center, eyeing it with greater affection than he ever showed me. "But I think they look beautiful as a set."

The men admired it, still ignoring me. "Quite beautiful."

"Yes, very," the other man said.

"How much?" one of the men asked. "I have a special someone I'd like to gift this to."

I saw his wedding ring, but I assumed that special someone wasn't his wife.

In the middle of the dinner party, Cauldron took offers, hosting a business meeting right in plain sight. He sold the necklace for five million dollars, and the money was to be deposited in Cauldron's account first thing in the morning.

Cauldron stepped away and grabbed another drink.

"I was just about to say this doesn't seem like your scene, but now it all makes sense."

He drank from his flute as he watched me.

"Always working, huh?"

He set the empty glass on a passing tray. "Now you know why I put up with your mouth."

My eyebrows furrowed because I didn't follow the statement.

"Because you're the one selling these diamonds."

I assumed he was the one who owned the house.

It was something about his mannerisms, the way everyone gravitated toward him for conversation. He was young like Cauldron, with dark hair and brown eyes, a muscular man stretching the stitching of his suit with his heavyset size. His arm was around a beautiful woman, holding her close like no proximity would ever be close enough. They both wore wedding bands, and it was the first time I'd ever seen a husband and wife who actually loved each other.

When he saw Cauldron, he finished his conversations and greeted him with a handshake. "Cauldron." He indicated to the woman he clearly cherished. "You remember my wife, Melanie?"

Cauldron greeted her with a kiss on each cheek, the first woman he'd ever greeted that way. "Of course.

Lovely, as always." He gestured to me. "This is Camille."

The man hardly looked at me and didn't seem confused by the lack of label.

"How are things, Fender?"

His handsome smile stretched with a grin. "My wife is giving me a child." His hand moved over her stomach, which was so flat it was hard to tell she was pregnant. His wife glowed, but he glowed too.

"Congratulations," Cauldron said. "To both of you." He raised his glass.

"Thank you," Fender said with a nod. "How's business?"

"Never better," Cauldron answered. They talked extensively about work. Fender was a young man, but he claimed to have recently retired. He never elaborated on what he did before.

"Do you have anything new in the pipeline?" Fender asked.

"My team tells me they've found a very large diamond just this morning. We're still investigating the clarity and carat size now," Cauldron said.

Fender's eyes narrowed, his interest piqued. "I'd like a first look."

"Consider it done."

My job was completed, apparently, so I left his side and found the restroom. I took my time, my feet aching in the heels and my interest nonexistent. The only good thing about the party was the food.

I looked at myself in the mirror after I washed my hands, seeing the way the diamonds around my throat sparkled in the low light. They really were beautiful. I didn't need to do anything to enhance that. When my fingertips touched the stones, I felt the coldness despite the heat of my flesh.

I left the bathroom and returned to the party. My eyes were down on the floor initially because the sky-high heels were painful on the arches of my feet, and I almost ran into someone because of my distraction.

"Hello, darling."

My blood turned cold as I looked up into the face that haunted my dreams. His obsession. His controlling nature. The way he kept my most valuable possession as leverage. My eyes shifted back and forth between his, the moment of panic paralyzing me completely.

"That dress is something else." He looked down at me just the way Cauldron did, but his look was far more possessive. Cauldron just eye-fucked me. Grave consumed me without even touching me, branded me with his kiss so everyone would know he owned me. "Let's go home so I can take it off." His hand grabbed me by the elbow. To an outsider, it probably looked like an endearing touch, but to me, it was a lasso around my neck.

His touch was like a hot iron, and I reacted like I'd been burned. I twisted out of his grasp. "Don't touch me."

He smirked, not caring what anyone thought of our dispute. "You think I won't throw you over my shoulder and march you out of here in front of everyone? Come on, darling. You came here hoping to see me, didn't you?"

I stepped back.

He stepped forward.

"Get the fuck away from me."

He moved forward again, undeterred by my rising voice. A slight smirk was on his handsome face, like he knew he was winning a game I'd never agreed to play.

Then Cauldron came out of nowhere. He didn't throw a punch. Didn't scream at Grave. His eyes locked on mine, and he extended his hand for me to take. That was it. No macho display of masculinity. It was quiet, but so loud at the same time.

Grave turned to regard him—and his blood went as cold as mine did. It was a look I'd never seen him wear before. The first time in my life I'd ever seen him look humble. That smirk was long gone, and a different expression I couldn't describe had replaced it.

Cauldron kept his hand there, eyes locked on me, waiting for me to take the lifeline.

When my hand dropped into his, his fingers immediately closed around me like tentacles. He guided me back to the party, our hands locked together, and he grabbed a glass of wine from a passing waiter and handed it to me as if nothing had happened. He didn't bolt for the door or call for the car. As if the interaction didn't happen at all, he continued his night like there had been no interruption.

He didn't say a word on the drive home. His eyes were focused out the window, watching the dark landscape turn into the bright lights of the city. His closed knuckles were propped against his chin, and sometimes he would rub his fingers along the bottom part of his jaw. He seemed to do that whenever he was deep in thought.

We'd been together for so long now that I picked up on his mannerisms.

We took the elevator to the top floor, and he stood there with his hands in his pockets, ignoring me.

My eyes were focused on the side of his face, listening to the hum of the elevator. "You knew he'd be there…"

After a breath, he turned to meet my gaze.

"I told you I didn't want to see him." I kept my voice low despite my anger. "But you did it anyway."

The doors opened, and he stepped out of the elevator, hands still in his pockets, a bored look on his face.

I followed him. "You have nothing to say?"

He entered deeper into the apartment before he turned around and regarded me, a hint of harassment in his handsome features. "I knew he might be there. But I'm not going to change my plans to avoid anyone. Not my style."

"But I told you——"

"Let's get something straight. Your thoughts and feelings don't matter."

I took an involuntary step back, as if his hand had actually struck my face. "Wow...fuck you."

"And you have no reason to be upset at all because I delivered on my promise to you. As long as you're with me, you're untouchable. Did you see the way that motherfucker tucked his tail between his legs and whined like the little bitch he is?"

My eyes shifted back and forth between his.

"Don't act like that didn't turn you on."

"*Turn me on?*" I asked incredulously. "Two seconds ago, you told me my feelings don't matter."

He came close to me, eyes sharp like a butcher's blade. "I've stripped that asshole of all his power. Now all he can do is stare——unless I decide to carve his eyes out of his fucking head." He was so close to me I could feel his breath fall on my face. "Now I'm going to fuck you while he's thinking about me fucking you, so you better be ready for me in three minutes." He walked off as he unfastened his bow tie, heading for his bedroom down the hall.

I watched him go, furious but helpless. I entered my bedroom and set the diamond necklace on the vanity. The teal dress was skintight and took some time to remove without stretching it or ripping it. I eventually got down to my heels and underwear, ripping off the tape over my nipples.

He stepped into the room bare-chested and barefoot, his black sweatpants low on his hips. "I told you to be ready for me."

"It takes a little longer——"

He lifted me by the hips and set me on the edge of the bed. As he stood between my knees, he lifted one of my legs and removed the heel secured around my ankle. He did the same to the other, the heavy shoe thumping against the rug as it hit the floor. His big hands lifted my hips to the ceiling, until his thumbs dug into the seamless thong. He yanked it down, treating the delicate fabric like it was a sturdy rubber band.

One thick arm scooped under my back, and he lifted me as he scooted me farther up the bed, as if I were nothing more than a pillow. As he settled on top of me, he pushed his bottoms down until his pulsing hardness emerged. One arm hooked behind my knee, and he positioned my other leg behind his shoulder before he tilted his hips and guided himself inside me.

It all happened so fast. My back had barely hit the bed, and now his thickness was deep inside me, stretching me like it was the first time. His face was directly over mine as he sank, his big size welcomed by wet slickness. He pushed until there was nowhere else to go, when he felt my body wince in resistance. A satisfied moan left his lips before he started to move, to thrust inside me with deep and even strokes. "Fuck…this is a wet pussy." He glided through my stickiness, his eyes looking down into mine with victory.

Folded underneath him, all I could do was take it, watching his lean and hard body work to fuck me into the sheets. My palms flattened against his chest for the first time, feeling the slabs of concrete that filled out his t-shirts so nicely. My hands dragged down, my nails catching the grooves of muscles of his stomach. I could feel them tighten with every thrust, feel his hard body flex that much harder. I circled his torso with my hands and felt his muscular back, feeling the lines that divided all the different segments of his strength. One hand moved down to his hard ass and gave a tug, pushing his dick farther into me even though it hurt to take any more.

He quickened his pace and fucked me harder, the red tint entering his tanned skin. His dark eyes hardened in arousal, his firm jawline getting even tighter. "That turned you on, didn't it?" His breaths grew shallow, his beautiful skin starting to glisten with sweat.

I could feel the ache between my legs, feel the tightness that was so deep it was almost painful. My knuckles dug deep into his ass as I guided him inside me, wanting more of him, wanting him harder.

His hand suddenly grabbed me by the throat, and he squeezed slightly. "Tell me."

All the animosity I felt for this man disappeared in the moment. The heat of passion was too much, burning everything else that didn't matter. It was just the two of us, man and woman, our bodies so slick together. My eyes locked on his, nails latched deep into his flesh, my body so tight it was going to explode. "Yes…" Once I gave in, my body writhed in pleasure, an explosion between my legs that set off aftershocks everywhere else. My nails dug deep, my hips bucked to meet his thrusts, tears blurred my vision.

His hand remained secured around my throat, his neck and face tinted with more blotches of red. His eyes were victorious and hungry at the same time, and he came with a sexy grunt. Our pleasure was synced for a moment, both of us in the throes of indescribable satisfaction. I could feel his dick harden as he released, feel his essence once it was deep inside me, the weight of an anchor.

We both came to a finish, our sweaty bodies still locked together, breathing hard. My body was folded and opened wide for him, and his eyes still burned into my face. When his dick didn't soften, I knew the night was far from over.

He started to rock again, his hard eyes possessing me with just his stare. "Let's see how much come this pussy can take…"

THIRTEEN
CAULDRON

I had breakfast on the terrace, the open newspaper in my hands, a cigar between my lips, booze poured into my black coffee. It was a cloudless morning, the traffic light on the street because the festivities of the day hadn't quite started.

Pius stepped onto the balcony with an additional plate of breakfast and another mug for coffee. Camille emerged behind him, wearing a lacy black-and-green robe, her feet covered with thick white slippers. Her heavy makeup from the night before had been washed away, leaving behind a face of natural beauty. She looked at me before she took a seat.

I looked at her.

Both of us were thinking the same thing.

She sat down and poured her coffee. She added milk and cream and skipped the scotch. "Those cigars are gonna kill you, you know." She brought the mug to her lips and took a drink.

I turned my attention back to the paper. "I'm aware."

"For a man who has everything, you don't seem to value your life much."

"I'm just not stupid enough to believe I'm going to live long enough to die from lung cancer."

"Then what are you going to die from?"

I lifted my gaze from the newspaper, seeing her pour a lake of syrup all over her waffles. "Something more exciting."

She held my gaze for a moment before she looked down at her food. "Are we returning to Cap-Ferrat?"

"Yes."

"You're done using me to model your diamonds?"

The ploy worked so well I would never stop. "No. I'll be doing it a lot more often."

"I'm sure you can sell diamonds without me. You were doing it before."

"You know why men buy diamonds?" I held the cigar between my fingers, my arm on the armrest.

She sipped her coffee.

"To show their status. And when they give them to a beautiful woman they own, that really shows their status."

"What are you saying? That I'm part of this fantasy?"

"Yes." This woman really had no idea that men wanted to display diamonds on a woman of her caliber. But she was mine—and I wasn't going to share.

She ran her fingers through her hair before she grabbed her fork and sliced into her waffles. Diamonds were still in her lobes because she'd forgotten to take them off last night, but they looked like they were made just for her. She seemed to feel my stare because she lifted her eyes once again.

I didn't pretend I hadn't been staring. Everything I did was intentional, without shame or embarrassment.

She took a bite of her food, her eyes on me. "Bones told me you were the only person Grave won't cross. But he wouldn't tell me why."

"Because he doesn't know. Nobody does."

She held her fork in her hand, but her attention was solely focused on me. "Why?"

"My business is my own."

"Well, this is my business too—"

"Your business is to fuck me and wear my diamonds. That's it."

She stilled at the interruption, her eyes showing their irritation. "Stop being rude."

"Not rude. Just blunt."

"Trust me, you're rude," she snapped. "Don't interrupt me—"

"Then don't interrogate me about shit that's none of your goddamn business."

We stared at each other across the table, both of us packed with visible anger. The only time we seemed to be compatible was when we were slick and naked, soiling the sheets with sweat.

She abruptly rose to her feet and tossed her napkin on the table. "I'm going to pack."

"Sit."

She ignored me.

I rose to my feet. "Sit your ass down."

She flipped me the bird and walked off.

I followed her into the apartment and gripped her by the arm.

She twisted her arm out of my grasp then aimed her palm right for my face.

I grabbed her wrist and steadied it before she could slap me again. I squeezed her so hard it hurt a little bit as I forced her hand back to her side. "I warned you not to fuck with me."

"Well, you shouldn't fuck with me either." She shoved me in the chest and headed to her room.

I went after her, abandoning my hot coffee and cigar.

When she got to her bedroom, she slammed the door in my face and locked it.

My temper was smoldering, so I slammed my body into the door and broke it right off the hinges.

She screamed and tripped backward, landing on the rug around the bed.

I moved on her fast, pinning her hands together above her head. "Listen to me."

For the first time, she didn't fight me. Watching me break down the door like a cannonball obviously got her attention.

Good.

"I own you in every way that you can think of. You seem to forget that fact every five minutes, demand information you have no right to know, run your mouth like anything you have to say matters. Know your place." Once I relayed the message and let it sink in, I released her.

"*Know your place?*" She sat up, her robe coming undone in the fight, showing her short white tank top that revealed her pierced navel and hard nipples through the thin fabric. She wore no bottoms, just a black thong. "I do know my place, and it's not putting up with your bullshit."

I got to my feet, in nothing but my sweatpants because it was too warm for a shirt, even this early in the morning. "As long as you want my protection, you're going to put up with my bullshit every fucking day."

On the floor of the bedroom with her nearly naked body on display, she looked up at me with unbridled anger in her eyes, like she wanted to slap me until she made me bleed. There was a special kind of loathing there, the kind that pierced deep under the skin. "Don't pretend you don't need me, Cauldron. You need me to sell your diamonds, so I suggest you stop being the world's biggest asshole."

Something about the way she looked drove me crazy. The way her hair fell over one shoulder, showing one of the diamond earrings in her lobe. The silk robe was open, exposing her almost naked body and making it look so vulnerable. But what turned me on most of all was her resistance. I didn't tolerate disobedience, had no patience for it, so this attraction made no sense whatsoever.

I dropped back to my knees and moved over her, the robe coming apart altogether. My hands slid up her loose shirt, and I gripped her tit, my thumb brushing over the hard nipple.

"What are you doing?" She lay back with me and didn't slap my hand away.

I yanked her thong over her ass before I pushed my bottoms down in a hurry. Nothing more was said before I shoved myself deep inside her, my knees cushioned by the thick rug on the bedroom floor.

The anger from our fight was channeled into passion—
and we fucked on the bedroom floor as if the fight had
never happened.

Camille and I could agree on one thing.

Neither one of us enjoyed Paris.

I preferred the privacy of my Cap-Ferrat estate, the
way nature and civilization coexisted in a peaceful way.
If I craved further solitude, all I needed to do was
board my yacht and take it out in the Mediterranean.

"So that's her, huh?" Laurent looked out the back
windows to the pool, where Camille was lounging in
the sun on one of the armchairs, wearing a pink bikini
with sunglasses sitting on the bridge of her nose.

"Yes." I brought the glass to my lips and took a drink.

He gave a nod in approval. "She's hot."

I ignored his words.

He turned to look at me, as if to gauge my reaction.
"Willing to loan her—"

"No."

"Damn, she must be good."

"We're monogamous."

My cousin cocked an eyebrow. "You? Monogamous?"

"It's not what you think."

"You're fucking one woman and only one woman—it's exactly what I think."

I ignored what he said. "Grave saw us together at Fender's event."

"Did you speak?"

I shook my head. "He had Camille cornered, and I intervened."

"How did you intervene without speaking?"

I shrugged before I took a drink. "Sometimes a look is more than enough."

"You think that'll be the end of it?"

"I hope it's not. I hope he spends every waking moment utterly enraged."

"Bet that makes the sex better."

"Oh, it definitely does."

The door opened, and Camille walked inside, standing in her bikini with her sunglasses pushed back on her head. "I thought I should come in and say hello since you two were staring at me so hard through the window." Her anger was sheathed, but only slightly.

Laurent exchanged a look with me before he extended his hand. "Laurent."

She took it. "Camille."

"I'm Cauldron's cousin."

"Really?" She shifted her gaze to me next. "Finally, something personal about this man." She walked off, her heels tapping against the floor as she went.

Laurent stared at her ass the whole way. "She's…not what I expected."

"She's got a mouth, that's for sure."

"And you like that?"

I took another drink. "It's taken some getting used to."

I was in my study when the phone rang.

It didn't have a number. Wasn't even blocked. It just didn't have a source.

I knew exactly who it was.

I answered. "I knew this phone call was coming."

There was a long stretch of silence. It was packed with rage, rage that he'd made the call, and rage that he knew I got under his skin.

"Yes?" I asked, being an asshole just for the fun of it.

"What do you want?" His voice was low, his anger barely controlled.

"You're the one who called. You tell me."

His jaw clenched. I could hear it over the phone. "I want Camille. Name your price."

"She gave me the impression she doesn't like you very much."

Silence.

"There's gotta be another whore out there for you."

"I said, name your price."

"I don't have one—because she's priceless."

Silence.

"I always get everything, don't I?" I smiled as I spoke, knowing it was ripping him apart, down to his core. "She says as long as I keep you away, she wants to stay forever. She's earning her keep too, not just from fucking me—"

"I'll kill you, motherfucker."

This was too easy. "Then do it."

Silence.

"Her beautiful neck sells my diamonds better than I ever could." I waited for him to say something, but nothing was forthcoming. I savored the silence, enjoyed it with a sickness.

"She hates you. I can see it written all over her face."

"But she hates me less than you—and that's all that matters." Bored with the conversation, I hung up.

FOURTEEN
CAMILLE

Days passed, and Cauldron and I hardly spoke.

He ran so hot and cold. He'd fuck me for days, and then pretend I didn't exist for the next several days afterward. I suspected he got busy with work, because on those days, he spent most of his time in his study and then his bedroom. Sometimes he would leave the house, and of course, there was no explanation as to where he was going.

I wondered if Grave had contacted him, but I suspected I wouldn't get an answer if I asked.

I was in my bedroom reading when the door opened.

There wasn't a knock, and I knew there would never be.

I looked up from my closed book, seeing him stalk into the bedroom in just his sweatpants. It seemed like he'd recently showered because his hair was flatter than usual. His thick arms had veins running down to his wrists, and his shoulders were broad and rounded because of the muscles he had there. He looked down at me, the darkness in his eyes announcing the reason for his presence.

"Long time, no see."

He sat beside me on the couch, his arms immediately stretching over the back. The stare he gave was authoritative, as if he'd just given an order and I missed it. "Ride me."

I stared at his handsome face and felt a flood of contradictory emotions. He'd ignored me for days, and I found myself resentful, even fearful that he got bored with me. My nights started to feel lonely, and my body ached to be touched. But I also felt a deep loathing for this man, for his arrogance, for the way he spoke to me with such little regard, the way he tried to order me around like I was another member of his staff. I knew what position I had signed up for, but I was tired of being treated like an object rather than a person.

And then there was desire...because I would never forget the way he chased off Grave with just a look.

That was all it took—just a single stare.

He commanded every room he stepped into, chased away all the monsters because he was the king of the monsters.

As much as he might have aggravated me, his home had become my home. Other clients had struck me in the past because that was what they were into, but Cauldron didn't have those dark desires. It was my job to please him, but he liked to be in control of everything, including the bedroom.

I never knew you could hate someone but want to fuck their brains out at the same time.

Turned out, you could.

I was in my pajamas because it was past nine, but as always, he didn't seem to desire me more or less depending on my appearance. I pulled the loose shirt over my head and felt the draft harden my tits. Then I slipped the little shorts off my body before I hooked my thumbs into my panties.

With his arms stretched out on either side of himself and his sweatpants tight against his crotch, he watched me, his stomach as tight as it was when he stood upright.

When I was fully naked, I lowered myself to my knees in front of him and watched the way his eyes betrayed him with a jolt of excitement. A breath escaped his lips too, quick and not subtle. I grabbed on to his bottoms and pulled, getting them over his ass when he lifted his hips.

There it lay, anxious to delve deep inside my mouth.

I grabbed him by the base and got to work, feeling the thick pipe block my entire airway.

He could never just sit back and enjoy it. He always had to have a hand in something. His hand reached for my neck, and he directed me at the pace he wanted, as if I didn't already know how he liked his dick sucked at this point.

When he was close, he steadied me.

With his dick out of my mouth, I could breathe, really draw air into my lungs. My hands clutched his shoulders as I straddled his hips. I lowered myself until my sex sat right on his shaft, feeling the wetness from my own mouth.

His hands immediately gripped my hips, his fingers reaching all the way to my ass to knead it. The silence was broken by the quiet breaths he took, his indication of excitement. He lifted me up as he pointed his head at my entrance.

I felt it push inside me, push past my tightness and become slowly sheathed by my wetness. Now I was used to his dick, ready for every sensation it gave me, craved it when I didn't have it. I felt the breath leave my lungs as I gasped.

He let out a quiet moan when he was buried inside me, like the sensation was just as addictive for him. His big hands squeezed me hard, and he pushed up with his hips, inching a little deeper inside me.

My hand dug into his hair, and I pressed my lips to his, ignited by that heat that seared our closed mouths. I'd only kissed him once, and it was fire, fire that got me to melt into a puddle on the floor.

He abruptly turned his head away and ended the kiss.

My body turned still, unsure what I'd done to warrant his rejection.

"I told you I would only do it once." His head turned back to me, his eyes still deep in arousal.

It took me a moment to understand what he was saying, to understand exactly what he'd meant that night.

He didn't kiss whores.

And I was a whore.

It shouldn't surprise me. Not the first time I'd heard that. It shouldn't hurt me…but it did. I wasn't sure why.

His eyes flicked back and forth between mine, his fingers still deep in my flesh.

As if I was paralyzed, I didn't know what to do.

The moment was over—at least for me.

"It's nothing personal," he said quietly, trying to coax me back into the passion.

I forced my head back into the moment, to fulfill the job that was required of me. Because that's what it was. Just a job…and nothing more. "Trust me… I know it's not."

Hugo knocked before he entered my room. "Mr. Beaufort would like you to join him for dinner."

I continued to read. "I'm not hungry."

"He didn't ask if you were hungry. He didn't ask you anything, actually. He told you to join him for dinner. Do so, or I'll have to return, and we both know how unpleasant my company can be." He walked out and shut the door.

I gave an annoyed sigh before I shut my book and headed downstairs. Cauldron was in the grand dining room, sitting at the head of the table with floral center-pieces down the middle like he was expecting to entertain. His eyes immediately moved to me when I entered the room, a glass of red wine in front of him.

I took the seat on his left and immediately snatched the bottle to fill my wineglass.

He stared at the side of my face, his eyes hot.

"What?" I asked, not looking at him.

"You're angry."

"Not angry." I took a drink, recognizing the hint of citrus.

"I told you it wasn't personal."

"And that's fine."

"If it's fine, why won't you look at me?"

I forced my stare on him, feigning indifference. "There. Is that better?"

He held my gaze, a subtle shift in his eyes as he took in my appearance. "I'm not sure what you expect of me."

"I expect nothing—as I should have done in the first place."

His arms went to the armrests, and he relaxed in his chair. After a long moment of holding my gaze, he spoke. "Talk to me."

"I thought my feelings didn't matter?" I snapped. "Why would I tell you a damn thing when you've made it perfectly clear I mean nothing? Less than nothing?" The words flew out of my mouth like fireballs. I was livid, with him as well as myself.

He held my stare and didn't react. "I shouldn't have said that—because they do matter."

My eyes were rigidly glued to his face because I couldn't believe he'd said that. It was the first decent thing he'd ever said to me. "I just don't like feeling this way, like I don't matter. I thought I'd left that life behind, but now I realize I can never escape it. Sometimes I forget my predicament, forget our arrangement, but then I'm cruelly reminded that I am a whore…and I'll probably die a whore. I'll never be anything more… a wife or a mother." My eyes drifted away, caught up in the sadness.

Cauldron stared for a long time, as if he didn't know what to say. "I know Grave. Give it enough time, and he'll move on to some other shiny toy. He'll forget about you, and then you can pursue the life you want."

"You may know him, but you don't know him the way I do." I gave a shake of my head. "Even if he does find someone else, the instant he realizes I'm available, he'll come right back. If I marry someone, he'll kill him. He'll kill my children too. I'm his as far as he's concerned."

"You're mine now, and he knows that."

My heart gave a shudder as I stared.

"You will be free of him someday."

His words gave me no solace because he had no idea of what he spoke.

"I know you're used to men growing attached. Infatuated. Obsessed. Falling in love. Don't expect that from me because it'll never happen. I suspect that's why you're offended, because a man has only wanted more from you, not less. You need to understand my indifference isn't personal. I'm just not wired that way."

Was that why I was offended? My ego? "Why is that?"

He grabbed his glass and swirled it gently. I'd expected an answer of silence, but miraculously, he actually answered. "I'm just incapable of deeper feelings. Always been that way."

"A woman broke your heart." It was the only explanation. He'd loved a woman—and she'd shattered him.

He stared into his glass. "I guess that's true. But not in the way you assume."

My eyes narrowed.

"My mother was raped, tortured, and murdered." He said it all matter-of-factly, like it was no big deal, ancient history. He finally took a drink before he set the glass back on the table.

A moment of shock gripped me. I was so still I forgot to breathe for a few seconds. It was a heavy confession, so heavy I wasn't sure how to react to it. Finally, something came to me. "I…I'm sorry."

He took another drink.

"When did this—"

"The details aren't up for discussion. Just be grateful I shared what I have. It's something I don't mention to anyone."

I stared at the side of his face, seeing no sign of harbored pain.

The silence stretched between us.

I had so many more questions, questions that would just anger him.

After another drink of wine, he turned to me. "What about you?"

"What about me?" I whispered, my voice subdued now that I knew he'd lost someone he cared about.

"I'm assuming your parents are no longer in the picture."

"My mom was really young when she had me, so my dad excused himself from the responsibility. She raised me on her own...single mom." Her smile would forever live in my heart. I still saw it in my dreams, heard the way she laughed. "She was my best friend."

He stared with kind eyes, as if this was the first time he could relate to me. "What happened to her?"

Sometimes the memories were too much. They hit me like a fly against the windshield, guts splattering everywhere. Just like him, I didn't want to discuss the details, relive those horrible months. "She got sick…"

His eyes narrowed slightly, almost imperceptibly.

"I'd just become a legal adult when she passed, so I was on my own after that. Hence my line of work…"

There was a depth to his eyes that possessed no bottom. It continued forevermore, his soul across the universe. Absolutely still, he absorbed those words with a hard expression. "I'm sorry."

"I know."

His eyes narrowed a little farther, turning guarded.

I'd rejected his dinner invitation because his presence was unbearable at times, but this evening had been different, had shed light on the darkest part of his soul. Contrary to what he said, he could feel, feel the same range of emotions I could.

"You never considered going to your father for help?"

At that moment, Hugo entered with our first course. A soup. Steam wafted from the surface, but we both ignored it.

When he departed the dining room, I answered. "No. He hadn't been a part of our lives then, so why should he be now? Besides, I wouldn't even have known how to find him at the time anyway. My mother left me the house, but without a way to pay for it, I lost it to fore-closure. I had a lot more stuff on my plate."

His attention was fully focused on me. The hot soup turned cold. His glass of wine was untouched. The bread in the center of the table was ignored. He rubbed his palm across his jawline then down the stubble at the top of his neck.

"Anyway…that's my life story."

"Have you enjoyed your profession? Or did you despise it the entire time?" He grabbed his spoon and took a bite, his eyes on the bowl in front of him.

For the first time, we were enjoying a real conversation, and I wanted it to last. "I know there's a stigma around it, but it was definitely preferable to other lines of work. I was well compensated, and I actually liked some of my clients. You know, young, rich, and handsome, like you."

His face remained hard despite the compliment.

"But I was young, no regard to my future. Once I realized what I really wanted in life, I knew this job was no
longer feasible. No way I could ever find the love of my
life if I was still fucking men for money." I felt a very
real fear that my past would forever compromise my
future, that if I was lucky enough to find a man I loved,
he would never love me once he learned the truth. "I
still might not find the love of my life because I used to
fuck men for money."

"I don't see why it would be an issue."

I finally took a few bites of my soup, which was now
lukewarm. "You're used to the lifestyle. Most men
aren't."

"The past belongs in the past, and if a man can't live in
the present with you, then he's not the right man for
you. If a man can't forget about your old lovers, or if
he's too weak to make you forget about them, then he's
also not the right man for you."

FIFTEEN

CAULDRON

The car pulled up to the restaurant, and once the driver opened the door for me, I walked right past the hostess podium as if I knew exactly where I was going.

Because I did.

I headed to the rear, the private room large enough to accommodate a party of fifty people, but now it had one lone table in the center, big enough for two. The chatter from the main room died away once I crossed the threshold.

He sat there alone, his eyes on me like he'd been watching the door for the last hour.

An hour because I was purposely late by an hour.

I lowered myself into the chair and enjoyed the irritated look deep in his visage. He tried to cover it as best he could, but his eyes were permanently scarred by his anger. The bottle of wine was open, so I poured myself a glass.

Silence.

Muffled conversations from the other room.

The distant sound of the violin and the cello.

He finally spoke. "You're unsurprised to see me."

I took a drink and wiped the remains with my thumb. "Micah is more loyal to me than you realize."

One arm rested on the white tablecloth. A single white rose was in the vase between us. It would look like we were on a date if the tension weren't thicker than humid summer air. He dismissed what I said by taking a drink.

"But I came anyway because I know this conversation needs to be had. Now say your piece so we can part ways and never speak again."

His fingers rested on the stem of the glass, his fingers rotating it on the white tablecloth. His dark eyes were focused on me, the cogs in his brain turning to figure out how he would play this. "You've had your fun. You've tortured me. Now give her back."

I took another drink.

"She means nothing to you."

"I wouldn't say that."

His eyes narrowed. "Then what is she to you?"

I gave a shrug. "A very good lay."

The wineglass halted on the table. It looked as if he might snap the stem with his fingertips. "What do you want, Cauldron? There must be something."

I gave another shrug. "I already have everything—especially now that I have her."

"A favor. I can do something for you, no questions asked."

"Unlike you, I do my own dirty work."

His hand left the glass entirely, like he knew a shard was about to impale his hand if he weren't careful. "I'm prepared to make this bloody if I have to."

"You mean you've grown some balls? Good for you."

A quick tremor shot through his body, making the veins stand out on his forehead. It was probably tempting to break that glass and stab me with it, but then there would be a retaliation, and we would both bleed to death in that restaurant. "She's to be my wife, the mother of my children, and I won't sit back while she's held captive against her will."

"Held captive against her will?" I asked incredulously, releasing a loud laugh. "Oh, trust me, she's not being forced to do anything…"

Ferocity burned in his eyes.

"She can walk away whenever she wants. She's the one who chooses to stay."

"She feels nothing for you—"

"It didn't seem that way last night—"

"*I'll fucking kill you.*" He threw the bottle of wine at the wall, where it shattered. Red liquid stained the white walls and splattered the white tablecloths stacked on the banquette along the wall.

I didn't flinch. Relaxed as ever, I remained in my chair and started drumming my fingers on the table. "I liked that wine."

He straightened his jacket. "Then you can lick it off the floor."

"Or I can lick it off—"

"I swear to fucking god." He gripped the table like he was going to throw that against the wall too. "Give her back to me, or you'll regret it."

I hadn't had this much fun in a long time. My fingers continued to drum on the table as I looked bored. But inside, I was grinning like the devil. I had the one thing he wanted more than anything, and I would exploit that to no end. "No."

"Then I'll take her from you—"

"She doesn't want you."

"She doesn't want you either—"

"Like every other woman I've been with, she's wrapped around my finger." I rose to my feet and smoothed out the front of my shirt with my palm. "She wants my dick as much as she wants my name. I've made her forget every other man she's been with—especially you."

With veins popping in his neck and skin the color of a ripe tomato, he was fuming. There was too much rage to channel into his movements. He didn't know if he wanted to smash my skull with a plate or pin me underneath the table. But whatever he decided, there would be consequences, and that was the only thing that steadied his hand. His breaths grew labored, pissed off but hurt at the same time.

Hurt that the woman he loved preferred me to him.

Revenge was so fucking sweet.

He could try to take her back, but what would be the point if she loved me instead of him?

I watched the hurt dance across his face, as if I'd fired a bullet made of sorrow.

He lost his temper and flipped the table to the side. Dishes crashed on the floor. The vase with the white rose shattered. Restaurant staff didn't come to check on the commotion, the music from the main room too loud. He stormed off, leaving me in the wreckage of his childish tantrum.

I took my seat once again—and smiled.

SIXTEEN

CAMILLE

In my leggings and a sports bra, I stepped into the on-site gym, a separate building on the grounds. Most of the walls were made of glass, and the back wall was a large sliding glass door that opened entirely to reveal the grounds.

Cauldron was there, lifting a bar stacked with heavy weights toward the sky before he lowered it back to his chest. He did a set of ten before he re-racked the bar and lay there, his bare chest shiny with sweat. He gave himself a minute to catch his breath before he benched over two hundred pounds ten times and returned the bar above his head. Then he sat up, his muscled back facing me. He wiped the sweat from his face with the white towel then rubbed the back of his neck.

I could see his back in greater detail than before because the sweat made every groove shine with a distinct reflection. Massive shoulders led to a strong back then narrow hips. He was in loose shorts and his workout shoes, looking out to the open grounds as he evened out his breathing. He seemed to be finished because he stood up and grabbed the bar so he could do biceps curls next.

He didn't notice me.

After he did his curls, he moved the bar to the back of his neck and did squats, his large body carrying the weight with fatigue but also strength. His form was perfect, his breathing irregular as he pushed his body to conquer his workout.

I was supposed to do some cardio, but I found myself thoroughly entertained.

He finally racked the bar, his shiny chest facing me, all the muscles plump and tight from his workout. His eyes lifted and locked on mine without a hint of surprise, either because he already knew I was there or he didn't care. His eyes made a quick glance at my tight little clothing before he grabbed the towel and wiped his face. "What are you doing in here?"

"You aren't the only one who needs to stay in shape."

He grabbed his bottle of water and took a drink, spilling a bit down his neck and chest.

I could watch him all day.

He wiped himself off with the towel again then came toward me, the little shorts low on his hips, a subtle happy trail down the center of his flat stomach. His arms were as big as my head, all the veins popping out of the tight skin. When he came to my room in the evenings to be serviced, it was usually dark and there was too much going on for me just to stare, but now I could see him clearly, bright in the sunshine. He flipped his towel over the back of his neck as he looked down at me. "Want me to spot you?" His chin was tilted down to look at me, his lips close to mine as if he might kiss me—even though I knew that would never happen.

"I'm more of a cardio kind of girl."

"Really?" His hand reached for me, his big fingers full of one of my cheeks. "Your ass fooled me." He gave it a smack before he headed to the door, six-foot-something of pure masculine sexiness.

I watched him until he was out of sight, thinking about that tight ass as soon as it was gone.

"I've packed most of your essentials, but here's another suitcase if there's anything else you'd like to bring." Hugo rolled the suitcase into my chambers and set it near the couch.

"Bring where?" I asked, dumbfounded by this announcement.

"Mr. Beaufort hasn't told you?"

"Does it look like I'm in the know?"

He gave a gloating smile. "I should have assumed." Without answering, he walked out of my bedroom.

"Dick." I pulled out my phone and texted Cauldron. *Where are we going?*

The three dots appeared immediately. *On the yacht.*

On the yacht? Did that mean there would be other women there? *Business or pleasure?*

For tax purposes, business. But it's always pleasure.

You don't seem like the kind of man who pays taxes.

Trust me, I don't.

I packed the rest of my things in the suitcase Hugo had provided me then made my way downstairs, in jean shorts and a white blouse that tied up above my belly button. A sun hat sat on my head, and I had my shades hooked in the V in my top.

The guys took my luggage and packed it in the back then I sat in the second row.

Cauldron wasn't there.

Under the shade of one of the large trees, we sat for nearly thirty minutes, waiting for the man of the hour.

He finally emerged, in blue shorts and a black t-shirt, every inch of his body perfectly chiseled with all those hours in the gym. His eyes were hidden behind his shades, and the seriousness of his expression made him look like he was going to the office rather than on a vacation.

We drove off once he was inside, and he immediately worked on his phone for the entire drive. Sometimes he made me feel like the only person in the room, and other times it seemed like he forgot I was there at all.

When we pulled up to the harbor, I asked the question that was on my mind. "Will your girls be joining us?"

He finished typing up his message before he looked at me, sunglasses still on the bridge of his nose.

I waited for an answer.

There wasn't one.

The doors opened, and we were escorted up the ramp to the enormous yacht that was several floors, far too big for a single bachelor. It was much bigger than the average dream home and required a crew of twelve to undertake a voyage.

It was the first time I'd stepped on to his ship as a guest instead of a stowaway. The luggage was stored in our bedrooms, and the ship was prepared to depart. I half expected others to join us, pretty girls in string bikinis who were getting paid just to have a good time, but no one ever showed up.

It was just the two of us.

I took a seat in the seating area at the front of the boat, and the second I sat down, waiters brought everything I could ever want, from a cheese board with delicate French cheeses to chocolate strawberries and cured prosciutto. There was Cristal champagne and cucumber water in a pitcher. All I had to do was sit there and watch them serve me like I was the one that ordered the feast.

The yacht departed from the dock, and Cauldron emerged thirty minutes later in his black swim trunks, his tanned skin already glowing under the sunshine. He took a seat beside me and skipped the champagne and went straight to the hard stuff.

"It's noon."

He added a few ice cubes and ignored what I said. He leaned back, his arm over the back of the couch, his eyes on the bright-blue ocean ahead. Other yachts were in the water, most of them much smaller than his. He ran his fingers through his hair and took another drink.

"So, it's just the two of us?" I'd waited for more people to board the ship, but it never happened.

"Yes."

"And what will we do on this voyage?"

"The usual. Fucking. Drinking."

"And eating?"

He took another drink. "You can do that for the both of us."

"Ha. I don't think you'd like my ass so much if I did."

"You're wrong about that." He set down his glass and grabbed a cigar. He had a lighter in his pocket, so he put the tip in his mouth and scraped his thumb over the dial so the flame would emerge.

"Nuh-uh, I don't think so." I snatched the cigar out of his mouth and tossed it back on the table.

The flame still burned in his hand as he turned to regard me. The sunglasses hid the thoughts in his eyes, but I could tell he didn't appreciate that stunt. He reached for the cigar again.

This time, I smacked it out of his hand. "None of this shit."

"What the fuck did you just say to me?" He raised his voice, loud over the waves that hit the hull of the ship below.

"I hate smelling it on your breath. And your clothes. Even your skin."

"Am I supposed to care about that?"

"Not to mention, it's bad for your health."

"Definitely don't care about that."

"Well, I do."

Instead of reaching for the cigar again, he stared at me, a sigh escaping his clenched jaw. He tossed the lighter onto the table then grabbed his drink again. He sat back, knees apart, and watched his yacht conquer the calm ocean.

I made myself a plate of snacks, a little self-conscious that he never ate anything while I devoured everything in sight. With my legs tucked under my ass, I enjoyed everything, from the crystallized oranges to the chocolate-covered almonds.

In silence, he stared at the ocean, perfectly content not saying a word.

I eyed the side of his face, his jaw clean because he'd shaved that morning. I liked the stubble, but I liked the fresh look too. It highlighted the strong bones of his jaw, the way its sharpness created a distinct shadow down his neck. "Have you ever done this before?"

He finished off his glass before he set it on the table. "Done what?"

"Brought just one woman on your yacht?"

"No. But don't feel special."

"Hard not to."

He looked forward again and ignored what I said. "I'll be working like normal. Nothing is different, except the location. I have a business meeting in a few days, so that's the real reason we're out here."

"On a boat?" I asked incredulously.

"Yes."

"Um…how does that work?"

"It's how rich men prefer to do business."

"It seems awfully inconvenient."

"Not if you want to stay off the grid."

"And why would you want to stay off the grid?"

He pushed his sunglasses up to expose his eyes, and he turned to look at me like he was annoyed with my slowness. "It's impossible to be traced out to sea, so if a deal's going down, no one can put out a hit."

"A hit?"

"You know, kill everyone and take the money." He looked forward again. "Looks like Grave shielded you pretty good."

"He didn't include me in that part of his life."

"You just stayed home?"

"Pretty much."

He gave a subtle nod.

"Honestly, I'm not even sure what he does for a living. It's criminal, I've gauged that."

"All rich men are criminals."

"I don't know about that…"

"Even if they earn an honest living, they don't pay taxes, which makes them a criminal. Trust me, when you're at this caliber, there's only temptation and no accountability. No reason to follow the law when the law doesn't apply to you."

"Do you know how he earns his money?"

He gave a nod.

"Drugs?"

"You don't want to know, Camille."

I'd slept beside that man every night for years, and I didn't know him at all. I'd been with Cauldron a short time, but I felt like I knew him so much better…even though I didn't know anything about him either.

I was dead asleep when I felt it.

Exquisite pleasure between my legs. Precise pressure against my sex. Hot breaths. Sharp stubble from thick facial hair. My thighs instinctively squeezed, feeling a head between my soft limbs. "God…" My back arched on its own, and my hips curled for me to press myself farther into his powerful mouth.

My eyes hadn't opened and I was still half asleep, but that made it feel even better. Every touch was unexpected, made my toes curl. My fingers reached for his hair, and I dug into the strands, my ankles locked around his head.

His tongue circled me harder, making me whimper and writhe.

When he pulled away, my thighs squeezed him tighter to lock him in place.

He had to grab my knees and force them apart. "Don't worry, sweetheart." His narrow hips separated my thighs as he shoved my nightshirt up to my chin to expose my tits. "Not going anywhere." His deep voice was quiet, barely above a whisper, but commanded so much authority without effort.

My eyes broke through the stickiness of my lids to crack open, seeing the darkness around me. It was easy to forget I was sleeping in a boat because the ship hardly rocked in the waves. His face slowly came into view, directly over mine, his eyes predatory. Then I felt it, his size push right into me.

I gave a jerk when I felt him hit me deep. My hands instinctively reached out and latched on to his muscular biceps as I gave an incoherent moan, my mind still partially asleep. His slender wrists hooked behind my knees, and he folded them into me, a moan so subtle issuing from his hard mouth that I wasn't sure if I'd dreamed it.

His thrusts started slow and even, his eyes locked on mine from above. His muscles were thick and tight from holding his body over me, but he didn't look remotely exerted. His slowness faded, his thrusts hitting me harder and deeper once he knew I was ready for it.

I was pinned to the bed, and he took me harder, his eyes looking down on me with ownership. His breathing deepened as he pounded into me, bringing our bodies closer together as he forced himself fully inside me.

My moans started off as quiet whispers, but they quickly progressed to something deeper and louder. My nails dug into his skin like anchors, and I felt the deep pull inside my core, the way everything tightened toward my center. When my breathing hitched as if the air had left my lungs, I knew it had hit me. The heat took control, pulled me into a fire that burned me from the inside out. Incoherent moans, digging nails, tight squeezes, it all happened together.

And he watched the whole thing.

My hips flexed, my back arched, my entire body writhed against him, my mind still caught in the tendrils of sleep. It was so good that it took my breath away, gave my body a wave of pleasure followed by one of numbness.

Fully inside me, he ground his hips, not wanting to pull out because he was so close to the finish. He came with a deep groan, similar to the masculine grunts he made lifting heavy things in the gym. Everything stopped when he felt his release. Our breaths, our movements, everything seized.

Then it all came back slowly. As he breathed his winded breaths, he looked down at me, that same intensity on his face as when we started. He pulled out of me and released my knees before he moved off.

Once my body relaxed, I felt the strain from being folded like an origami paper. I gave a sigh once my body came loose again, but my core was still tight from the aftershocks of pleasure. It all felt like a dream.

Without saying a word, he walked out of my cabin buck naked.

When I turned over to look at the clock on the night-stand, I saw the time.

It was 2:03 a.m.

When I stepped into my cabin, I found the black dress on the bed, along with the jewelry he wanted me to wear. Diamond earrings were in one box, and a heavy diamond necklace was in the other. I'd spent the day sunbathing on the deck while Cauldron was cooped up in his study. Now my skin had a deep glow, a beautiful tan unlike any I'd ever had in my life. I examined the dress, which had open slits across the abdomen and underneath the breasts.

I immediately knew the purpose of the business meeting.

I was on the clock.

I showered and washed off all the tanning oil then did my hair big and nice and my makeup dark, the way Cauldron preferred. Then I carefully put the necklace around my throat, feeling the weight the second I secured the clasp. The diamond in the center was like a heavy rock on the side of the road. The earrings came next, so large they hid my lobes entirely.

The dress was so scandalous that I couldn't wear a bra, so I did what every other woman did before they went to the club—taped down my nipples. After I checked my appearance in the mirror, I stepped into the hallway and approached the deck.

It was almost sunset, the blue water growing calm with the setting sun. The sky was a mild blue, slowly transitioning into the pinks and purples. The seating area with white cushions that I had occupied early in the day had been transformed for a business meeting, booze and cigars on the table, Cauldron sitting alone in a black t-shirt and jeans. The only time he ever got dressed up was when he went to a fancy party with a dress code.

I walked across the deck and approached him.

His mind seemed to be elsewhere because his eyes were focused on the horizon, his features rigid with concentration. His body was shifted forward, elbows on his knees, the vices on the table ignored.

When I came into his vision, he finally shifted his eyes to look at me. The stare lasted for only one second, but it was enough to show his approval. It was practically a glance, but the intensity was so focused it was like a laser from a sniper's rifle.

I took the seat beside him. "Do boats drive in the dark?"

His eyes were on the horizon again. "No."

"Then how are they going to get here?"

He didn't need to answer because the hum of the rotors became audible. A dark spot appeared on the horizon then drew closer, the silhouette of a chopper more apparent.

"Where's he going to land?"

Cauldron ignored the chopper and looked straight ahead.

The wind picked up, blowing my hair all over the place and scattering everything on the table. The staff immediately ran forward to gather everything that toppled over onto the deck. Slowly, the black chopper lowered until it landed on the top level of the yacht.

Never seen that before.

The engine was killed, and the rotor blades finally stopped. All the chaos died away. The staff corrected everything and then assisted the visitors to the yacht.

Cauldron opened the decanter and poured himself a glass of scotch.

I'd never met anyone who drank like him. He tolerated a potent amount of alcohol without becoming intoxicated. Or he was always drunk, and I just couldn't tell.

He took a drink before he got to his feet.

I did the same.

A heavyset man in a pinstriped suit walked across the deck, swinging his arms unnecessarily, lacking the tight posture that Cauldron exuded. A bushy moustache hid most of his upper lip from view, and he had a fat neck that glistened with a hint of sweat. He came around the seating area and approached Cauldron with his hand extended. "Cauldron Beaufort, we finally meet."

Cauldron shook his hand wordlessly.

His accent wasn't French. It was Afrikaans, which explained why the chopper came from the south. Must have come from a yacht that was parked somewhere off the northern coast of Africa.

The man glanced at me next, looking at everything except the diamonds I showcased. His dark eyes were innately creepy, telling me he was a real monster, not the kind I once assumed Cauldron to be.

We all took a seat.

The man lit up a cigar first and then poured himself a glass of booze. He took a puff then a drink. "These are them?" He took a deep puff then let the smoke explode in a cloud before it was carried on the wind.

"Yes." Cauldron grabbed his glass and took a drink.

I wasn't a fan of hard liquor, so I just sat there.

The man looked at me again. Not the diamonds. Me.

No pleasantries were exchanged. No small talk. Criminals got straight down to business because there was no such thing as ass-kissing in their world. Networking wasn't a social transaction, but a financial one.

The man continued to smoke.

Cauldron didn't light up. Wasn't sure if it was because of me or not.

The man hadn't taken his eyes off me. Not once. Kept drilling into me like I wasn't wearing that black dress. "I'll give them a go."

What did that mean?

"I don't loan my diamonds," Cauldron said quietly.

"I wasn't asking you to." He gave a gesture with his hand. "Take off the dress."

Both of my eyebrows jumped up my face. "Excuse me?"

"I want to see how they look on bare skin." A grotesque smile moved across his face. "Want to see how they dance in the light when I'm fucking you."

What?!

He got to his feet and extended his hand. "Come on, baby."

"*Baby?* How about I shove this diamond up your ass, fucker?"

He wasn't the least bit intimidated, judging by the way he laughed uproariously. "You like them feisty, huh? Got some ropes for me to borrow?"

Ropes? What a worthless piece of shit.

He moved forward and reached for my wrist.

Cauldron got to his feet. "She's not part of the deal, Hector."

Damn right, I'm not.

"If she's wearing the diamonds, she is." His eyes lingered on one of the slits in my dress, seeing the bare skin.

I unclasped the necklace and set it on the table then did the same to the earrings. "There." I sat back down and crossed my legs, feeling violated even though he hadn't touched me.

Cauldron remained standing. "Let's talk numbers."

"Numbers?" Hector finally stopped gawking at me and looked at Cauldron. "You shouldn't negotiate with a man who's hungry. Only when he has a full belly. And right now, my belly is empty." He looked back at me again.

"Doesn't look empty to me," I spat.

Finally, his smile dropped.

"This has been a misunderstanding." Cauldron remained calm the entire time, not the least bit ruffled by this man's disgusting behavior. "Camille's only purpose in this conversation is to showcase the diamonds."

"Misunderstanding?" He looked at Cauldron again. "You've let me use one of your girls before."

"Not this one."

Hector was like a child. The more Cauldron said no, the more he wanted me. "You want me to give you a number? Give me her first."

Cauldron didn't flinch. "No."

"You really want to lose this sale over a whore?"

Cauldron met his stare. "I don't need your money, Hector. If you don't want to lose these diamonds, you better get your shit together. Or leave—doesn't make a difference to me. And she's not my whore. She's my lover."

That was the wrong thing to say because Hector reached behind him and pulled out a gun.

I gasped.

Cauldron moved in front of me, the gun aimed at his chest. Fearlessly, he looked at the man who held him at gunpoint. "Your stupidity just cost you an additional five million dollars. Push me, and it'll go up to ten."

He had a gun pointed at him, and he was negotiating.

"I know how much you want these diamonds, Hector. Your wife's birthday is coming up."

Another pig…of course.

Hector lowered the gun and returned it to the back of his pants.

Cauldron moved quicker than I could see, throwing a punch and sending Hector to the floor.

I gasped again, not expecting it.

Hector blacked out for a second, and that was enough time for Cauldron to remove the gun and point it at his face.

Hector opened his eyes, staring straight down the barrel.

"Don't fuck with me." Cauldron pointed the gun at his shoulder and pulled the trigger.

Hector let out a howl and gripped his arm, clenching his jaw tight in agony.

Cauldron righted himself and returned to his seat, the gun still in his hand.

I watched the blood drip all over the deck. When Hector sat up, he got it on the white cushions. He continued to put pressure on the wound, but it was gushing everywhere.

Cauldron made no move to help him.

He winced as he sat down, his palm flat against the gushing wound. "Fucking asshole…"

"You want the diamonds or not?"

He was seething in pain, breathing hard and breaking out in a noticeable sweat. Now he didn't stare at me at all.

How do you like that, bitch?

After a couple breaths, he gave a nod.

"Good." Cauldron waved his men over.

The laptop was placed in front of him, and after he typed in some information, the laptop was turned to Hector.

He took much longer to enter the information, getting blood all over the keys in the process. One of the guys presented gauze and wrapped up his wound underneath his shirt to reduce the loss of blood.

When Cauldron took the laptop back, he entered in some kind of passcode and read the information on the screen. "Funds have been transferred. Congratulations, Hector." The men boxed up the diamonds and escorted Hector back to his helicopter.

Cauldron didn't turn to watch him leave. He refilled his glass and took another drink, unaffected by all the blood that had spilled across his immaculate white cushions.

I was still disturbed by the whole thing. A gun had been pointed at me momentarily. "Is that how your business deals usually go down?"

"He's just an idiot."

"Why didn't you have a gun?"

"I've never needed one. No one has ever been that stupid." He dropped a few ice cubes into his glass, shook it, and then took a drink.

As if the meeting had never taken place, he looked exactly the same as before Hector arrived. "I was surprised you stood in front of me like that."

"Why?"

"Uh, because he had a gun?"

"Hector would never shoot me. But he wouldn't hesitate to shoot you." He took a drink. "If he can't have you, then he'll kill you so no one else can."

"Real mature."

"You'll never have to see him again. Our business relationship is finished."

"You still sold him the diamonds."

"Because they're tainted now."

"Tainted?"

"Diamonds absorb light and reflect it as prisms. According to African legend, they absorb other things too. Blood. Evil. Bad energy…all kinds of things. Wouldn't want to sell them to someone else at this point."

He was such a callused man it seemed unlikely he would believe in bedtime stories. "And you believe that?"

"So what if I do?" He set the glass down and turned to me.

I gave a minuscule flinch when he looked at me head on, unprepared for the intensity of his gaze. Hector's creepy stare was easy to combat, but this look…it made me feel weaker than I ever had.

"So what if I do?" he repeated, challenging me.

The stare was too difficult to hold, so I looked away. "Why did you tell him that?"

I heard the ice cubes tap against the glass as he took a drink. Heard the way they clinked against the sides when he gave it a swirl. "Tell him what?"

"That I'm not your whore."

"You told me never to call you that."

I lifted my chin and looked at him, surprised he would honor that request when he owed me nothing.

"And a whore accepts money. You accept nothing."

"I accept protection."

"Even if you didn't need it, would you leave?"

Unsure if it was a real question or a rhetorical one, I just stared.

"You wouldn't."

"I would leave and start my own life…"

He stared at me long and hard. "I don't think you would."

SEVENTEEN

CAULDRON

We docked the yacht and returned to normal life at my Cap-Ferrat estate. I was holed up in my study, badmouthing Hector every chance I got. Made sure the world knew what happened when you crossed me.

A bullet to the shoulder was just the beginning.

After I hit the gym first thing in the morning, I worked in my study all day, Hugo coming by several times to refill my coffee and bring lunch. My business was in another country, so I spent a lot of my time on video calls to stay abreast of the work being done there. I could move to Botswana instead, but France had always been my home. I was a Frenchman—and I preferred to stay that way.

When the sun had set and the heat had receded, I left the house and played poker with some friends in the back of one of the restaurants they owned, then came home smelling of booze and cigars.

Camille wouldn't like that.

That didn't stop me from walking into her bedroom for our nighttime ritual.

She was sprawled on the couch, her feet up on the opposite armrest. She was in little pajama shorts, and her skin had a deep glow from our days out to sea. My eyes followed her sexy long legs to her long-sleeved sweater, which was bunched up at the front, revealing a little bit of her skin and her belly button piercing. Her blond hair was over the armrest, and she held a paperback in her hand, something she must have taken off the bookshelf.

Just looking at her turned me on.

The hair. The pink color of her toenails. The way she looked even more beautiful without makeup. Even her attitude, which was in full flex right now because it was almost ten in the evening and she was winding down.

She shut the book with a distinct thud. "Haven't seen you in a while."

I came around the couch, barefoot and shirtless, just in my sweatpants with nothing underneath. I lifted her slender legs and took a seat before I returned them across my lap. My fingers felt the smoothness of her skin, even let a finger graze over one of her bright toenails. "Been busy."

She sat up and came closer to me, leaning sideways into the back cushions. Soon, her nose scrunched up, and her eyes flashed in disappointment. "Busy drinking and smoking…"

I continued to feel her legs, cracking a slight smile. "You weren't kidding."

"It's so disgusting."

"You'll fuck me anyway."

"Maybe if I face the other way."

My eyes moved to her face because that suggestion was perfectly acceptable.

She caught my look, and the second we made contact, she stiffened, intimidated or uncomfortable.

Maybe both.

I left the couch and moved to the bed, dropping my bottoms along the way. I lay flat and propped myself up on a pillow, my large dick against my stomach.

She left the couch and stared at me, feigning indifference when she was anything but. The sweater was pulled over her head, catching some of her hair in a sexy way. Then her little bottoms were pushed down her long legs, revealing a black thong.

Fuck.

She teased me and took her time, knowing exactly when to make me ache and for how long. Her thumbs hooked under the fabric, and she pushed them down, bending over as she got them off. When she stood upright, her pussy was perfectly groomed, always ready to take the stage.

I sat up against the headboard, my back cushioned by the pillows she'd left untouched on her side of the bed. Without direction, she straddled my hips, facing the opposite way, her peach of an ass right in my face. She tilted her hips, slipped my thickness inside, and then sank.

My fingertips dug into her hips once I felt myself push inside, giving an uncontrollable moan because she always felt so damn good. Wasn't sure how I ever forgot.

She arched her back, her feet tucked close into my sides, and she started to rock her hips in the sexiest way, taking me in all the way before releasing me and doing it again. It was her shining moment, showing me how she earned her premium status.

My hands moved to her tiny waist and guided her faster, setting the pace that I liked, my eyes hypnotized by that fine ass. Her bleached asshole looked right at me. With every rock, I felt the pull in my stomach, wanting to blow my load before she even got started.

She was just so damn hot.

My breathing turned uneven almost immediately, breaths shaky and weak. My dick ached for release, my balls tightening against my body because they were ready to explode. My hands had to slow her down because it was all too much.

Like a horse responding to the pull on the reins, she did as I asked. "Come inside me."

I closed my eyes because it took all my strength not to.

"I know you want to."

I clenched my jaw tight because I didn't want it to end. I felt like a teenager who couldn't conduct himself with a woman. But any man with an ass like this in his face would be in the same predicament.

Against my wishes, she rocked her hips faster, plunging my dick into her creaminess over and over. I could see it build up around the base of my dick and right behind the grooves of the head.

"Come."

That was the trigger that made me come undone. I closed my eyes briefly as the pleasure started at my stomach and moved down my length. It exploded from my tip, pumping all my desire right into the object of my affection. With a loud groan, I finished, her beautiful ass still right in front of me.

She sat back, right on my dick, and looked at me over her shoulder. "I've never had a man last longer than a minute when I do that."

The anger came out of nowhere, having the bite of a snake. "Don't talk about other men with me." My dick was still hard inside her, coated in our mutual arousal.

Her eyes remained locked on mine. A breath passed between us. She didn't know what to say.

I pushed her off me, making her back hit the mattress, her feet toward the headboard.

I was on her instantly, my hips separating her knees and thighs, my dick burrowing its way back inside her once more.

She inhaled a deep breath in surprise, her palms flattening against my chest.

With one hand fisted into the back of her hair, I took her roughly on the sheets, fucking her like I hadn't had her in weeks. With every thrust, I claimed her as mine, made her forget the men she teased, the men who used to pay for her services.

She was mine now.

EIGHTEEN
CAMILLE

Outfits were given to me out of thin air. Hugo would lay a new dress across the back of the couch with matching shoes and the jewelry Cauldron wanted me to wear, and I was expected to put it on for whatever event we had that night. Tonight, it was a dark blue dress with a single strap. It was a cocktail dress, tight on my waist and hugging my hips so perfectly it seemed tailored.

We got into the car and left, Cauldron in a gray button-down shirt and black trousers. As with the rest of his clothes, he filled it out perfectly, his shoulders and arms stretching the material. He rolled the sleeves up to his elbows, showing all the cords down his forearms.

"Where are we going?"

"A friend has invited me to dinner."

"When you say 'friend,' do you mean customer?"

He kept his eyes out the window. "No."

The jewelry he'd given me was much more discreet than the usual diamonds he had me wear. It complemented my outfit appropriately.

We pulled up to the house fifteen minutes later. It was just like Cauldron's, like all billionaires'. After a while, all the properties looked the same. We were escorted inside then came face-to-face with the owner of the house. "Cauldron, it's lovely to see you." He shook his hand.

"You too, Oscar." After he shook Oscar's hand, he moved his arm around my waist.

I nearly jumped because he'd never touched me like that before.

"This is my girlfriend, Camille."

His girlfriend? I snapped out of it and shook Oscar's hand. "You have a lovely home."

Oscar smiled at me before he introduced his wife, Martine, who was twenty years younger and super-model status. She was nice, giving me a kiss on each cheek and a genuine smile. We were escorted to the dining room, where the servants waited on us hand and foot.

"How's business?" Oscar asked.

"No complaints," Cauldron said. "I'm due to make a trip out there soon. Keep everyone on their toes."

Did that mean I would tag along?

"I do the same with my employees," Oscar said. "You gotta make sure everyone stays honest. Am I right?"

Cauldron nodded. "Always."

Martine sipped her wine as she looked at me. "How did you two meet?"

Like a deer in the headlights, I just sat there, unsure what to say. Memories of me climbing over his lime-stone wall to get to his front door came back to me. I snuck on to his yacht and slept aboard until I confronted him far out at sea. If I told them the truth, they'd probably think it was a joke. A very bad joke.

"An art auction," Cauldron said. "Instead of bidding on the paintings, I bid on her."

Oscar gave a chuckle like it was a joke.

Even though it kinda wasn't.

Cauldron moved his arm over the back of my chair, his fingers lightly touching the back of my neck.

I almost gave another jerk because he never shared any kind of intimacy with me. It was always straight down to business—fucking. The only foreplay we had was when I was on my knees with his dick in my mouth. We'd never shared a single kiss after that first time.

Now, he touched me like this, called me his girlfriend, made me feel a lot more special than a whore.

Oscar raised his glass. "Cheers."

We all did the same before we clinked our glasses together.

"The moment I saw Martine, I knew she was the one," Oscar said. "Would have asked her to marry me on the spot if I hadn't been a complete stranger."

Finally. A man who wasn't a pig.

Martine smiled and gave his arm a squeeze. Despite their age difference, it seemed like she did care about him.

We dined for the next hour, had a raspberry torte for dessert, and then said our goodbyes before we got back in the car. It was a short drive back to his estate, and that time was spent in silence, him on his side of the car and me on mine.

When we entered the house, Hugo was there to greet him. "Anything I can get you before you retire for the evening?"

Cauldron didn't cast a backward glance. "No." He headed up the stairs.

Hugo looked at me next but didn't dare offer the same courtesy.

Fine by me.

Cauldron stopped halfway up the stairs. "Hugo?"

His servant whipped around to face him. "Mr. Beaufort?"

"Camille is the lady of this house. It's time you treated her as such."

Whoa.

Hugo was thunderstruck. He turned to me, as if I would supply an explanation.

I was just as shocked as he was.

Cauldron continued up the stairs.

He'd just earned himself a nice blow job.

I followed him up the stairs, making it to the third floor. His bedroom door was cracked and a streak of light flooded into the hallway, but I didn't dare go inside. I headed to my bedroom down the hall, pulling down the side zipper to my dress as I went. Once it came loose, I could draw my first deep breath. The four-course meal had bloated my stomach and made it difficult to remain squeezed into that little dress. I let it fall to the floor at my feet before I slipped off the closed-toe heels.

I picked up the shoes and the dress, and when I righted myself, he was standing there. His evening clothes had been shed, and now he was in his signature sweatpants and intense gaze. The stubble along his jawline was thick and dark, matching the color of his eyes.

I was just in my thong, my nipples taped down.

He stared at me hard, like he wanted the bundle of clothes in my hands to disappear.

I carried everything into my closet. The shoes went on a shelf, and the dress was returned to the hanger. I hadn't spilled anything on it, so I didn't see why we needed to waste the energy getting it dry-cleaned.

When I returned to the bedroom, he was sitting at the edge of my bed, his bare feet on the rug as his hands gripped the wooden bed frame that surrounded it. Despite eating the same dinner that I did, his body showed no hint of bloating. It was slender and tight, the deep carving of his abdominal muscles casting shadows. Perhaps he ate nothing during the day, reserving his calories for his evening meal.

I held his gaze as I drew closer. "I'm your girlfriend now?"

His eyes remained as guarded as ever. "Do you prefer a different label?"

"Just doesn't seem like your style…"

"You're the only woman I fuck. Isn't that the definition?"

I grabbed the tape over the first nipple and slowly pulled it off until my nipple came free. I did the same for the other, handling the tape delicately because it could tug on my breasts too hard and make me wince.

He crossed his muscular arms over his chest as he watched me. "Why do you do that?"

"So you can't see my nipples through my dress."

"I don't think anyone would care, Camille."

I rolled the tape into a little ball before I set it on the table near the couch.

"You should be proud of your tits." His eyes dropped to look at them before he looked at me again. "I know I am."

I felt my tits harden, but I didn't know if it was because of the cold or his words.

He beckoned me toward him with an almost imperceptible nod.

I drew near, feeling the heat the closer I came.

When I was close enough, his hands moved to my waist then curved around to my back. My cold skin was engulfed in heat that made bumps appear all over me. My breathing had been rhythmic and regular, but now it veered off course and turned shallow. His arms cocooned me, bringing our faces closer together than they'd ever been. His head was tilted down slightly as he looked at me with those espresso eyes, his enormous arms covering nearly every inch of my back like a warm blanket.

My eyes met his as my stomach tightened. It was the same sensation I felt right before I came, my body preparing for the greatest sense of pleasure I'd ever known. He used to intimidate me, but now he made me nervous…really nervous.

He kept up his stare, one hand moving to my ass and giving it a squeeze. "My woman. Is that better?"

My breathing hitched again. "Have you ever had a woman before?"

His long stare was his answer.

I knew it was coming, but an eternity wouldn't be enough time to prepare for it. My heart skipped a beat. My palms turned cold and clammy. My knees felt weak, as if they might buckle underneath my weight.

The arm hooked around the small of my back pulled me deeper into him, bringing our lips together.

I felt his strong mouth, felt the coarse stubble of his facial hair when my lips moved, tasted the three glasses of wine he'd had that evening. I knew he was a good kisser because I'd kissed him before, but this was different. Packed with the highest voltage of chemistry, it electrified all my nerves. It was familiar but also brand-new territory because he'd been a stranger at the time. But now...he was the man between my legs every night.

His hand squeezed both of my cheeks in a masculine grip as his other hand dug into my hair and pushed it back from my face. His large fingers cradled my face gently as his other hand continued to grip my ass like he wanted to smack it.

The sex had always been good, but it felt empty. A means to an end. A one-night stand on repeat. But with this kiss, it shifted from black-and-white to full color. The silence turned to music.

He pulled me closer into him while he deepened the kiss, tilting his head as he took in my bottom lip between his. There was a playful bite. A breath. And then he kissed me again, stealing my breath away while adding his own.

I had touched his body everywhere, had climaxed in the past just by feeling those large biceps. But now, I ventured into new territory, sliding my hands up his neck until I cupped one of his cheeks. My thumb swiped over his thick stubble, and I felt my skin nearly break because it was so rough.

I took his mouth with the same enthusiasm he took mine, our audible breaths growing louder as the passion rose from warm to scalding hot. My fingers stroked his short hair, and I let my tits press against his chest.

His fingers dragged my panties over my ass to my thighs before they curled around my ass toward my opening. Two fingers pushed inside me, immediately coated in the arousal that dripped from my entrance. He moaned into my mouth as he slid them inside, soaked to the bone.

He turned me on, and I was not ashamed to show it.

His kiss turned hungry, taking my mouth with the dominance he always showed. There was tongue, hot breaths, masculine grabs all over my body. He gripped one of my tits hard as he fingered me, pulsing his fingers deep inside me and curling at the perfect spot to make me writhe against his mouth.

He'd make me come at this rate.

My lips struggled to meet his demands because it was too hard to focus when his fingers were pushing me to the brink of exhilaration.

He ended the kiss and lifted me into his arms so he could lay me across the bed.

I cupped the back of his head with my palm and brought his lips back to mine like I needed them to breathe.

He held himself up on one arm as he pulled down his sweatpants, kissing me at the same time.

I helped him, yanking them down so he could be free and plunge inside me. Our bodies immediately wrapped around each other, and he shoved himself inside me with a single thrust.

I gave a breathy moan against his mouth, my fingers slicing into the muscles of his back.

He breathed against my mouth as he rocked, his dick harder than it'd ever been, pounding into me over and over.

I was already on the threshold from just his fingers, so I exploded immediately, my tightness squeezing his thick length with the strength of a boa constrictor. "Cauldron…" My nails scratched into his back as my hips bucked against him. A climax unlike any other gripped me around the throat and took away my breath. Swept away in the current, I writhed incoherently, the pleasure between my legs so damn exquisite. "Yes…" Tears blurred my vision then streaked down my cheeks to my ears.

He pumped into me hard as he chased his own climax, his dick slick with the copious arousal between my legs. The bed rocked with his movements, the wooden headboard tapping against the wall because he fucked me so hard. He reached his completion with a satisfied moan, his dick twitching inside me as he finished. "Camille."

I'd felt him inside me before, but now I really loved the way it felt, the way I carried his arousal like a souvenir. He'd said my name before, but never like that, never thick and breathy. Never with that same tone of unquenched desire.

After heavy breaths and stares, he pulled out of me.

I didn't want to let him go. "Wait." I grabbed on to his biceps and pulled him back to me. "Again."

He looked down at me, his breaths heavy, his eyes intense.

"Please…"

That seemed to be the magic word because he was as hard as a piece of wood again. He shoved himself inside me once more and started to rock. "Goddamn, Camille."

When I looked out the back window, I saw Cauldron.

But he wasn't alone.

Three other men were with him, all wearing sports coats. Just like in Paris, they were gathered on the white couches near the pool, all smoking cigars while the table was covered with booze and the snacks Hugo provided.

Cauldron was smoking right along with them. He brought it to his lips and took a deep drag before he let it rest between his fingertips as his arm relaxed on the armrest of his chair. He must have said something humorous because the other three broke into laughs… or they just laughed at his joke to kiss his ass.

He never said anything funny to me.

I was about to lounge by the pool. In my bikini and open silk robe, I stepped through the back doors and approached their seating area.

Cauldron's eyes immediately shifted to me and remained there. Instead of being annoyed by my presence, he seemed infatuated by it. His relaxed expression immediately hardened into one of mild intensity.

I walked past the men and let them discuss business.

His deep voice carried over to me. "Camille." He raised his hand and gave a subtle beckoning with his fingers.

My eyebrows arched high when he called me over like one of his servants. I stayed put, my hands on my waist.

"Camille," he repeated. "Come over here."

"Ask me. Don't tell me."

The men in his company all got a kick out of that. "You've got a feisty one on your hands, Cauldron."

Cauldron ignored them. "Come. Here. Now." He didn't raise his voice, but his tone showcased his ferocity.

He wouldn't lose this game in front of his buddies, so I chose to de-escalate the situation by walking over.

"She sounds like a lot of work, Cauldron," one of the men said.

"Oh, she is," Cauldron said before he brought the cigar to his lips and took a drag. "But nothing I can't handle."

One of the guys chuckled at that.

I joined their table, standing in a black bikini and heels with an open cover-up.

Cauldron made the introductions, sharing names I would never remember, calling them associates.

"Nice to meet you." I grabbed the cigar out of Cauldron's hand and put it out in the communal ashtray. "I'm Camille."

Cauldron didn't move for another cigar, but he explained my significance. "The woman of the house."

"Looks like the woman of the house hates cigars," one man noted.

"No," I said. "I just hate it when he smokes them." I walked off, heading back to the other side of the pool where I could lounge in the sun, well out of earshot from whatever the men were discussing.

Cauldron faced me, and his eyes never left me. Even when he spoke to them, he watched me lounge in the armchair and absorb the sun. He never reached for another cigar, but he downed more booze to replace the other vice.

I took a dip in the pool, and even then, I had his full attention. He seemed uninterested in his own guests.

Their meeting eventually wrapped up, and the men said goodbye before they walked inside.

Cauldron remained in place, watching me float around in the pool as he enjoyed his scotch on the rocks. His fingers curled until his knuckles were displayed, and he propped those against his hard face. He was under the shade of the umbrella, so his sunglasses hung at the top of his shirt.

I splashed around as I looked at him. "Yes?"

He didn't move.

"You wanna get in? Water feels nice."

"No."

"You sure?" I reached for the string at the top of my bikini and pulled. It immediately came loose and floated on the surface of the water. My nipples automatically hardened when the material was gone, no longer keeping the warm water from me.

He remained still, but his interest was piqued.

"Who were those guys?"

"Associates."

"I know, you said that. But that didn't answer my question." I slipped off the bottoms under the water and watched them rise to the top, too. I grabbed both soaked pieces and tossed them onto the pool deck to dry.

The bait worked, and he got to his feet. He pushed the jacket over his big shoulders and let it slide down his arms before he folded it on the back of the chair. Then he unbuttoned his shirt, starting at the top and working his way down, revealing more of his tanned chest as he went.

Now I stared at him as hard as he stared at me.

Piece by piece, his clothes came off until he dropped his underwear.

There it was, hard as usual.

He walked to the steps and made his way down until everything but his chest was submerged. Then he came closer to me, his eyes intense but his mouth playful. "You need to stop with the cigars."

"No. *You* need to stop with the cigars."

His hands groped me under the water, bringing my naked body up against him. My legs circled his hips, and I latched on, my arms hooked around his neck.

He moved into deeper water, submerging our bodies until only his shoulders poked out of the water. His hands held on to my bare ass, his big fingers spanning each cheek. "You're lucky people think you're cute when you do that."

"Not trying to be cute. I told you to stop smoking."

"You don't tell me what to do."

My eyes shifted back and forth between his. "Yes, I do."

His hard face took in my appearance, those dark eyes armored walls that kept out everyone, including me. His thoughts were a mystery, a hand of cards held close to his chest.

"I'm the woman of the house, aren't I? I'm *your* woman."

"Like every dictator who ever lived, you're letting the title go to your head."

"Dictator, huh? That's rich coming from you."

A glimmer of a smile moved on to his lips.

It was infectious, reaching my own mouth because it was so boyish and handsome.

"I'll make a deal with you. I'll stop smoking if you do something for me."

"Do something for you? I don't have any disgusting habits."

The grin remained. "Never said it was. It's just something I want."

"You want to make a trade? Fine. What do you want?"

"To make a video of us."

"A video of us doing what?"

He grinned.

"Why would you want that?"

"That's my business."

"Why would you watch a video when you can just—"

"We have a deal or not?"

I stilled at the way he cut me off. "Are you going to show it to anyone?"

"Is this really the first time anyone's asked you to make a video?"

"Yes."

"Really?" He cocked an eyebrow.

"Yes."

"That's surprising," he said. "I'll stop smoking if we make a video. Deal?"

"I'm just looking out for your health…and you're being a pervert."

That grin was back. "I love cigars, so the abstinence is going to cost you."

"Fine."

He continued to smile. "It's a deal."

"You know, you're really handsome when you smile."

My words immediately chased it away. The corners of his lips dropped, and he was back to his usual demeanor—brooding and moody.

"I wish you would do it more often."

"Happy people smile. I'm not a happy person."

"You're a billionaire in paradise, and you're still miserable?"

"Miserable is a strong word and not the one I would use."

"Then what word would you use?"

His fingers kneaded my ass under the water, and his eyes dropped down to my lips like he was bored with the conversation.

"What word would you use?" I pressed, finding myself more concerned about his happiness than I realized.

He drew close, his lips coming for mine.

"Tell me," I whispered, tilting away from his mouth.

He started to glide us across the water, the cool water hitting my back as he moved forward. With his eyes on mine, he guided me to the edge of the pool where my back gently came to rest against the wall. "Empty."

It was just a word, not a fist to the face or a knife in the back, but it hurt like hell.

My face must have been contorted in a painful expression because he didn't kiss me again. He held my stare, those dark eyes hard like his closed knuckles. His fingers didn't dig deep into me anymore.

"I—I wish you didn't feel like that." I said it with emotion I didn't feel until the words were out of my mouth. I'd snuck on to his boat, and he hadn't hesitated to try to shoot me, and here I was, wrapped up in his emotional well-being. When did that happen?

"I don't always feel empty."

My tits were right against his chest. My heartbeat thumped against his body and reverberated against mine. It felt strong enough to make ripples in the pool.

"At least not when I'm with you."

I steadied my breath as best I could. Otherwise, he would feel it, feel the way I nearly gasped in response. It took everything I had to hold his stare and bottle my reaction, to hide the wings that sprouted from my heart.

He leaned in and took my mouth. The kiss was slow but full of his dominance, the way he always took the reins every time we were physical together. His body pushed mine against the wall, and his heat made the surrounding water boil. Breaths. Tongue. Ass-grabs. He made me feel like he was the only man I'd ever had.

He lifted me out of the water then brought me back down, sliding my tightness over his thickness. We inched together until we were fully connected, followed by a quiet moan from both of us. With me pinned against the wall, he took me with the same slowness as the other night, our lips locked together, our slick bodies moving in perfect synchrony.

Like every other night, he came to my bedroom and made me scream his name. He gave me passion I hadn't felt in years, probably ever. The marks on his back would remain for days, and the indent in his shoulder from my teeth would be there until he woke up the next morning. But as always, he dismissed himself when we were through.

"Cauldron."

He pulled on his sweatpants then turned to face me, his eyes a bit sunken because he was tired from the long day of working and the long night of fucking.

"Stay." I was naked on the bed, and as the sweat had evaporated, I grew cold, so I pulled the sheets to my chest and propped myself on my shoulder. My makeup was a mess and I should wash it off before bed, but I'd rather go straight to sleep—with him beside me.

He stared for three long seconds before he gave his answer. "No."

I was stung and could barely hide it. "Why——"

"Because I don't do that."

My head snapped from the whiplash. I was the only person who made him feel less empty, but then he dismissed me so coldly anyway. "Why?"

He walked out without answering.

I continued to stare at the closed door as if he might come back, realize he was being an asshole and issue an apology, but then I remembered Cauldron wasn't the kind of man to issue apologies. I didn't recall getting one after he shot me.

I lay down and went to sleep—alone.

***

I knew he was having a bad day when I heard him yell from inside the house.

"If you don't want the bag, I suggest you figure it out."

The bag?

I sat at the table at the poolside. Hugo had just delivered my lunch, and not a single backhanded insult was uttered. He seemed distracted, like he was listening to his master's heated conversation.

"Hugo!"

He lost control of the platter and nearly dropped it, but I helped him grab it. He didn't issue a thank-you before he ran off. "Yes, Mr. Beaufort?"

Cauldron emerged onto the terrace, shirtless and in just his sweatpants. The only time I ever saw him get fully dressed was for company. He didn't even wear shoes. There was something terrifying about watching him come at Hugo with swinging arms and tense shoulders. "We leave for Botswana first thing in the morning. Make all the arrangements."

"Of course, Mr. Beaufort." He hurried into the house, actually running. "Right away."

Cauldron continued to the table, looking so angry it seemed as if everything was my fault. He dropped into the chair across from me and leaned back. His hands gripped the armrests, and he looked over his property as if he hated that too.

He was so sexy when he was angry, his hard jawline even harder, his dark eyes focused. His body was tighter too, all the muscles clenching so the lines that separated the different muscle groups were more distinct.

"I want to ask if everything's okay, but I have a feeling you won't respond."

He continued to stare elsewhere as if he hadn't heard me speak.

"Cauldron?"

His mind was so far away it was on a different planet.

I decided not to bother and ate my lunch.

He sat there, one elbow on the armrest, his fingers resting against his lips, his mind deep in thought.

Hugo emerged with a tray of food and set it in front of Cauldron. His meal was different from mine. While I had a veggie wrap with produce from the market and freshly made hummus with a cup of onion soup, Cauldron had a green salad with shrimp on top. He basically didn't eat carbs, and I couldn't think of a worse life than a keto one.

Once the scotch was on the table, he filled the glass and took a deep drink.

"What's the bag?"

It must be important because his eyes immediately shifted to mine.

"It sounded like a threat when you were on the phone."

"Because it is."

"What does it mean?"

He considered the question for a long time before he grabbed his fork. "You don't want to know, Camille." He poured the tarragon dressing over the bed of lettuce and began to eat, elbows on the table, hunched over his food like a bear.

"Why did I ask, then?"

He took another bite before he directed his eyes on me. He chewed his food, debating his response. "I tie a plastic bag over someone's head before I bind their wrists and ankles behind their back with zip ties. Then I watch them watch me as they suffocate and die."

The warm day suddenly felt like a winter morning.

He held my stare for a while before he continued his meal. "When I say you don't want to know, take my word for it."

I walked into his study upstairs.

It was the first time I'd ever walked in there. It was a big room, a full sitting area in front of a large hearth. There were windows all along the wall, and a big ornate desk was in the rear. A large painting hung on the wall behind him, Cap-Ferrat with sailboats in the bay. He worked on his laptop, his chin tilted down to look at the screen.

He didn't seem to realize I was there until I was right in front of his desk.

His eyes flicked up.

"Hugo normally brings me clothes he wants me to wear, but he hasn't delivered anything. Am I not coming with you?"

"No."

The disappointment was like a rock that dropped into my stomach. "How long will you be gone?"

"I don't know. A few days. A week, maybe. Depends on the bullshit I have to deal with." His attention moved back to the laptop.

"That's a long time."

His eyes flicked from left to right like he was reading.

"What am I supposed to do while you're gone?"

He turned his attention back to me. "I have a lot more to think about than how you'll keep yourself entertained in my absence. Swim. Shop. Drink. Whatever the fuck you please." And just like that, he was back to his laptop.

Instead of snapping, I managed to release an agitated sigh. "I meant because I'll be here alone without you. What if Grave realizes you're out of the country and comes for me?"

He released a sigh, and this time, he shut his laptop. "Just because you climbed over my walls and harassed my butler at the front door doesn't mean my security is lax. They just didn't shoot you because you weren't a threat. If you were, you would have been shot on sight. Don't worry about your safety. I can still protect you whether we're in the same room or on opposite sides of the world."

"That wasn't our deal."

His face hardened in both confusion and irritation.

"He's afraid of *you*. Not armed men with guns. If you aren't here, there's nothing stopping him from pulling up with his own crew and blowing yours to hell. I'm not staying here without you, so I'm coming."

"Camille, it's not the right place for you—"

"I said, I'm coming."

The second his eyes flashed with agitation, I knew shit was about to hit the fan. He got to his feet, towering over me, reminding me who was in charge. "Trust me, you don't want to be there when I conduct business."

"I model your diamonds all the time—"

"Not the same thing. This is all business—no pleasure."

"I still feel uncomfortable being here alone. I go where you go."

His jawline was sharp like broken glass, and his eyes shone like bullets.

"Why don't you want me there?"

Silence.

"You have another lover there—"

"Is that what this is about?" He came around the desk, his eyes on me the whole way until we were face-to-face. "You think I'll bed other women while we're apart? My word means nothing to you?"

"Every associate I've met of yours is a massive pig, so…" I didn't realize the root of my unease until he figured it out himself. Being left unprotected was only part of my fear.

"Their wives are aware of their promiscuity. And if I were like them, I wouldn't hide it either. I will tell you the truth straight to your face and feel nothing as you cry rather than lie to keep your cheeks dry. That's a promise."

My arms locked across my chest.

"Don't insult me again."

"I didn't insult you——"

"Yes, you fucking did." He raised his voice. It filled every corner of the room and spilled out into the hallway. "Don't question my fidelity ever again."

I looked away.

"Apologize to me."

"What?" I asked incredulously, looking back at him. "I am not——"

"Yes, you fucking are." He stared me down, his eyes becoming angrier with the passing time.

I turned on my heel and walked out.

He grabbed me by the arm and threw me on the couch.

My back hit the cushions, and my head landed on one of the decorative pillows.

He was on top of me, hiking up my dress and pulling down my panties. "Camille."

I shoved him as hard as I could, but it was like throwing your body against a solid wall.

My legs were folded against me, and then his sweat-pants were pushed down. With a quick thrust, he was inside me, pinning me deep into the cushions. His face directly above mine and with that possessive look, he took me, one hand sliding into my hair like reins to a horse. "Say it."

The instant he was inside me, the fight left my body. My hands pulled him closer rather than push him away. My knees pressed into his torso and squeezed him to me like a snake that wouldn't release her prey. He was my drug, getting me off better than anything else in this world. With every hit, I needed more of him as the addiction worsened, and I certainly couldn't stop. Not now. Probably not ever. "I'm sorry…"

Cauldron walked down the stairs in dark jeans and a black t-shirt. Members of his staff were behind him, carrying his bags for his travels. His eyes locked on me when he saw me standing in the foyer, my rollaboard suitcase beside me. His look intensified as he came closer, until he was directly in front of me.

"I'm coming with you." Our dilemma hadn't been solved last night. We'd fucked on the couch then his desk. We'd somehow made it upstairs to my bedroom, and then he'd left me there. Exhausted, I just went to sleep.

"I thought this was resolved."

I gave a slight shake of my head. "I meant what I said before. The only place I truly feel safe is with you." Bones's advice had been dead on. I could go anywhere in the world and Grave would follow me, but ever since I'd come into Cauldron's possession, I was untouchable. A crowded room had never stopped Grave from pursuing me, except when Cauldron was in that room too.

His eyes shifted back and forth as he looked at me. "I have matters that require my attention. I don't have time for you."

"I understand."

He turned to Hugo and gave a nod.

My luggage was taken with his and packed in the car. We sat side by side in the back and left the estate and headed to the private airport where his jet was waiting. He was on his phone the entire time, ignoring me just like he said he would. Then we were on the plane and, soon after, in the sky.

I looked out the window and watched Nice disappear as we headed across the Mediterranean. When I looked back at Cauldron, he was still typing on his phone, and the flight attendant had just brought us drinks and appetizers.

I saw the way she looked him over, trying to be discreet, but not discreet whatsoever.

It bothered me when it shouldn't.

Hours later, we landed in Botswana, a place I had no knowledge of whatsoever. Lots of kids in school went on safari in Tanzania and South Africa, but none of them mentioned coming to the territory known for its diamond hoard.

We were ushered from the airport and into the countryside outside the city, where a private home was surrounded by a big wall. It reminded me of his French home, an oasis away from everyone and everything. Just like in Cap-Ferrat, there was staff to attend to our every need.

Cauldron didn't stick around. He grabbed a gun and stuffed it into the back of his jeans before he headed to the door. He didn't say goodbye to me. Didn't say a word. Just disappeared out the door and headed to his next location.

Without him, I had no purpose, so I went upstairs to my bedroom.

TWENTY
CAULDRON

The armored tank traveled across the open landscape until it reached the rocky crevasses where the mines were tucked away. We came around the bend and spotted our site, the cargo trucks ready to sift through the dirt already shoveled in case anything was missed. Before the car came to a full stop, I got out and headed straight for Jeremiah. "Where are they?"

He turned to the peak of the mountain and nodded. "They're on the north side. They dug straight into our tunnel in the middle of the night then caved ours in."

"Did they now?" I stared at the mountain as if I could picture it all.

"They've been working all day to dig it out."

"And we still don't know the culprit?"

"They shoot on sight."

I stared at the tunnel, my blood boiling underneath the surface.

"We could call in more men and have them ambushed from the north. But since we don't know who we're dealing with, wasn't sure if that was wise."

"Whoever it is, they have a death wish."

"Perhaps they don't realize it's us."

I scoffed. "Oh, they do."

Jeremiah stared at the mountain for a moment before he looked at me again. "What do you want to do?"

"Pull all our men out. Cave in the entire mountain."

Jeremiah stared at me as if he didn't quite understand. "I'm sorry?"

"You heard me."

"We'll lose all our progress—"

"So will they. And do it when their men are inside."

"They're just villagers looking for work—"

"Well, they should have come to me if they were looking for work. Do it."

Jeremiah continued to stare.

I turned to meet his look, showing him how little patience I had today.

"You aren't thinking clearly—"

"Maybe if I shoot you in the head, I'll be able to think more clearly."

He stared, his eyes shifting back and forth. "We'll do the demolition at nightfall when the excavation sites are empty. They'll lose all their progress, just as we'll lose ours, but innocent people only trying to feed their families won't be sacrificed. I know that's what you really want."

I wanted to pull out my gun, but I let it sit in the back of my jeans. "What I want is to kill this motherfucker. So when he comes to the excavation site to see the destruction, I'll put that bag over his fucking head."

We wired the caves and the external parts of the mountain, and during the deepest part of the night, we pulled the trigger and demolished the entire thing. The destruction was so loud I was certain everyone in the city could hear it. The mountain shifted and crumbled underneath, releasing a thick cloud of dust that blocked out the sky completely.

It was the perfect cover.

My men positioned on the north side moved in, and after a short battle of gunfire, everything went silent. Their gunners were taken out, and the excavation site was secured. The unarmed men were spared, their ankles and wrists bound in zip ties.

The dust slowly cleared, carried off in the midnight breeze. Starlight returned. The full moon was visible once again. The spotlights were shifted and pointed to the center where the three men sat on their knees in the dirt.

I examined the tunnel they'd built themselves and was pleased to see it was gone. A small pile of bodies had been made twenty feet away, and after a gallon of gasoline was poured on top, they were set on fire.

Burning flesh at midnight.

The men on their knees weren't mercenaries. They were commanders, running this whole operation in the stead of their employer. I stood in front of the three of them and watched them avoid my eyes, watched them tremble because it was the end of the road. They took the payday and assumed they would be invincible, but their boss obviously didn't tell them I was a bigger boss.

I almost felt sorry for them. *Almost.* "Look at me."

They all did so immediately, as if obedience would spare their lives.

"I'm sure you know how this is going to end."

The one on the far left started to breathe hard, the panic overwhelming him.

I could feel the heat of the flames from the bonfire. I nodded toward it. "Each one of you will end up there. Your families may figure out what happened to you if you have good dental records. If you don't…shit out of luck."

That sank deep into their flesh because two of them breathed hard. The first one had no reaction, the strongest of the three.

"But I'll offer you some respite. Identify your employer, and your death will be painless." I looked to the man on the left, the one who looked like he would cave the quickest. "Who are you working for?"

He trembled under my stare, shaking so much he almost tipped over. "He'll come after our families——"

I snapped my fingers.

One of my men tied a plastic bag over his head.

He sucked in a deep breath but only got plastic. It bent into his mouth and stuck there. He toppled over, suffocating, the bag crinkling as it was pushed and pulled by his receding breaths. Then it stopped.

I looked at the next guy. "He can't come after your families if I kill him first. After I leave here tonight, that's the first thing I'll do. He'll die the same way your comrade just did. Spare yourself."

He considered the offer a long time before he gave a nod. "Grave."

The shock was like a bullet to the skull. Didn't see it coming. Didn't feel it either because it killed me instantly.

My man shot him from behind, and he face-planted.

The other received the bag.

He tried to fight it, but the bag was secured within a second. He flailed on the ground, rolling around like a worm after a heavy rain. He went still a minute later.

The bonfire continued to melt flesh off bone, and death was in the air.

Jeremiah stared at me.

I stared back.

It was sunrise when I returned home.

Wasn't tired or hungry.

Just pissed off.

I took a shower then sat on the couch in my living room, wearing my sweatpants and nothing else. My mind raced, thinking of the next course of action. Foolishly, I'd assumed this was just another player in the game, but none of them would fuck with me the way Grave did. Should have known.

My phone rang.

His number wasn't saved in my phone, but I recognized it.

I gritted my teeth before I answered, knowing how unpleasant this would be. In silence, I held the phone to my ear.

"Give her back, or I'll sabotage all your mines."

"I'll kill all your men."

"You think that matters to me? They're expendable, and they're paid to be expendable."

Motherfucker.

"You'll never find diamonds if you're too busy dealing with me."

Grave always stayed in his lane, and I always stayed in mine. It'd been that way for a very long time. Peaceful coexistence, if you could call it that. But now, all of that was over. "She's really worth a war?"

"You tell me, Cauldron."

***

I sat with Jeremiah in my office downstairs. Barely slept a few hours before he came over, but my mind was sharper than a tack, fueled by rage. "We need more men. A lot more. And our security protocols need to be changed. Our perimeter needs to extend to a full mile radius. Our sites need to be monitored from every point around the mountain."

Jeremiah took those notes as he gave a nod. "I agree."

"Nothing can compromise our schedule. We've already had a major setback."

"Of course."

My phone rang, and it was Hugo—again. I finally answered because I was tired of him trying to reach me. "In case you haven't figured it out, I'm busy. Don't bother me unless it's—"

"Urgent. Yes, I know. But this is urgent, Mr. Beaufort."

"What's happened?"

"Grave is on the property."

I sucked in a deep breath and felt my tendons ache when my hand made a fist. "Why hasn't he been shot?"

"Because you told us not to, Mr. Beaufort."

My clenched fist released, and I felt another dose of rage.

"Unless your orders have changed."

I breathed into the phone.

"Mr. Beaufort?"

"What does he want?"

"Camille. I've informed him she's not here, but he doesn't believe me."

"Has he threatened you?"

"No. He's unarmed."

"Where is he now?"

"Standing right in front of me."

The fucking audacity. "Put him on the phone."

"Yes, Mr. Beaufort." The phone changed hands.

His smirk was so loud I could hear it in every word. "I'm going to find her. And I'm going to fuck her in your bed."

Thank fucking god Camille had insisted on coming with me. "She's not there."

"I'll search every room in this house until I find her."

"She's. Not. There."

Grave turned silent, his disappointment heavier than his previous smirk.

"I don't go anywhere without her. So if you want her, you'll have to come directly through me next time. Now, leave my butler alone and get the fuck off my property, or I'll have my men fire." I hung up and threw my phone at the wall so hard the screen shattered and pieces scattered. I paced, my hand rubbing over my beard, raging behind my clenched teeth.

At that moment, Camille appeared in the open doorway and looked at me. She looked at the broken phone then at me again. Her mouth opened. Closed. Opened again. Then she made the right choice and walked off.

I turned to Jeremiah. "Call Hugo. Tell him he's not to mention any of this to Camille."

Camille and I didn't exchange more than a few words until we returned to France. She must have felt my seething anger every time she was in my company and was smart enough to let me boil in silence.

When we returned to my Cap-Ferrat residence, it looked exactly as it had before. An assault on my property was invisible to everyone except those who knew about it. I thought I knew Grave better than Camille, but she'd proven otherwise.

When I came face-to-face with Hugo, we exchanged a long look, both thinking about the same transgression.

He was the first one to speak. "I hope you enjoyed your trip, Mr. Beaufort."

I ignored him and took the stairs.

"Lunch will be ready in twenty minutes."

I kept going.

When I entered my bedroom, I took a shower to wash off the plane and then headed back downstairs. Camille was already seated under the umbrella on the deck near the pool. She didn't look like she'd sat on a plane for several hours. Whether she was in her leggings with a loose shirt and no makeup or in full cocktail attire, she looked just as refined.

I was in my sweatpants and nothing else, letting the sun hit my bare skin.

She took a drink of her iced tea then studied my face, trying to determine whether it was safe to speak yet.

I would be angry for a very long time, but the worst had passed—for the moment.

"I missed you."

I was already still before she spoke, but I felt my body tighten just a fraction more. The confession was totally unexpected, and the sincerity in her voice was even more unexpected. Stoic, I said nothing.

She didn't seem hurt by my rejection. She drank her tea again.

"I'm here now."

"I prefer you when you aren't angry."

"I'm always angry."

"Then less angry…"

Hugo brought the plates of food and departed. Salad wraps with a side of fruit. The garden was in full bloom, and the birds sang from their homes in the trees. It was quiet otherwise, an oasis from the outside world.

"Did you…resolve everything?"

No. I'd entered a war. "Yes."

"Your home is nice."

I ate my food, enjoying my scotch the way she enjoyed her iced tea. Most of the meal was spent in silence, but the good kind, the kind that didn't feel awkward without conversation. "Have you ever fallen for a client?"

The question brought her to a standstill. She was about to take a bite of the salad wrap in her hand when she hesitated. "I thought you didn't want me to talk about other men."

"Unless I directly ask you about it."

She put down the wrap, as if her answer was more than just a simple no. "I've never loved any of my clients."

"That wasn't what I asked."

She stared.

"Have you grown attached? Had feelings? Ever felt like more than just a job?"

She continued to stare, her bright eyes shifting back and forth between mine. Her relaxed posture suddenly turned tense, the comfortable intimacy we'd just shared shattered by my interrogation. "Why don't you just ask what you really want to know."

"I already did."

Her confidence disappeared the moment she spoke. Her eyes dropped down to her food, and she grabbed her salad wrap once more. With her eyes on anything but me, she ate her lunch. "Only once."

She was ready for me when I walked in.

Her pajamas were replaced by lingerie. Black. Lacy. Crotchless.

On top of her, I sank deep inside and felt how ready she was. She'd been thinking about me long before I walked in the door, daydreaming about this moment with her eyes closed and her fingers between her legs.

She gasped when she felt me, her nails deep in my back, her ankles hooked around my torso.

With my lips to her ear, I thrust inside the wettest pussy I'd ever fucked. "You really did miss me."

She squeezed me tighter in response. Her fingers slid up the back of my neck and into my short hair. She writhed underneath me, rocking her hips back into me as we moved together across the bed. With heated breaths and sexy moans, she made me forget all the bullshit. "Cauldron…" Her whispers were deeper than before, almost painful, as if she didn't just want me but needed me.

It didn't take much to bring her to the edge; she was so hot before I even walked into the room. I felt her explode around me, felt the strength of her tight pussy as I pounded her into the mattress.

"Yes…"

Watching her get off got me off. I'd never cared much about the woman's pleasure, but hers really made me hot. The way she was so desperate and unafraid to show it. Maybe this was all just an act to earn her keep, but I suspected it wasn't. It was sincere. Every moan. Every thrust. Every tear.

It was real.

I'd been writing letters my whole life.

Letters I never sent.

Letters that were only meant to be written but never read.

It helped me release all the things I could never say. Helped me express my remorse or my rage. Helped me feel something as deeply as I possibly could so it would pass and I could move on.

So I wrote one now.

In my scribbled handwriting, I wrote a simple paragraph, read it back, and then ripped it out of the notebook before I crumpled it in my closed fist. Permanently wrinkled and resembling trash, I threw it in the wastebasket in my bathroom and forgot all about it the second I was done.

A knock sounded on the door before Hugo stepped inside. "Mr. Beaufort wishes for you to join him for dinner."

I shut the notebook and left it on the couch. "Downstairs?"

"No. You'll be dining at Mr. Beaufort's favorite restaurant in the village."

That meant there would be other people there, probably people interested in his diamonds. "I'll be down in a second."

He nodded before he left the room.

Hugo wasn't sunshine and rainbows when he interacted with me, but he wasn't rude anymore. It was a major improvement. I grabbed a black dress out of my closet and slipped on some heels before I went downstairs.

Cauldron sat at his desk in his study, his eyebrows furrowed as he read the screen of his laptop. He was in a dress shirt and dark jeans, looking as handsome as ever. He was so good-looking he could have all those beautiful women on his yacht for free. He finished typing before his eyes flicked up to meet mine.

I usually felt like the jewel in the room, felt endless stares directed my way, but next to him, I felt ordinary.

His look suggested he didn't feel the same way. He shut the laptop and approached me near the doors. One arm moved around my waist, and he pulled me in for a kiss, his hand inching for my ass until he had a big handful. He squeezed it before he ended the kiss and headed to the door.

I remained behind, my lips on fire and my knees weak. He'd never done that before, kissed me just because he wanted to, not in the heat of sex. When he'd first kissed me, that was a shock, but this was an even bigger one.

He opened the door and turned back to me, his eyebrows furrowed by the holdup.

I snapped out of it and walked with him out the door.

Instead of a blacked-out SUV waiting for us, it was a sports car. Cauldron opened the passenger door for me before he got behind the wheel and drove away. It was clearly one of his toys because he took off like a space-ship and put the engine to the test. He drove fast down the winding roads, and if it were anyone else, I'd ask them to slow down. Not because I was scared of him, but because I trusted he knew what he was doing.

Once we were in the village, he slowed down and gave the car to the valet.

It didn't seem like he had a reservation, but they got him a table anyway, giving him a prime spot away from the kitchens and the hostess stand. Whenever we were in public, he was a gentleman, pulling out the chair for me and selecting the wine we would have for the evening. He did that now before he looked at his menu.

I held my menu in my hands, but my eyes were on him. The low light hit his handsome face perfectly, cast a deep shadow under his jawline. The top button of his collared shirt was undone so more of his tanned skin and muscles were visible. I hadn't appreciated his good looks in the beginning because I was too busy trying to survive. But now, I really took him in, appreciating that my lover was the best-looking guy I'd ever seen.

He seemed to have decided what he wanted because he put his menu down.

I quickly looked away, trying to hide my blatant stare. "What are you having?"

"Florentine steak. It's better here than it is in Florence."

I looked down the menu, my stomach in such knots I wasn't even hungry.

"And you?"

"I'll try the same." I put the menu aside.

"Good choice."

When the waiter came over and poured the wine, Cauldron ordered for both of us. The bread was placed in the middle, and then we were left alone again. Never-ending silence passed like cars on the freeway, and for all that time, Cauldron stared at me. Sometimes he sipped his wine, but most of the time, he resigned himself to openly staring at me like it didn't matter if it made me uncomfortable.

It didn't.

But it did make me feel hot all over. Made me feel lucky that I got to be the woman he stared at. "Have you ever done this before?"

He didn't speak, but his eyebrows furrowed slightly.

"Taken a woman to dinner."

He drank from his glass again. "Why would I?"

"Then why did you take me?"

He set his glass aside and continued his stare. When enough time had passed, it was clear he wasn't going to answer the question. He was the only person I knew who could be so comfortable in silence, who could refuse a question without unease.

I drank my wine then grabbed a piece of bread from the basket between us.

"The same reason I kiss you."

I lifted my gaze from my bread in surprise.

"The same reason I fuck you and only you."

I felt the heat move into my cheeks, and it had nothing to do with the wine. "And what reason is that…?"

Another bout of silence stretched, even longer than last time. "Time will tell."

He drove back home, taking the turns at dangerous speeds like he was used to the road. One hand was on the steering wheel, and the other was free.

Like a teenager, I left my hand there, hoping he'd take it.

Lights from passing cars filled the windshield and brightened his handsome face, casting long shadows under his jawline. As with all other times of the day, he wore that focused look, like he was thinking about more than just driving. I wondered if he looked like that even when he slept.

We arrived at the house, and his staff was waiting to take his car to the garage somewhere else on the property. It wasn't attached to the main house, and I wasn't sure where it was.

We entered the estate, taking the long walk up the stairs to the third floor. Some of the windows were open, the sound of the fountain in the roundabout audible. The flowers still carried their scent, and the hint of summer wafted on the air throughout the house even though the sun had been gone for hours.

He pulled his shirt over his head as he entered my bedroom, the rippling muscles visible underneath his tanned flesh. His jeans hung low on his hips, and they hung even lower once he unfastened them.

Bumps formed on my arms. My throat had gone dry. My heart wasn't calm anymore. My body was no longer my own, at least when we were alone together. When he turned to look at me, my world was set on fire. Flames erupted in my belly and burned me from the inside out. I was so hot it felt like an inferno in my chest.

He crossed the room toward me, barefoot with the button of his jeans undone. He crowded me, his face tilted down to regard me, the shadow from his hard jawline stretching down his neck. Dark eyes were on me, more commanding than Napoleon.

I forgot to breathe.

His hands went to my thighs then slid up, gathering the material of my dress until he pushed it over my hips to my waist. The material bundled there, my black thong exposed. His eyes remained on mine as he gripped either side of my thong and pulled it down to my thighs.

The second the material left me, I could feel the string of arousal from my sex as it clung to the bottom of my panties. It stretched until it snapped, hitting the heat between my legs when it bounced back. His eyes remained on me so he didn't see, but he would feel it in a second.

Instead of hitting the bed, he took me to the couch, pinning me in the corner. His jeans dropped to his thighs, and he positioned my body to slide inside. It was a smooth entry, so smooth that the pleasure was detailed across his handsome face. It was accompanied by a moan, a sexy and deep one.

I was pinned against the back of the couch with one leg over the back, and he fucked me deep and close, his face directly in front of mine, his hot breaths washing over me, the hint of red wine on his lips.

My arms locked on to him, holding on for dear life because I didn't want to let go. Everything felt so good. The closeness. The strength of his body as it domi-nated mine. The way he looked at me like I was the sexiest thing he'd ever seen. He made me feel like a woman. Made me feel like a lover, not a whore. "Caul-dron…" I said his name without him having to ask. I dug my nails into his skin to leave my mark, to claim him as mine because I didn't want another woman to ever have him. I never wanted to share this man.

His face moved into my neck as he gave a moan, as if it took all his strength not to let go. His struggle only spurred me on because it was so sexy to watch his weakness, watch him fight to fulfill my pleasure first.

"Fuck…this pussy." His deep voice was right at my ear, deep and powerful, sexy with its innate command.

My teeth sank into his shoulder as I released, a flood of tears burning my eyes before they streaked down my cheeks. My nails pierced his flesh. I gripped his dick so tightly I probably bruised it. The greatest pleasure hit me like a ton of bricks. It was my job to make him writhe, but he was the one who gave me the best sex of my life.

It took less than a few seconds for him to follow me, to pump me with his seed. His thrusts came to a standstill, and we clung to each other on the couch, our hot breaths bouncing off each other's skin.

Instead of feeling him pull away from me, I was lifted from the couch with my legs straddling his hips. He carried me to the bed and laid me down, his jeans and boxers still around his thighs. He cherished my body with a few kisses before he pulled up his pants and turned to leave.

I didn't know what came over me, but it came hard and fast. "Don't go."

He turned back to me, part of his chest and shoulders blotchy and red from his arousal.

"Please." Every night, I was left alone in this bed. Silence accompanied me all throughout the night. Sometimes I reached for him beside me, but all I felt were cold sheets. This man had all of me, but I still had very little of him.

He stared for a moment longer before he dropped his jeans and came to the bed.

I couldn't believe it.

He got under the sheets beside me.

I stared at him for a moment, unable to believe this was real, and then I pressed my body into his, draped my arm over his stomach, cradled my head into his shoulder.

He didn't pull away.

His hardness was more comfortable than the soft mattress and French linen sheets. My eyes closed, comforted by his heat and his smell. He didn't touch me, but he let me touch him, and that felt like a win.

TWENTY-TWO
CAULDRON

The second she fell asleep, I slipped from her grasp and left the bedroom.

It was like lying on a bed of needles. It'd been a long day and I was ready for bed, but all I did was lie there with my eyes wide open. I stared at the crown molding around the ceiling, listening to her breathe as I waited for her to drift off.

I woke up bright and early the next morning and took care of my workout. It was the only way I knew how to start my day, by straining my muscles and getting the endorphins going. It was another sunny day in a French paradise, but my anger burned just beneath the surface of my exterior.

It was always there.

"Mr. Beaufort?"

I returned the bar to the rack and wiped my face with the towel. "What is it, Hugo?"

He stood there in his butler's tuxedo, his arms behind his back, his features slightly strained like he had bad news. "Is this a bad time—"

"What is it?"

He came forward and withdrew a piece of paper from his pocket. It was badly wrinkled, like it'd been smashed inside a closed fist and abandoned at the bottom of a wastepaper basket. "The maids were cleaning Camille's room and came across this. Wasn't sure if it would be of interest to you."

I studied the folded paper before I took it and began to read.

When did this happen?

I climbed his wall and talked shit to his butler out of survival. I snuck on to his yacht and pulled a gun on him because I didn't have a choice. But now...I forget the reason I came here in the first place.

Now I'm here because I want to be.

I'm used to doing all the work. Studying my clients, discovering their fantasies without interrogation, being exactly what they want without having to ask. But his fantasy is to take me, to fuck me, to make me watch him as he makes me come. I mean...I've never had a man like that.

I don't want to leave.

Even if he killed Grave, I still wouldn't want to leave.

How did I get here...?

I finished reading her flowy handwriting then folded it back the way it was.

"I thought it'd catch your interest."

I gave a slight nod. "Bring me all the notes you find."

"Yes, Mr. Beaufort." He took the paper and returned it to his pocket before he gave a slight bow. "I'll prepare breakfast."

I watched him walk away before I returned to my workout.

Hugo brought breakfast to my study. He placed it on the desk beside my computer, another Americano on the tray. He assembled everything for me as I continued to work on my laptop. "Can I get you anything else, Mr. Beaufort?"

"No."

He dismissed himself from the room.

A moment later, Camille walked inside, wearing a single-strap dress and a fedora. She approached the desk as her heeled wedges clapped against the hard floor. They were muffled by the rug when she drew near.

I lifted my gaze and met hers.

Hurt was in her eyes.

I knew the source.

We stared at each other, back and forth, the silence continuing.

Finally, she spoke. "How long did you stay?"

"Until you fell asleep."

She seemed a little taken aback by my honesty, showing a slight wince. "Why didn't you stay?"

"You know why."

There was an armchair, so she lowered herself and crossed her ankles. "Yes, you told me you prefer to sleep alone—"

"It's not a preference. I don't sleep with people."

"I understand. But why is that?"

I had shit to do and my breakfast grew cold, but I didn't snap the way I would if she were someone else. "That's my business—"

"I think we're past that, Cauldron." Her eyes drilled into mine with confidence, like she wouldn't stop until this battle was won.

"You have your secrets. I have mine—"

"I have no secrets. You know everything about me."

My hand reached for my laptop and closed it. "I don't let my guard down. It's nothing personal."

Her eyes narrowed as if wounded. "I'm your woman, so it is personal."

My woman. First time I'd heard that.

"You think I'd ever hurt you?" she asked, her voice breaking in offense.

"No."

"Then why——"

"You have as much of me as I can give. Why do you need more?" Now I did lose my patience, did lose the calmness to my voice.

"Because…" She shook her head, trying to find the words. "Because I want all of you." Her eyes avoided mine as she said it. Embarrassment flooded into her cheeks as a rouge.

I stared at her face as I waited for her to meet my look. It took a long time for her to find the strength. When our eyes were locked together once more, I continued. "As I already said, it's nothing personal. Nothing you say will change my mind."

Her stare was so subtle, but it conveyed everything she didn't say. It showed her anger. Her deep disappointment. "Then tell me why. Tell me why you're afraid——"

"I'm not *afraid* of anything. I just don't let my guard down for anyone. Period."

She released a frustrated breath then looked at her hands in her lap. A couple strands of hair fell forward from behind her ear.

"I have a lot of work to do."

She continued to stare at her hands. "I feel like I know you…but then I realize I don't know anything about you."

"You know everything that matters."

She raised her chin and looked at me once more. The unease in her eyes told me she didn't agree whatsoever, but she didn't press an argument. She rose from the chair and departed. "I'm going shopping."

"In the village?"

"Yes." She turned back to look at me like she anticipated a protest.

No way in hell would I let her out without me. "Not today."

"Excuse me?"

"I said not today."

"But why? You're busy, and I need some things——"

"Because I said so."

She turned her body back toward me, one hand on her hip like a cocked gun. Her eyes smoked like a hot barrel after pulling the trigger. She inched closer to the desk, and the stalk in her step reminded me of an opponent on the battlefield. "Because I said so?" She spoke slowly, enunciating every single word. "I can put up with some of your bullshit, but not all of it. Let me tell you right now, '*Because I said so*' ain't gonna fly. You don't tell me what to do. *I* tell me what to do, and I'm going shopping."

I'd never been more infuriated and more aroused at the same time.

"See you when I get back." She marched off.

I released a growl under my breath before I left my desk. "Hold on."

She headed to the front door.

"I said, hold on." I grabbed her by the elbow.

She twisted out of my hold like she'd anticipated it, but her palm didn't slap me in the face.

Kinda disappointed. "Just let me change."

"Change?"

"I'll come with you."

"You." Her eyebrows furrowed. "Shopping."

"Yes."

"Why?"

I ignored the question and headed off to get dressed.

It was a quiet day because it was Tuesday. There were some tourists, but they were at the beach or lounging at their resorts. Camille bought a couple tops and some dresses, and then grabbed some hair essentials.

"Give Hugo a list next time."

"I need to get out of the house once in a while." Her hands were full of shopping bags as she walked. "As nice as your place is, it gets old."

I grabbed the bags out of one of her hands and carried them.

She gave me a double take in disbelief.

"You were having a hard time."

"Was not. Just admit you're a gentleman."

I'd rather die.

"Sometimes, at least."

While we enjoyed the shops with the ocean as our view, I watched for unfriendly eyes. From what I could tell, no men were tailing us, none that were camped out down the road, waiting for one of us to leave. My actions were the result of paranoia, but after all the shit that had happened, it wasn't really paranoia at all.

Grave wanted what was mine—and he wasn't going to get it.

When she'd bought everything she needed, she rubbed her stomach. "Now I'm hungry."

"You want to eat somewhere?"

"Sure."

Like a regular couple on a shopping day, we went to a restaurant with an outdoor patio and took a seat. All her bags were on the empty chairs beside us, and she adjusted her hair underneath her fedora before she looked at the menu.

We sat under the umbrella in the shade, but my eyes still narrowed because it was so bright. The sunshine was so brilliant, it reflected off the water and made me squint slightly.

She looked through the whole menu like it was a book. "What are you getting?"

"Salad."

"All you ever eat is salad and steak."

"Creature of habit."

The waitress came over and took our order, and once that was done, we were resigned to stare at each other. I had a lot of shit waiting for me when I got home, but I tried not to think about all the stuff I'd have to catch up on.

She took off her sunglasses and set them next to her purse on the table. "I know shopping isn't your thing, so why did you come?"

"The reason you came to stay with me in the first place."

It took her a moment to draw the right conclusion, and when she did, her face fell. "Sometimes I forget."

Her feminine handwriting was imprinted on my mind like a picture on a table in the hallway. I felt no remorse for violating her privacy, not when her confession was stuff I'd already surmised on my own.

A long stretch of silence ensued, so long, our food was brought to us.

She'd ordered a pasta dish with minestrone soup, and I ate my salad with shrimp. Other couples were in the restaurant, some holding hands on the surface of the table, others laughing or grinning.

Her eyes caught mine then would flick away.

I stared at her or the ocean, the only two things worthy of my attention.

"So, how long is this going to go on?"

Having no idea what she meant, I gave her a quizzical stare.

"You won't kill him, right? You don't want to look over your shoulder forever either."

"I always look over my shoulder."

"Doesn't that get exhausting?"

"I don't know another way of life."

She hesitated with her meal, as if my words really struck her core. She stared at me for a moment before she returned her spoon to her bowl. "How did you get into the diamond business?"

"I did my research. Knew there was a lot of money in it."

"But you do more than sell diamonds. You're in this criminal underworld... How did that happen?"

"Guess I was born into it."

Now she seemed uninterested in her food altogether because she stopped eating. "You've never told me about your father."

"Because there's not much to tell."

"Is he still alive?"

I gave her a long stare, my heartbeat suddenly absent. Her eyes were so bright, reflecting the beautiful day, and they were absorbing everything around her, including my darkness. "No."

"I'm sorry."

"I couldn't care less, so don't be." I meant it with every fiber of my being, felt more hatred than my body could contain. Just thinking about him made me angry, and it was too beautiful of a day to be so angry.

"Is he the reason your mother was—"

"This discussion is over."

Her chin immediately dropped, and her eyes were on her food once more. "I'm sorry. I just...I just want to know you."

"Trust me, you don't."

Her head lifted again. "I've heard it all, Cauldron. My clients confess their deepest and darkest secrets all the time. Nothing you could say would faze me."

When I pictured some faceless man beside her in bed, smoking a cigar or drinking a scotch after a night of passion, it made me angry. Imagining a connection strong enough to make them confide their darkest fears made me even angrier. Picturing her with anyone, in any context, made me angry.

She knew me well enough now to pick up on my silent hostility. Instead of apologizing, she abruptly changed the subject. "Thanks for coming out with me today. It's nice to do stuff with you, other than...you know."

Fucking. "I'll always uphold my end of the deal and keep you safe."

She looked down at her food again. "Yeah...I know you will."

"Cami, where is it?" She sat at my bedside, the lamp on the nightstand illuminating her beautiful face. Her hand went to my wrist, where she gave me a gentle squeeze. "Cami?"

My hand immediately went to my throat, feeling for the necklace that wasn't there. I was a small child in a twin-size bed, my duvet cover a rose pink. There were posters on my walls of horses and boys.

"Cami?"

"I-I had it."

"Where is it now?"

My hand slid down my chest and dropped into my lap. "He—he took it from me."

"Why did you let him take it?"

I started to cry.

"Why did you let him take you? Why did you let all those men take you?"

"Mom…I'm sorry."

She pulled her hand away. "I'm so disappointed in you."

Now I sobbed.

She left my bedside.

"Mom, I'll get it back."

She moved to the bedroom door.

"Wait…wait."

The lamp went out. The bedroom was dark. And then…there were things. Things in the dark. "Mom…" They came at me, moving all at once, ready to pull me down to hell where I belonged. "*Mom!*"

I jerked upright in bed and clasped at the necklace that wasn't there. I was coated in so much sweat, I felt slippery against the sheets. I climbed out of bed and tumbled to the floor, and I felt my back hit the wall with a thud.

My bedroom door flew open. "Camille?"

I screamed at the sight of him, holding a shotgun across his bare chest.

He did a quick walkthrough of the bedroom, checking the bathrooms and then the windows for intruders.

I hyperventilated on the floor against the wall, his dark figure just like the monsters in my nightmare. My dreams and reality merged into a haunting existence. I gripped my chest to make sure my heart continued to beat, and I felt it race as if it might explode.

Cauldron put the gun down on the table and came to me on the floor. "Are you okay?" One hand went to my thigh while the other grabbed me by the arm.

I slapped him away. "Don't touch me."

He abruptly pulled his hands away and left them hanging in the air. "What happened?"

I continued to pant deep and hard. Hot flashes came and went. My knees came up to my chest. "Nightmare…"

He watched me for a while before he leaned against the wall beside me, arms on his knees, wearing nothing but his boxers.

I breathed and breathed until the remnants of the dream finally faded. The monsters felt so real, like hyenas descending on an injured animal to feast. They didn't have faces, didn't really have appearances, but they were terrifying.

Cauldron turned to look at me. "Do you want to talk about it?"

I could still see her face, her earnest face as she gripped my wrist. "My mother...she asked for her necklace. I didn't have it."

"What necklace?"

"A necklace she gave me when I was young..." I stared at the bed that I'd toppled out of. "I don't have it anymore."

"You lost it?"

"No...he took it from me."

His features slowly hardened as he realized of whom I spoke.

"He took it so I wouldn't leave. It worked for a while. But then I realized I had to escape, even if that meant I had to leave it behind. I tried to go back and get it, but...that didn't work."

His handsome face was set in darkness, his eyes quietly angry.

"She told me she was disappointed in me. Not just because of the necklace...but how I've chosen to live my life." The tears rekindled and watered my already wet eyes. "She left me...and then these monsters came." Tears fell down my cheeks to my lips, coating the skin with salt that I could taste without moving my tongue. I could still see her perfectly, see the way she left me behind...again.

"She's not disappointed in you, Camille."

"I'm a whore. Of course she is."

"No one should ever be ashamed of what they do to survive—including you."

I sniffled and wiped away the tears.

"And no mother is ever disappointed in her children. It's just not possible."

I sniffled again.

"Just a nightmare. Means nothing."

"Maybe...but I still feel like shit." My arms crossed over my body, suddenly freezing cold when I'd been sweaty just moments ago.

His hand slowly reached out and stopped several inches away, as if waiting for permission. When I gave a nod, his hand rested on my knee, his calloused thumb brushing my soft skin. It remained there for a while before it slid up my thigh to cup the inside of it. "Come on." He got to his feet then extended his hand to pull me up. "Get some sleep."

I let him pull me to my feet, but I didn't slide back into bed. "I can't now. I'll just watch some TV for a while." I moved to the couch in my long t-shirt and plopped down before I grabbed the remote. I turned on the TV, the bedroom flooding with blue light, chasing away the monsters hidden in the shadows.

Instead of leaving the room, he took the seat beside me, pretty much naked in his small shorts. His muscular legs were covered in dark hair, but his chest and back were nothing but tanned skin. He relaxed against the cushion, one foot propped on the table.

"You don't have to stay with me."

Quiet, he watched the TV.

"I'm sure you're tired."

He grabbed the blanket hanging off the back of the armchair then patted the cushion beside him. "Come here."

The last thing I wanted was to be alone right now. There was no greater feeling than lying in his arms. I knew how it felt, briefly, and I still missed it. Even if his actions were solely out of pity, I couldn't reject the opportunity. I slid to his side and felt the blanket cover me. My face rested against his shoulder, and my arm hooked through his without invitation. The heat from his body was sweltering, like midday at the beach. My legs rested over his, and I felt his arm curve around me, bringing me close.

Now, it was like the nightmare had never happened.

His chin rested on my head while his fingers lightly stroked my arm. For a man who claimed to be incapable of so many things, he was awfully gentle. In a still moment like this, he made me forget the need for survival. I hadn't felt this content since the moment before I found out my mother was sick—the last time my world felt whole.

"Why is this necklace so important to you? Other than the fact that your mother gave it to you." His voice was quiet, but still audible over the sound of the TV. The volume was on low, and it was a rerun of an old show.

"It's all I have of her." I curled into his body more, no longer needing the TV to chase away the horrors in my mind. "When she passed away, I couldn't afford to pay for anything, so it was all lost. Creditors took all the furniture. That necklace is all I managed to keep. It's like a family heirloom now…a memory of when life was good."

Heavy silence passed, lasting for an eternity. "Where does he keep it?"

"His bedroom. I snuck in when he had a party and managed to get it in my hands, but he caught me. That was when I came to you. I hoped that if I convinced you to kill him, I could get that necklace back."

His fingers continued to caress my arm, his calloused fingertips tender and loving against my skin. He brushed the hair from my neck, and the slight touch to my sensitive skin made me break out in bumps. "I'll get it back for you."

It took a second to accept his words, to convince myself I hadn't imagined them. My body moved from his so I could get a look at his handsome face, to study the sincerity in those dark eyes. "You will…?"

He pulled me close again, his lips brushing across my temple. "Yes."

When I woke up the next morning, the usual coldness I felt was absent. I was still wrapped in a bundle of warmth. My eyes opened, and I saw that the TV had been shut off sometime in the middle of the night. I also realized the hard surface underneath my head wasn't the armrest—but his powerful chest.

Slowly, my head rose and fell with his breaths.

My hand rested on his stomach, my fingertips sprawled out to feel the hardness of his abs.

I raised my head slightly to get a look at his face.

He was fast asleep, his normally focused face calm. His edge was gone. So was his hostility. Now he was just a man.

I couldn't believe he'd stayed.

He'd stayed with me.

My head returned to his chest, and I went still, careful not to wake him. I could lie there forever as long as he was beside me. With the patience of a monk, I lay still and watched him breathe, watched the patch of sun slowly move across the floor as the sun rose higher above the horizon.

How much time had passed, I didn't know. Time moved so quickly when we were together, even when he was unconscious.

He finally stirred, his hand immediately dragging across his face as reality set in. He blinked a few times, regarding the bedroom as he tried to remember how he got there. A quiet sigh left his lips before he turned to look at me. His eyes said it all—that he didn't plan for this to happen.

Before he could storm off, I moved on top of him and planted my palms against his chest. My sex sat right on his length, which was naturally hard from the morning. I gave him a gentle grind through our underwear, and that seemed to chase away the anger about to break through.

I tugged his boxers down as he grabbed my thong and pulled the fabric over to reveal my entrance. Our bodies came together instantly, his hardness ready for my slickness. He groaned as he felt me and tugged on my underwear a little tighter, making the fabric fray at the seams.

I took him fully, moving all the way down until there was nowhere left to go. My breath hitched, my core tightened in a slight wince, but it felt so good, I didn't care about the discomfort of his size.

His intense stare had returned, mixed with the sexy look of his sleepy gaze. His short hair was matted from sleeping on the couch, and his big hand gripped my hip with crushing force as he started to guide me.

I rocked my hips as I moved up and down, going nice and slow because morning sex was about sensuality. It didn't take much to release, not when a dreamlike haze was cast over your eyes. Every touch was amplified. Every breath was loud in the silence. I watched his skin slowly darken with the red tint he exuded when he was turned on. It spread from his chest to his shoulders and up one side of his neck.

He tugged me harder and harder, pulling me down his length with greater intensity.

Everything came together to make me release. The pleasure on his face, the size of his dick as it hit me over and over, the way my clit dragged against his pelvic bone. It was all so good. With my nails deep in his chest, I came, moaning as I ground my clit hard against his body.

He'd been waiting for this moment, gripping me harder and harder as he resisted the compulsion to explode. But now, he released with a sexy moan, smacking my ass hard with his big palm. "Fuck."

We writhed in mutual passion until the high hit its crescendo then came back down. Our sweaty bodies came to a gradual standstill, and our breathing masked the morning birds outside the window. We stared at each other as we caught our breath, and now that the fun was over, reality returned to his features.

His anger could only be delayed, not prevented. Now it took up his handsome features once more. The anger didn't seem directed at me specifically, more at himself than anything else.

He guided me off him then left the couch.

I didn't try to stop him. Didn't thank him for staying with me. Didn't say a word.

He grabbed his gun and walked out without saying a thing.

TWENTY-FOUR
CAULDRON

We hadn't exchanged more than a few words since the other day.

I had nothing to say and was relieved she didn't press me to say anything. Everything happened so suddenly. Once I heard her scream, I barged in with my loaded shotgun. The rest was a blur.

I threw on my sports coat then headed to the hallway.

"Cauldron."

I turned around at the sound of her voice. She stood in a white dress, her hair pulled up like she'd spent the afternoon by the pool. Disappointment was in her gaze, as if my distance was unwarranted and unfair.

"Are you leaving?"

"I have a meeting." I adjusted the sleeves.

"That didn't answer my question."

"It's on property." I turned away.

"I don't appreciate you ignoring me——"

"Can we do this later?" I turned back around, snapping.

Her eyes shone with anger. "Don't act like I'm nagging you. If you think you can ignore me without consequence, then you're an idiot." Now she was the one to turn around and walk away, and she slammed the bedroom door just for good measure.

I headed downstairs just in time because the doorbell rang. Hugo opened the door and revealed Marie Delacroix, one of my biggest clients. Earrings she'd purchased from me dangled from her lobes, and the diamond that hung from her necklace was both subtle and flawless. Her face lit up when she saw me, and she came close to give me a kiss on each cheek. "It's been a while, Cauldron."

"It has." I kissed her back. "Too long."

Her arm hooked through mine, and we entered the back patio, where we took a seat surrounded by the trees and flowers. The sun was setting, so the temperature was cool and comfortable. She was in a short black dress with heels, one shoulder exposed, her hair thick and curled.

We stared at each other for a while.

"How's work?" I asked, initiating the small talk I despised.

"Just had a shoot with *Vogue* in Istanbul. It's beautiful this time of year."

"It is."

"What's new with you, Cauldron?" She grabbed the wine that Hugo had brought her and took a drink, smearing her lipstick on the rim of the glass.

"Business, as usual."

"You ever think of anything else?" Her leg moved underneath the table, sliding right up against my calf. At first, it seemed like an accident, but when she continued to do it, it became clear it was intentional.

"Occasionally."

She smiled as she withdrew her leg. "So, what have you got for me?"

I gave a slight wave to my men.

The first came over and set the box in front of her. He unlocked it and revealed a beautiful diamond necklace, simple in its size but brilliant with all the little diamonds along the platinum.

"This is stunning." She lifted the necklace from the box and examined it, resting it against the back of her wrist to see how the diamonds looked on her flawless skin. With her eyes on the jewelry, she said, "First time I've been here for business."

We'd met many years ago at the Cannes Film Festival. She wasn't my client then, just a lover who frequented my yacht a few times. She became interested in my diamonds later, and sometimes business and pleasure mixed. "I've been busy, so this is more convenient." I'd meet her off property, but I feared if I left without Camille, Grave would decide to pull a stunt. And I knew taking Camille with me would be a big mistake. Marie would definitely lose interest in my diamonds if she saw the woman in my life. I gestured to my men again, and they brought more diamonds for her to peruse.

"Beautiful," she said as she examined them all. "Just gorgeous."

"This is the one for you." I secured the bracelet to her slender wrist. "If you want my opinion."

Our touch lingered, but I felt nothing. No heat. No electricity. No desire whatsoever.

But she clearly did.

She examined it with a smile before she looked at me again. "I trust your taste, Cauldron."

I gestured to the men again, and that was when they brought the laptop. She and I did business, exchanging the funds before the other diamonds were whisked away back to the vault. The two of us continued to enjoy our wine. She probably expected more than just the transaction, so I'd have to spurn her advances without outright rejecting her. Telling her I was taken would guarantee the loss of her as a client.

Hugo presented canapés, and we talked about her life in Paris as we drank a bottle of wine together. Her foot made its way up my leg several times, despite the fact that I had no reaction to it.

When the wine was drunk and the night had deepened, I tried to get rid of her. "I'll walk you out, Marie." I stood and ignored the subtle confusion on her face.

It took her a moment to rise to her feet, and when she did, she slipped her arm through mine. "That jacket looks very nice on you."

"Thank you," I said with a smile. I walked her into the house and to the entryway. The valet already had her car out front.

Marie pressed her chest right into me, her hands moving to my biceps, where she squeezed them through the jacket. Her eyes settled on my lips like she wasn't going to leave until she got what she wanted. "I'm in town for a week. Maybe we can take your yacht out for a couple days?"

"I'll let you know."

She moved in to kiss me on the mouth.

I made a subtle turn and kissed her cheek, acting like I'd misunderstood her intention. "I'll call you." I walked her through the door then waited on the doorstep, my hands sliding into my pockets.

She gave me a flirtatious wave before she got into the car and drove away.

Thank fuck that was over.

I walked back inside and headed to the stairs. When I looked up, I spotted her at the next landing, one hand on her hip and the other gripping the rail so hard she might break it. Her eyes were spotlights right on me, white-hot and angry.

I sighed before I walked up the steps to meet her. "Camille—"

Smack.

She hit me harder than she ever had. This time, she meant. Really meant it.

The heat in my cheek was like an inferno. I slowly turned back to her, swallowing my anger as best I could before I did something I couldn't take back. "It's not what it looked like—"

Smack.

I turned again, clenching my jaw to suppress my rage.

"Don't insult me." She marched off, taking the stairs to the third floor.

I stayed behind, letting the rage circulate through my veins before it left my nostrils. When I got my bearings, I went after her. "Camille." I came up behind her in the hallway and grabbed her by the arm.

She tried her old trick of spinning before elbowing me in the face, but I was tired of getting smacked around, so I grabbed her like a steel cage and shoved her against the wall. She fought me hard, fought me like it was life-and-death, but I got her pinned in place. She tried to knee my groin, but I used my leg to block it.

"You're going to shut up and listen to me."

She tried to throw her body against mine, to no avail. "Bite me."

"It's not how it looked—"

"Her foot was so far up your leg, it was practically up your ass." She was vicious, throwing her body against me, looking at me like I was a traitor. "And you did nothing."

So she'd watched the entire thing. "There's a reason for that."

"Is it the same reason you're taking her out on your yacht?" she snapped. "The same reason you let her kiss you?"

"I turned my cheek."

"Didn't look like it from my angle."

"I. Turned. My. Cheek."

"You should have told her you're seeing someone. Plain and simple."

"I'm not seeing someone." Her jealousy only made me angry because this started off as an arrangement, and now it was fucking complicated. "You're my whore. That's it."

All the fight left her body. Her wrists went limp in my grip. Her eyes glazed over with a misty fog. There was no bite of anger, just raw devastation.

I regretted the words the second I spoke them.

She turned her head and avoided my look. Then she walked away, no longer caged by my grip. With drooped shoulders and a bent back, she walked down the hallway to her bedroom, her pace slow, her appearance defeated.

I felt like shit.

She went into her bedroom and gently shut the door behind her.

After a long night of tears and a crumpled note, I packed my things and walked to the front door.

"Camille, what are you doing?" Hugo walked beside me, seeing the suitcase I pulled behind me and the bag on my arm.

"Could you call the valet? I need a ride."

"Mr. Beaufort——"

"Mr. Beaufort has no issue with me leaving. So, please grab me that car."

Hugo looked at me for a moment before he walked off. He didn't head to the valet or to pick up the phone. He went in the direction of Cauldron's study.

I released an annoyed sigh. "Fine, I'll walk." I went out the front door and pulled my luggage behind me. His security team watched me, watched how ridiculous I looked walking by the fountain and to the large iron gates.

"Camille."

I didn't look back. "Fuck off."

His feet hit the pavement as he jogged to catch up to me. "Camille—"

"Leave me alone." I made it to the gates and stared at the attendant to let me through. "Come on, open it."

He glanced at Cauldron before he looked at me again, like he wouldn't do a damn thing until his boss told him to.

I rounded on Cauldron. "You've tried to get rid of me for so long, so here you go. I'll fucking climb the wall like last time, but I took all the clothes you bought me, so the damn bag is too heavy. So just open the fucking gates."

He was in nothing but his sweatpants. No shirt. No shoes. And he stared at me like there would be no cooperation. "Let's talk inside."

"Fine. I'll leave the fucking clothes." I left the suitcase and walked to the wall.

He snatched the bag off my arm. "Camille."

"Just let me go."

"Give me five minutes, and if you still want to leave, my driver will take you anywhere you want."

"*If?*" I asked incredulously. "Trust me, my ass is gone." I marched back to the house and left my luggage behind so he could carry it.

Of course, one of his men came forward and took everything so he didn't have to. Barefoot, he walked up the roundabout beside me and back into the coolness of the house. My arms locked over my chest as we moved through the house and entered his study.

He shut the door behind him then looked at me.

I stared him down, disgusted by that handsome face.

He clenched his jaw as he tried to find the right thing to say. His eyes shifted back and forth before he looked down and rubbed the scruff of his jaw. He didn't shave this morning. He looked tired too, like he hadn't slept. "I'm sorry."

"That's it?" I asked, eyebrow cocked. "You're sorry?"

"It was an asshole thing to say…and I didn't mean it."

"I told you not ever to call me that——"

"I know. I lost my temper because you wouldn't let me explain." He examined my face, seeing if there was a rebuttal before he could continue. "Marie is a good client. She buys a lot of my diamonds. Her girlfriends buy my diamonds. It's like free advertising. I didn't want to offend her."

"Saying you're involved with someone isn't offensive."

"She wanted more from me, so if I tell her I'm giving that to someone else, she'll never speak to me again."

"Is that all that matters to you?" I asked incredulously. "Money?"

His jaw clenched, like he was processing his rage as calmly as he could. "Money. Power. Sex. They all matter to me."

"I'm not on that list?" I asked quietly.

His eyes shifted back and forth between mine.

I felt my heart in my hands. Felt myself reach out and hand it to him.

"You're taking this too personally. I could have Marie whenever I want, but I don't want her at all. I could have any woman I want, but you're the only one I desire. Marie is beautiful, but I felt nothing for her. Her advances were fucking obnoxious. I just wanted to do business and then have her leave."

"Now she's waiting for you to call—"

"And I won't because I'm too busy fucking you. It's just business, Camille. We've talked about this before. There's no reason not to trust me. When have I ever said what you wanted to hear just to make you feel better? When have I ever done anything other than give you the cold, hard truth?"

"I want a man who tells the world I'm his."

"You are mine—"

"That's not what you said to Marie."

He looked away for a while, visibly struggling with his anger. "Let's not forget what this is, Camille. It's a deal. You give me what I want, and I give you what you want. I'm not your man. I'm your clandestine lover— nothing more."

It was like a knife between the ribs that sank deep enough to puncture my lung. "And that's all I am to you?"

He held my gaze, stoic.

"You save me from my nightmares, and I mean nothing to you? You sleep with me, something you said you would never do, and that means nothing? You kiss me like you love me, but it's just for show? I don't believe that, Cauldron. You don't either."

He didn't blink, his look was so intense.

"Treat me like that again, and I'm gone."

He continued to stare.

The conversation seemed to be over, so I stepped around him to leave.

"Sit." His arm reached out for me, barring me from the exit.

I stared at him for a few seconds before I took a seat.

He pulled his phone from his pocket and made a call on speaker.

I had no idea what he was doing.

A woman answered. "Ready to set sail?"

He looked at his desk across the room, the phone sitting in his hand. "Marie, I should have told you this last night, and I'm sorry that I didn't. I'm seeing someone, so nothing can happen between us."

Marie must have been in shock because she didn't say anything.

"I'm sorry I didn't mention it sooner. Take care." He hung up and returned the phone to his pocket. "Does that make it better?" He turned to look at me, standing there like a chiseled statue.

"A little…"

He took the seat beside me, his hand moving to my thigh. "Next time some woman shoves her foot up my ass, I'll tell her."

An uncontrollable grin cracked across my face.

That made him smile too—a little bit.

It was hard to hold the grudge when my wounds were healed. It was hard to stay angry with his hand on my thigh, with that handsome smile on his face. When he looked at me like that, it was as if nothing had happened.

TWENTY-SIX

CAULDRON

I walked into that same restaurant.

He was at the same table, in the private room in the back. One ankle rested on the opposite knee, and his arms were squeezed by the gray sports coat. An Omega watch was on his wrist. Arrogance was in his eyes.

He thought he had me in the palm of his hand, and he kinda did.

I took the seat across from him. The decanter of scotch was already there, along with two glasses of ice. He'd started without me. The sneer on his face was obnoxious. Hadn't changed since I'd known him.

"Where is she?"

I filled my glass.

"I assume you've come to your senses."

Far from it.

"Don't pretend your business isn't hurting, Cauldron."

"I have so much money, I don't need more money." I swirled the glass and took a drink.

"Then I guess I have to hit you harder."

"Likewise."

His smile dropped. "Then what's the purpose of this conversation?"

"The necklace."

His eyes narrowed at the request. "She told you about that?"

"She tells me everything."

His rage was subtle, storm clouds obscuring his eyes.

"Give the woman her dead mother's necklace, you fucking asshole."

He sank back in his chair, his arms crossed over his chest. "She knows what she needs to do to get it."

"She's made it pretty clear that nothing is worth coming back."

The breath he took was quiet, but it filled his lungs with smoke from the fire in his chest.

"I'll pay you for it. What's your price?"

"Her."

"Are you deaf?" I snapped. "She doesn't want you. Get over it."

"She doesn't want you either, asshole."

I smirked before I took a drink. "Oh, she does."

The volcano spewed lava in his eyes. "I'm not her first choice, and neither are you."

"That's not what she told me. Not what she wrote in her diary."

Now he was quiet, afraid if he said more, I would just supply more evidence that would torture him into insanity.

"Give me the necklace and move on, Grave."

"You're the one who needs to move on, Cauldron. I know what you're doing."

"I'm trying to get her necklace back—"

"You only want her because I want her."

I grabbed the glass and took another drink.

"And that's fucked up."

I set the glass down and stared at him, feeling no remorse whatsoever.

"Not to me—but to her."

I ignored the tug on my heartstrings.

"If what you say is true, at least."

I centered the conversation back on the purpose of this meeting. "Give me the fucking necklace."

He ignored the command and reached for his glass.

"You think you're the only one who can sabotage a business?"

The glass hadn't reached his lips when he stilled. His dark eyes pierced me from across the table. He returned his scotch to the table and stared at me hard. "Is that a threat?"

"It's not if you give me the necklace."

"It seems to me that you're the one obsessed with her—not the other way around."

"Just not a monster. Not a monster that holds her mother's necklace hostage. What the fuck is wrong with you?" I'd stormed into her bedroom, assuming Grave had broken through one of her windows, but I found something much worse. Her lifeless body crumpled on the floor, tears like rivers.

"I won't change my mind."

"Fine." I slammed the glass down and got to my feet. "Two can play that game, Grave."

"Are we really doing this?" The backs of his knees pushed his chair back as he sprang to his feet. "Are we really going to rip our lives apart for a woman you don't even love?"

I turned back to stare at him.

His arms were stiff at his sides, and his eyes were so angry. Frustration was packed deep inside his body with nowhere for it to go, like steam under the lid of a pot. He trembled in his anger, fingers rolled tight into fists.

It was all worth it to see him like this.

"I told you I was sorry for what happened—"

"That doesn't mean shit to me." It was anger that couldn't be conquered, a grudge so deep it was like roots from the oldest tree. "But making your life a living hell does."

"Why are you so angry?"

My eyes focused on the woman across from me. She'd been a blur up until this point, my mind plotting evil schemes. "Who said I was?"

"Uh, the look on your face."

She sat across from me on the back terrace. Surrounded by flowers with buzzing bees, we listened to the waterfall as the sun trickled down. The blue of the ocean slowly faded, turning gray as the sunlight disappeared. I was in paradise, with a beautiful woman who wanted me, but all I wanted was to make heads roll.

"You want to talk about it?" She picked at her dinner with a fork as she looked at me.

I grabbed the wineglass and took a drink. "I'm still trying to get your necklace back."

When she heard what I said, she stiffened. "What does that mean?"

"First, I asked for it. That didn't go anywhere."

"You asked Grave? Yeah, not surprised he said no. It's the only thing anchoring me to him."

"I'll have to try something else."

"Like what?"

"Hitting him where it hurts—his business."

She set her silverware down altogether. She fidgeted slightly, visibly uncomfortable. "I really appreciate what you're doing, but I don't want you to get hurt."

I insulted her words by grinning, but I couldn't help it. "You don't have to worry about that."

"Why?"

I drank my wine again.

"Why?" she repeated, as if I hadn't heard her. "Will you ever tell me what happened between you two?"

"We're enemies. I told you that."

"More like frenemies."

I sank into my chair, hands gripping the edges of the armrests.

"I think it would help if I understood—"

"It's beyond your understanding. Our world is small. Only a few key players. For the health of the ecosystem, it's better to find a way to coexist."

"So, you're in the same line of business?"

"It's complicated."

"Well, I'm pretty smart——"

"I'm done talking about him." The only time I wanted to think about that motherfucker was when I was taunting him, not enjoying my grand estate and the woman who served as my trophy. "I will get your necklace back. It'll just take me some time."

She wore that look on her face that told me she wanted to charge through my walls until she got what she wanted. But she withdrew, letting the topic fade. "Like I said, I don't want anything to happen to you. You're more important than that necklace."

My eyes locked on her face, reading all the signs of sincerity that came so naturally to her. She wore her heart on her sleeve, bravely shared her feelings without fear of rejection. She made me feel wanted, but she did it in a way that wasn't claustrophobic and needy. She didn't want me for the same reasons the others did—because of money. It made me feel like shit, but not shitty enough to stop.

———

"Here you are, Mr. Beaufort." Hugo placed the folded letter on my desk, smoothed out as much as possible to get rid of all the creases. It'd been crumpled up like the other, thrown to the bottom of the wastebasket to be forgotten. He departed my study and left me alone.

I unfolded it and started to read.

———

How many times have I heard the girls say that the men will leave their wives? That they just need more time. Need to get their affairs in order. Speak to the lawyers before pulling the trigger. And how many times did I just nod along and keep my mouth shut? I thought they were stupid for believing their lies. Men said anything in the heat of the moment and never kept their promises.

But here I am…doing the exact same thing.

He called me a whore. Cared more about preserving his business partnership than his commitment to me. Told me that our relationship wasn't a relationship at all… just a symbiotic compromise.

I don't believe that. I don't believe a man can kiss me like that and not mean it. I don't believe a man can rescue me from my nightmares when his heart doesn't beat for me. Sometimes he grabs me and kisses me for no reason...and if he weren't holding me, I might fall to my knees. A man can't do those things and feel nothing, right?

Right...?

I hardly think of Grave. I have a new life now, living with a man who's my protector and my lover. He's all I ever think about now, the single most important thing in my life. Grave could be dead, and I would still be here.

Would he want me here?

Am I the stupidest person alive for falling for someone like Cauldron? A man who fights his vulnerability with the strength of steel.

Or am I the most romantic person alive...for believing he's worth fighting for?

It was the middle of the night.

The clock read 3:34 a.m.

I sat in my study and looked out the open window. The grounds were lit up, ancient trees illuminated across the estate. The world was still. The wind was absent. I should be asleep, but I couldn't sleep at a time like this.

My eyes glanced back to the phone on the desk.

The screen was black.

My eyes shifted back to the window.

With my fingers tucked under my chin and my elbow on the armrest, I pierced the night with my eyes, my mind envisioning the carnage I'd caused. Grave had crippled my business, and now I would do the same to him.

Crack.

My head snapped to the open doorway of my study.

A dish had fallen in the kitchen and shattered. The sound traveled all the way to me on the other side of the silent house. I grabbed my gun from the drawer and shoved the phone into my pocket before I went to investigate.

"Shit…" Camille was squatting on the floor, doing her best to pick up all the little pieces of the shattered plate without cutting herself.

"What are you doing?"

She jumped up with a yelp. "Jesus!" Her hand clutched her chest, and she backed into the kitchen island. "How did you get down here so fast?"

I turned on the safety and set the gun on the counter.

"And why do you always have a gun?"

"So I can shoot people."

She breathed through the hysteria before she rolled her eyes.

"What are you doing?" I repeated.

"What does it look like?" she snapped. "I was hungry." She kneeled back down to pick up the pieces.

"Stop. You'll cut yourself."

"It's fine." She continued to pick up the little pieces.

"*Stop*."

She gave a sigh packed with attitude and backed away.

I grabbed the broom and the dustpan and swept up the mess she'd made. The pieces were tossed in the trash, and the kitchen floor was pristine once again.

"I'm surprised you knew where the broom was."

"It's my house, isn't it?"

"Still…"

I checked my phone. It was still black.

"What are you doing?"

I returned the phone to my pocket and leaned against the counter. I was barefoot and bare-chested, comfortable in my gray sweatpants. I hardly wore anything else when I was home. "You want me to make you something?"

"You can cook?" she asked in surprise.

"Why is that surprising?"

"Because you have a house full of servants who do everything for you except wipe your ass."

Her feistiness tugged a smile across my lips. "It wasn't always that way. What do you want?"

"What's on the menu?" She leaned against the kitchen island, wearing a baggy shirt that reached her thighs.

One of her shoulders was exposed, and her hair was in a messy bun. Her beauty was natural, and most women couldn't say the same. Her face was angled and beautiful without that contouring bullshit, and her lips really were that plump and supple without fillers and makeup.

"How about a peanut butter and jelly sandwich?"

"Is that your idea of cooking?" she asked with a laugh.

"Fried eggs with white truffle?"

"I thought truffles were black?"

"They are. But the white ones are better and rarer." I moved to the pans. "Is that a yes?"

"Sure."

I got to work, setting my phone on the counter beside me so I wouldn't miss the call.

She stood behind me, watching me cook. "Smells good."

I grated the white truffle on top of the eggs and set the plate on the island in front of her. The pan and used dishes were left behind for Hugo to deal with later.

She cut into the first piece, the yolk dripping across the plate. She took her time with her first bite, savoring the taste. Then she gave a nod in approval. "Damn, this is good."

I pulled out my phone from my pocket and took a peek.

Nothing.

She continued to eat at the counter. "Waiting for a call?"

"Yes."

"It's four o'clock in the morning."

"Work never sleeps."

She finished the plate and left it in the sink. "Thanks for making me something."

My phone vibrated in my pocket. Her presence in the kitchen was forgotten, and I answered the phone. "Yes?"

"It's done."

The satisfaction had a numbing effect. I wished I could see his face when his biggest job went to shit, but my imagination would have to suffice. "Good." I hung up and returned the phone to my pocket.

She continued to stand there. "You stayed up until four for that?"

My arms crossed over my chest as I looked at her. "You didn't enjoy dinner last night?"

"Wasn't that hungry, so I didn't eat much. My stomach woke me up in the middle of the night. Thought there was a wild animal outside, but then I remembered I was on the third floor."

I cracked a smile as I left the kitchen. "Let's go to bed."

"Won't Hugo be mad that we left his kitchen a mess?"

"I couldn't care less." We took the steps to the third floor and walked down the hallway to where the bedrooms were located. Mine was before hers, so I stopped to let her pass.

Instead of going on her way, she stopped in front of me, her eyes dropping to my chest. "I'm not tired…" Her eyes lingered there before they moved a little farther down to my abs. She drank me in like I was the finest wine she'd ever tasted. "Are you?" Her eyes flicked back to mine.

This fine-ass piece of woman was practically begging me when she didn't even have to ask. My sweatpants had been snug since the kitchen, and they became even more snug after that phone call. My hand reached for her neck, getting a grip tighter than necessary as I moved in.

She took a deep breath and didn't resist me, letting me conquer her body like it belonged to me. Her head automatically tilted in anticipation of my lips, and when she felt my kiss, an involuntary moan released into my mouth.

My other hand gripped her ass underneath her shirt and tugged her close. Her little body was crushed into mine as our kiss turned from delicate to hungry. I lifted her into me and carried her into my bedroom, her sexy legs wrapped around my waist. We fell onto the bed together, undressed each other, and then our naked bodies were combined in a euphoric moan.

I had her folded underneath me with her pussy so slick it felt like a tight bottle of lube, and I fucked her into the mattress, nails deep in my back, hungry eyes locked on mine. She tugged on me when she needed more, and her moans were heavy with the sound of my name. "Cauldron…"

"Camille." I got lost every time we were together, swept up in the unbridled passion that consumed us both. Good sex was easy to come by if you could afford it, but this was free, and it was so much better than the dirty shit I paid for.

The sound of her name made her come, made her buck against me with wet eyes and sharp nails. She got so tight it was like her hand squeezed my dick as hard as she could. She hit the crescendo before she came back down…slowly drifting from her high. When her eyes focused once again, she looked at me like I was a king for making her feel so good.

She made me feel like one.

She tugged on my ass and brought me deep inside her. "I want it…"

I fisted her hair, hooked my arm behind one knee, and pounded her so hard that the crashing headboard must have woken up the rest of the house.

"Yes…" Her sexy whispers filled my bedroom and inflated my ego. "Yes." She wanted to watch me come, got off on the sight of my pleasure just as I got off on the sight of hers.

My body went white-hot before it was set aflame. Then I released with more pleasure than I'd ever felt, filling her with every drop of desire she evoked in me. "Camille…"

Her hand dug into my hair, and she kissed me, kissed me as she felt me fill her completely.

Hot and sweaty, I rolled off her, every muscle in my body loose in relaxation. She was on me instantly, one arm hooked around my waist, her head on my shoulder, her leg tucked between mine. Her body was just as hot as mine, but I didn't push her away.

The second my eyes closed, I was gone.

Beep. Beep. Beep.

"Oh my god, turn that shit off."

Cauldron reached for his phone and turned off the alarm.

I closed my eyes again and drifted away.

His weight shifted then he left the mattress.

I groaned then cracked open my eyes, seeing the morning sunlight through the curtains. There was a clock on his nightstand showing 7:08 a.m. "Are you Satan?"

With a voice deep and just a little bit raspy, he said, "I have shit to do."

"Well, I'm not moving." I closed my eyes and lay still. I heard him move about his bedroom, changing his clothes and brushing his teeth in the bathroom. He didn't seem to mind my sleeping there because he didn't ask me to leave. I heard the door shut a moment later, and then it went silent.

I went right back to sleep.

When I woke up, it was lunchtime.

I sat up in his four-poster bed and took a look around. It was the first time I'd been all the way inside, and I saw that the suite was just as majestic as he was. It had a grand sitting room with a large TV on the wall. A private wet bar, which he seemed to use often, judging by all the half-empty decanters. A private balcony that could easily accommodate twelve people. His private bathroom was probably as big as my bedroom—which wasn't shabby by any means.

I was tempted to go through his things just to get to know him better, but it wasn't worth violating his trust. When we'd met, he told me he didn't let anyone in his bedroom, but here I was, wrapped up in his sheets. It would be stupid to jeopardize how far we'd come. He claimed not to trust anyone, but from where I sat, he trusted me more than anyone else.

The bedroom door opened, and he stepped inside, wearing pants and a short-sleeved shirt. He rocked his sweatpants all the time, so that must mean he had company that morning. He looked at me in his bed, his eyes combing over my appearance wrapped in his sheets.

"I just woke up." I rubbed the sleep from my eyes and realized my hair was down. My hair tie must have come loose in the night, and now it was lost somewhere in the enormous bed.

"Lunch is ready."

I half expected him to yell or throw a fit. "Alright." He walked out and shut the door behind him.

In disbelief, I sat there for a while before I got out of bed, went to my room, and threw something on. A sundress from my closet was yanked down and pulled over my head before I went downstairs. He was on the back terrace, talking on the phone.

When I approached the table, Hugo pulled out the chair for me then scooted it in as I sat down.

Cauldron's conversation was clearly dire, given the look on his face. "That was fast." He listened, a man's voice somewhat audible over the line. He talked quickly, as if afraid he was wasting Cauldron's time. "I'll leave this afternoon." He hung up like that was an appropriate way to end the conversation.

"Leave for where?"

He set the linen napkin across his lap then leaned forward with his arms on the table. "Botswana."

"But you were just there."

"It is what it is." He cut into his food and ate, his expression dark with irritation.

"I'm coming with you?"

"Not this time."

"But—what about Grave?"

"Trust me, you're staying here."

"I don't understand—"

"I'm not an idiot." He lifted his chin and looked straight at me. "He knows the mines require my attention, and he knows you accompany me wherever I go, so once I arrive, he'll hit the house there and try to take you."

"How does he know about your mines? Does this have something to do with last night?"

"It's a small world, Camille." He cut into his food and took a few bites. "Of course it does."

"You think it's safe to leave me behind?"

"I know how his mind works."

It made me uneasy to know he would be in another country, but I trusted his judgment at this point. "Be careful."

He ignored what I said and kept eating.

"Your bed is really comfortable…"

"It's the same as yours."

"It doesn't feel the same." It was soft and warm, the best night of sleep I'd ever had. Or maybe it was just the man beside me who made me feel that way. "How long will you be gone?"

"Depends. But not more than a few days."

"What's happened to your mines?"

"An asshole is drilling into my mines and taking what belongs to me. Now he's collapsed my existing mines. Time and resources wasted. A lot of men will die for this."

"It's Grave, isn't it?"

His face remained stoic.

"Because you won't give me up."

He never answered, and I knew he never would.

I watched him pack his suitcase.

"It'll be dark by the time you get there. Can you wait until morning?"

He zipped up the suitcase then set it on the floor. "Why should I wait?" He faced me, wearing dark jeans and a sports coat. He was back to business, making money and killing the men who crossed him.

"The longer you stay, the longer I don't have to say goodbye."

The stare he gave me was hollow, his feelings so deep down they were invisible at the surface. His look continued for seconds. "I guess I can wait."

It only bought me time, but it was still elating. The smile that lifted my lips lifted my heart too. "Thank you." I moved into his body and felt my hands grip his arms. "Maybe I can cook for you."

"What's on the menu?" His arms circled my waist.

"Peanut butter and jelly." I grinned.

He grinned back—and he'd never looked so handsome.

He lay beside me in bed, his chest shiny with sweat after our rendezvous. Dinner was in our bellies, the gourmet peanut butter and jelly sandwiches I whipped up. When Hugo had spotted me in the kitchen, he'd looked horrified.

Cauldron seemed amused.

He leaned into me and kissed my shoulder then my collarbone, his warm arm pressing against mine as he maneuvered back on top of me. It was one of those nights where the sex never ended. There were only pauses in between, rest breaks where we lay together in silence. His hips moved between my legs, and he held himself over me, his strong arms powerful enough to hold up his frame. "Beautiful." His lips kissed the corner of my mouth as he slipped inside me, and it felt so good it was like it hadn't happened several times already.

I gave a moan of pleasure and sank my nails into his back like teeth into flesh.

The moment was shattered by the alarm.

Cauldron was off me in a flash. One moment, he was naked. And the next, he had his sweatpants on. Then he had a gun, a loaded shotgun that he cocked.

"What's happening?" I stumbled out of bed and grabbed my clothes.

"There's a pistol in my nightstand. Stay here." Unafraid, he marched out of the bedroom and into the hallway.

I stumbled on my way to the nightstand and almost smacked my head against it. With a shaky hand, I reached inside and grabbed it. It was heavy in my palm, slippery against my sweaty fingertips. I assumed it was loaded. I found the safety and clicked it off.

The alarm suddenly turned off.

Maybe it was a false alarm.

With the pistol in my hand, I headed into the hallway and ran to the stairs.

There were a dozen men down there, holding Hugo and the other staff at gunpoint. Hugo's gun had been confiscated. The security team outside was gone, so something must have happened to them. It was just Cauldron, standing there with his shotgun in his hands.

The leader of the mercenaries had a gun aimed right at Cauldron's head. "You aren't supposed to be here."

"Sorry for the inconvenience," Cauldron said through gritted teeth. "Now get the fuck out of my house."

"We're here for the woman—"

"I know exactly why you're here, and you aren't getting it." Cauldron cocked the gun and stepped forward. "Now get the fuck out before I stain the plaster with your brains."

All the men raised their weapons and pointed straight at Cauldron. Twelve to one.

The leader kept the gun pointed straight at Cauldron's forehead, the barrel just inches from his face. "I have my orders—"

Blood sprayed the wall, and he crumpled.

Cauldron wasn't the one who fired.

Grave appeared in the doorway, holding the smoking handgun. "Lower your weapons. Now."

The remainder of the men all returned their guns to their holsters.

Grave stared at Cauldron.

Cauldron stared back.

It lasted for seconds, nearly a minute.

What the fuck?

Grave finally nodded to his men.

They all left the premises, leaving the hostages unharmed.

Now it was just the two of them, staring at each other in the dark, both furious with the other.

Cauldron lowered the shotgun. "You have Jeremiah."

"Or he betrayed you."

"I don't buy my men's loyalty," Cauldron said. "I earn it."

Grave seemed to feel my presence because he raised his chin and looked up at me.

I stared back, my heart like a stone in my stomach. It was the same look he always gave me, like his possession had never changed. He owned me then and he owned me now, and a change of hands wouldn't alter that fact.

He turned his head back to Cauldron.

Another long stare ensued.

Silently, Grave walked out. His back was turned to Cauldron, giving him the perfect shot.

But Cauldron didn't take it.

Hugo brushed off the whole thing like it was another day in the life and immediately got to work on the bloody wall. Security removed the dead body that leaked blood all over the hardwood floor. It all happened wordlessly, like everyone had done this before and was paid well enough to put up with it.

I stayed at the top of the stairs, still in utter shock.

"You okay?" Cauldron came to my side, his hand reaching for my arm.

"I'm fine. But—what happened?"

"I know how he thinks. But he also knows how I think."

My eyes shifted back and forth, confused by the statement. "What?"

"He has Jeremiah somewhere. I need to get him back." Cauldron walked past me down the hallway toward his bedroom.

"Whoa, hold up."

He kept walking.

"I'm talking to you."

He turned back around, no longer patient but visibly annoyed.

Instead of bursting with all the questions I'd already asked several times, I had an epiphany. "He's family."

His poker face was strong.

"That's why he won't hurt you. And that's why you won't kill him."

He gave nothing away. "I have more important shit that requires my attention right now——"

"Why won't you admit it?"

"We'll talk about this later." He continued to his bedroom.

"You don't look enough alike…so he's not your brother."

Cauldron quickly changed his clothes then grabbed his suitcase.

"He's your cousin. Is that it?" I followed him as he walked out, one bag over his shoulder with the handle of the suitcase in his other hand. "Why won't you just tell me?" I followed him all the way down the stairs to the entryway. His men had already pulled the car around for him, were probably gassing up the plane as we spoke. "Cauldron——"

"He's my half brother." He finally turned to look at me with rage written on his face. "But that doesn't make him family."

TWENTY-EIGHT
CAULDRON

Three days later, I had Jeremiah back.

Grave's men had taken him a week ago, forced him into being a snitch. He was bruised and battered now, his face so swollen he looked like he'd been stung by a hive of wasps. The dead men were stacked in the other room, and the lock to his cell was opened.

He remained on the floor against the wall, either too afraid to move or physically unable. "I'm sorry...they tortured me."

I couldn't hold a grudge, couldn't hold him accountable for his betrayal, not when he wasn't in the game like I was. After a pitiful stare, I extended my hand to him.

He studied it timidly before he took it.

I pulled him to his feet, listening to him grimace the whole way up. "We'll get you to a hospital."

"You—you aren't going to kill me?"

"No." I threw his arm over my shoulder and walked him out of the building.

"But you should kill me."

"Do you *want* me to kill you?"

"No," he said quickly. "I just... I was the one who told them you were coming."

"Given the circumstances, I understand." We made it outside, where the men and the cars were waiting.

"You do?" He pulled his arm away and swayed slightly on the spot.

"I'm sorry this happened to you."

His eyes shifted back and forth between mine in disbelief.

"If you didn't talk, they would have killed you. And I wouldn't have wanted that." I gave him a gentle pat on the shoulder. "Let's get you to the hospital."

"Nothing happened, then?" he asked. "Is Camille okay?"

"We're both fine. When Grave realized I was there, he left."

Jeremiah gave a nod. "Good. Glad no one got hurt."

I got him in the car and watched them drive off. My work here was done. I appointed someone else to take Jeremiah's position so I could return home, but my circumstances were still dire. Bombs would continue to fire back and forth, and at some point, there would be nothing left.

I took the plane back to France, but the second I landed, he called.

Almost didn't answer.

I took the call and let my silence do all the talking.

"This can't go on forever."

"It'll go on until someone caves—and it won't be me."

Just like in the foyer of my estate when we stared at each other, the silence stretched into infinity.

"Haven't you tortured me enough?" he whispered.

My answer was quicker than a bullet leaving a gun. "No."

He sighed.

"An eye for an eye. You tortured Jeremiah. Now I'll torture Pierre."

"I didn't torture him for the fun of it——"

"Well, I will."

Another pause. A heavy one. "My client is dead because of you, and I didn't get paid——"

"So sorry to hear that."

"And I know you're running out of diamonds to sell. Soon, you won't be able to meet demand."

"Then the ones I have will become more valuable. It's called economics."

He was so pissed off. It was audible in the silence. "And if I cave, what then?"

I looked out the window from the back seat of the car, seeing the blue sky between the branches of the olive tree.

"Her only value to you is that I want her, so if I don't want her, you won't either."

"Then cave."

He breathed over the line, probably gritting his teeth until they were filed down just a little more.

"You can't do it."

Silence.

"It kills you that I have her. Fucking kills you." Truth be told, I didn't want him to cave. I wanted to keep torturing him. Every single night I fucked her, I fucked him too. I could do this forever, suck on the sweet nectar of revenge for eternity. The loss of my diamonds was minor compared to the joy his torture brought me. "And it'll keep killing you."

TWENTY-NINE
CAMILLE

Five days later, he finally came home.

His imminent arrival was reflected in the staff. They hurried around to change the flowers, make sure the estate looked brand-new before he even walked in the door. The sheets were changed, appetizers were prepared and placed in the entryway. It was ironic because Cauldron didn't care about any of those things. He'd ignore the canapés the chef prepared, hardly say two words, and then head straight for his bedroom.

That was exactly what he did when he walked in the door.

His men carried his luggage up the stairs to his bedroom, Hugo greeted him and presented the canapés and a cold glass of water, and one of the maids took off his jacket and hung it by the door.

Cauldron powered through them and headed straight upstairs.

I stood there as I waited for him.

The men with the luggage walked by first. He came afterward.

The hardness to his features told me he had a sour attitude. He didn't like traveling, even in a private plane, and he didn't like being interrogated when he first walked in the door. There was a warning in his look like he wasn't in the mood.

I decided to interrogate him at a later time. "I'm glad you're home."

His expression softened.

"I missed you." The days passed with painful slowness. My meals were eaten in solitude. I spent time in the pool, but without him sitting on the patio, it was lonely. The homemade jams and jellies tasted bitter, and the wine was weak. He didn't call. He didn't text. It sucked.

He tilted his lips down and caught my mouth. He gave me a short and sweet kiss, his hand gripping me around the waist briefly. After a gentle squeeze, he walked off and left me standing there, winded by that man's touch.

———

Summer was officially over, but it didn't feel that way.

The sun was still out past eight, and the heat continued to warm the land even when it was low in the sky. I sat on the terrace alone to eat dinner, but there were two place settings. Hugo set a basket of bread on the table and filled the two glasses with wine.

A moment later, Cauldron emerged from the house, in pants and a t-shirt. The scruff on his jawline was gone, and the hardness of his face was replaced by a subtle brightness. He took a seat across from me and immediately went for the wine.

Hugo brought our dinner a moment later, grilled fish with seasonal vegetables and potato purée.

We ate in silence for a while, his eyes on me most of the time, as if waiting for all the questions to start.

"How's Jeremiah?"

"He'll live."

"And your mines?"

"Backlogged. But we'll get it figured out."

More silence.

I swirled my glass before I made my move. "Half brother, huh? Which parent do you share?"

He took his time chewing his bite, his eyes studying me. "Father."

"You don't look that similar, but I guess I can see it. You have the same eyes."

"A gift from our father."

"His last name isn't Beaufort."

"I took my mother's name." His eyes were down, his fork absentmindedly stirring his food around. The second his mother was mentioned, he seemed to lose his appetite.

"When she died, your father remarried?"

"Yes." His eyes lifted to mine.

"Was he the one who killed her?"

Still as a mountain, he stared at me. He was cold, not moving, not even breathing. But then he answered. "No. But he's responsible, nonetheless."

Finally, I got to look behind the curtain. "What happened?"

"His line of business was dangerous. He was aware of that fact, aware of the threats against his family, but that didn't stop him. They came to our home when he was gone. Middle of the night. I was just three years old at the time, so she hid me in the closet and told me to cover my eyes until she came back for me." His eyes drifted away, looking at the estate behind me. "She never did. I kept my hands over my eyes, but that didn't stop me from hearing everything."

"Oh my god…"

"They raped her first. Then they stabbed her to death." He said it all matter-of-factly, as if he'd gone numb a long time ago. "When they couldn't find me, they assumed I was with the nanny and left."

Now I was sick, so sick I couldn't eat another bite. "Cauldron…" I didn't know what to say other than sorry a million times. "I'm so sorry." Cancer took my mother, and I was so angry. It was so unfair, watching her die far too young. I was left alone, legally an adult but still a child. But this…this was something else.

His expression remained impassive as if I hadn't said anything.

Every aspect of his character made perfect sense now. He preferred whores to lovers because he didn't have to feel anything. He didn't hesitate to shoot me because violence against women was perfectly normal to him. His constant anger…was like a second skin.

"He had an odd way of showing it…but he genuinely loved my mother. The loss hit him hard. He didn't remarry intentionally, but he knocked up a woman and thought marrying her was the right decision. Hence, Grave."

I listened to every beat of the story, afraid if I inter-rupted him, I would never hear the full tale.

"My father came to love Grave and his mother, but I was always the favorite. Neither one of them liked it. I heard them fight in their bedroom sometimes, where his wife would insist that he preferred me to her son—and he fully admitted it. As time went on, their resent-ment grew. The only time Grave and I got along was when we were young. But after that, our irritation for each other was palpable."

I knew something more had happened, something caused their deep-seated rift.

"They tried to get me killed. Grave insists it was her plot, but he was still aware of the scheme. She underestimated me, so it backfired in her face."

"What did your father say?"

"He was upset at first, but then he bought into her lies. It was an accident. A misunderstanding. No ill intent. That was when I abandoned the family surname and took my mother's. I told my father to fuck off and never spoke to him again." The story concluded when he grabbed his glass and took a drink. He'd relayed a story so full of malice with a stone-cold face.

I didn't know what to say…other than I was sorry again.

He grabbed his fork and took a few more bites of his food.

My appetite was long gone. "I guess she wanted Grave to inherit his fortune?"

"Yes. And to take over the business."

"What kind of business is he in?"

He looked at me across the table.

"Drugs? Prostitution?"

"Human trafficking."

"Like…sex trafficking?" Grave gave no indication he captured innocent women and forced them into a fate worse than death.

"No. Totally different."

"Then what is human trafficking?"

He continued to eat. "You really want to know? I promise you don't."

I took a couple breaths, meeting his steely gaze. "I do."

He gave a quiet sigh before he set down his fork. "He sells organs on the black market."

"Organs?" I asked in complete confusion. "As in… bodily organs?"

"Yes."

My blood turned ice-cold. "For…what reason?"

"Mostly transplants. But some people like organs for other reasons."

"Transplants?" I asked. "Like heart transplants?"

"Hearts, kidneys, lungs, everything. The recipient list can be long, and it's easy to be excluded from it altogether. A lifelong smoker is banned from a lung transplant because the damage was self-inflicted. This is a way to get around that."

"I-I've never heard of anything like that."

He drank his wine again.

"And what about the other uses…?"

"Sacrificial. Religious. Some people eat them—"

"*What?*"

"The world is a dark and twisted place, sweetheart."

And to think I'd slept with that man. No amount of money was worth that. "And that's your family business…?"

His eyes lacked all remorse. "Yes."

"I thought a family business was supposed to be upholstery or carpet cleaning."

His only response was a shrug.

"I'm glad that you sell diamonds."

"If my mother hadn't been killed, I would probably be in that line of work now."

The thought was sickening. "I choose to believe otherwise."

"A lot of people volunteer themselves as candidates."

"Why on earth would they do that?"

"Money."

"What's the point of money if you're dead?"

"Support their family."

I shook my head in disgust. "There are other ways——"

"Like their daughter sleeping with men for money? A lot of men would prefer this over that."

"Was that an insult?"

"Just saying. And if they've been diagnosed with cancer or some other disease, wouldn't they want to make some money before they go? They may have lung cancer, but that doesn't mean their heart isn't in perfect condition."

This conversation was making me sick. "I don't want to talk about this anymore."

He fell silent.

Tension infected the space between us. It made it humid, made it hard to breathe. "So, he won't kill you because he feels bad about what happened?"

"There's a lot more to our relationship than that, but yes. He was always jealous of me, jealous of the love my father showed for me and not him. He would steal my toys, fuck the women I'd already fucked to make me jealous, take my Christmas presents from under the tree and hide them so it looked like I had fewer gifts than him. I know he wanted me gone, and I think he had a hand in my assassination attempt but got cold feet at the last second."

I asked the obvious question that he hadn't answered. "Then why haven't you killed him?"

A long stare ensued. His eyes were locked on mine, but I wasn't the recipient of his stare. He was in another place, in another time. After a lifetime of silence, he spoke. "Because I can't."

———

Our time apart made him want me more than usual. Not long after he was sheathed inside me did he release with a loud groan, but his dick remained hard as ever and he continued on. On top of me with my body folded underneath him, he took me over and over, his eyes locked on mine with that possessive edge.

Anytime I dropped my gaze or closed my eyes, his commanding voice pulled me back. "Eyes."

I obeyed, watching this man claim me as his over and over. Lean and muscular, his body was like a heavy blanket that trapped the heat right next to my skin. Slick with sweat, his body rubbed against mine and made me slick too. All I had to do was lie there and feel the man ravish me like he never had me before. My job as a courtesan had never been easier, had never been more pleasurable.

He lay beside me when he was finished, his powerful chest rising and falling deeply with his breaths. His hair was a bit sweaty, and his handsome face was still hard from his exertion. He looked at the ceiling before he ran his fingers through his hair.

I lay beside him, my fingertips resting against his ribs. "You missed me."

He cracked a smile, a small one. "You missed me too."

"Well, I always miss you." I wore my heart on my sleeve, said things too fast to take back. Every other lover I'd had felt like work. I put on a production every moment we were together, checking his reaction to make sure it was exactly what he wanted. But I dropped that whole charade with Cauldron and chose to be myself. I didn't have to fake the climaxes. I didn't have to pretend to be interested in what he had to say. I didn't have to do anything at all.

Did his other girls go through the same thing? Did they fall for him just the way I had?

Cauldron continued to stare at the ceiling, unaffected by my affection. After a minute, he prepared to leave.

"Does it make sense for us to have separate bedrooms?" It flew out of my mouth like a cannon that couldn't be returned to the barrel.

He sat up against the headboard and looked at me. His expression was always enigmatic.

"I mean, we're always together."

He continued to stare.

I suspected I'd pushed things too far.

"I told you something I've never told anyone before. Don't ask for more."

I did appreciate his confidence, but I was still disappointed.

"I assumed that story would help you understand my need for space."

It was like a boot to the stomach. "You think…I'd ever hurt you?"

His hard stare continued, his thoughts locked behind the vault of his stare. "It's nothing personal."

"But it is personal because I'm the woman who sleeps with you." I should just let this go, but he didn't fuck me like a client fucked a hooker. He'd made love to me on and off for an hour, our eyes locked, our bodies writhing in passion. The connection between us was undeniable, but he continued to dismiss it.

"Camille, I am who I am, and I'm not going to change."

"You've changed everything else…for me."

He broke eye contact, as if ashamed. "But not this. Like I said, it's nothing personal. I just have issues. You'd think you'd understand after I told you my entire family has betrayed me at some point."

"I didn't mean to sound insensitive——"

"Selfish. That's the word you're looking for." He left the bed and pulled on his bottoms.

I winced like I'd been slapped, and then I was out of bed and at the door. "I just care about you so much, Cauldron—"

"*Camille.*" Somehow he silenced me just by saying my name. There was so much power in his voice, undeniable power. "I've never slept beside a woman. I can't remember the last time I kissed a woman before you. You have more of me than anyone else ever has. Don't demand more of me than I can give—because I've already given you what I can."

"I-I'm sorry."

His stare lingered for a moment before he walked out the door.

I let him go.

THIRTY

CAULDRON

Camille left me alone for most of the day.

I went about my daily routine, hitting the gym first thing in the morning then having breakfast before I started my workday. She kept herself busy as I stayed in my office, getting all the details from Jeremiah's replacement. I hit Grave's business hard, and he hit mine back just as hard. We were both in free fall but neither willing to hit the brakes.

World's biggest pissing contest.

Toward the end of the afternoon, she stepped into the study. In a red skirt and ruffled top with sandals, she approached my desk and took a seat. She waited for me to finish typing and meet her gaze. "You're still mad at me."

"Mad, yes. But not at you."

"What are you mad at?"

"Everything." I sat back in my chair and propped my elbow on the armrest. My fingers curled into a fist and slid underneath my jawline. Still, I stared at her, enjoying the sight of her face with minimal makeup. Her eyes were bright on this warm fall day.

She let the word echo in our minds for a while before she spoke. "I'm sorry about last night."

I continued to stare. Her looks always hypnotized me, the way she could express so much with so little. Her features were delicate, but her eyes could burn hotter than a bonfire of banned books.

"I just…" She looked down at her intertwined hands in her lap before she met my look again. "I want more."

I knew exactly what she wanted.

"We've become so close. I don't mean to rush things, but we've become inseparable, and I guess…I want you as often as I can have you. If I'm the woman you sleep with, I don't see why I can't be the woman you go to sleep with every night."

Instead of an apology, it seemed like another request.

She looked at me expectantly because it was my turn to say something.

"This started as an arrangement, and I haven't gotten past that yet."

Her eyebrows furrowed, turning her beautiful appearance into a quizzical one. "We've established this is a lot more than an arrangement—"

"But that doesn't mean I know what it is yet."

A glimmer of fire moved into her eyes.

"Pushing me isn't going to get you your answer any quicker."

She kept her silence, but her look suggested she had more to say.

We sat there for a long time, the tension like a heavy perfume that burned the nostrils.

"I'll be gone for a while this evening."

"Where are you going?"

"To a dinner party."

"Why aren't you taking me?" she asked, the accusation audible.

"Because I'm going to get your necklace back."

Grave was hosting a dinner party as a fundraiser for some disease awareness.

Ironic, huh?

I knew the real purpose of these events—to get clients. It was France's best-kept secret that Grave was in the trafficking business, and anyone who needed a kidney or wanted to display a set of eyeballs on their mantel knew who to call. Surgeons left their practices because they were paid triple their previous salary.

After a quick flight to Paris, I pulled up to the front of his home. The lit chandeliers were visible in the high windows, and the music from the piano was in my ears the second the car door cracked open. Couples in cocktail dresses and tuxedos crowded the enormous front doors as they made their way inside. It was just like any other fancy party. After a while, they all started to look the same.

I slipped inside among the wave of guests without suspicion and found myself in the crowded entryway. Standing tables were erected for couples to enjoy their flutes of champagne and the appetizers passed around. It wasn't hard to spot Grave, his handsome face etched into a charming smile while a pretty woman hung on his arm.

She was a piss-poor replacement for Camille.

I felt myself get hard when I imagined going home to Camille, naked except for the necklace I fetched for her. I'd fuck her senseless, knowing Grave was thinking about the same thing as he screwed his unremarkable date.

The crowd was distracted by the energy of the party, so the staircase was unwatched. I knew there would be another set of stairs toward the back of the house, so I walked down a few hallways until I found the stairs used by the servants. The music dimmed the farther I ventured into the enormous house, and soon I could hear my own footsteps again. With my hand on the rail, I moved to the second floor and then the third.

But then I came across trouble.

Grave had some security guys posted at the top of the stairs.

Seemed to learn from his previous mistakes.

I kept going, acting like I belonged there.

Both immediately barred the way for me to progress. "The party is downstairs."

"There's a dozen people in line for the bathroom. You expect me to wait that long?"

They continued to stand there, and just when they turned to glance at each other, I kicked one hard in the knee then punched the other so hard he hit the floor. Their groans were masked by the noise of the party, so no one heard the commotion. The one with the broken knee was still conscious and reaching for his radio, so I slammed my foot into his face and put him to sleep.

Now it was quiet, the third floor vacant. The staff was off the floor because they were too busy running the party downstairs, so I headed straight to his bedroom without interference.

Dark furniture. A four-poster bed. An enormous mantel around the fireplace. I could feel his presence without him being in the room. Camille told me her necklace was stored in his closet and protected by an alarm. I walked through the double doors and found the glass over the case of jewelry that housed his collection of watches. Her necklace was easy to spot because it was made of iridescent pearls and made me think of her right away. A little red light flashed from inside the case, a warning of what would happen once my fist broke the glass. I took out my gun and smashed into the case, glass shattering everywhere.

The alarm immediately sounded.

I pocketed the necklace and took my time walking out of there.

Instead of taking the stairs, I stepped into a guest bedroom and pressed my back to the wall. Several sets of feet ran up the stairs and exploded into Grave's bedroom. That was when I moved back into the hallway and took the stairs down to the bottom floor.

Guests were all looking around and shouting over the sound of the alarm. The musicians stopped their music because nothing could be heard over the obnoxious beeping. Not only did I take his leverage against Camille, but I also ruined his stupid little party.

I pushed through the crowd and headed out the front door without delay.

"Cauldron."

I walked up to the valet and extended my ticket. "Bring my car around."

The valet immediately took off.

I turned around to face Grave, my hands sitting in my pockets.

He was so livid that his face was red and blotchy, like he'd been in the gym instead of a cocktail party. When he marched up to me, it looked like he wanted to hit me but found the restraint not to. The fuming stare continued, as if there were no words to describe the betrayal.

We stared at each other until the valet showed up with my car.

"Nice party." I walked around to the driver's door so I could take off. "It's a shame I couldn't stay longer."

THIRTY-ONE
CAMILLE

I left my bedroom door open so I could hear him down the hallway. I sat on the couch, the TV on low, another crumpled-up note in the wastebin. It was long past dinnertime, and as the hours trickled by, I wondered when he'd return. He had to take his plane back from Paris, so I really had no idea when he'd walk in.

I heard his footsteps on the stairs a moment later.

His dress shoes tapped against the hardwood, and then the steps turned muffled once they reached the long runner down the hallway.

I jumped off the couch and hurried to the open door.

His tie was undone and in his closed fist, and the top buttons of his shirt were already undone like he couldn't wait to get the tuxedo off. The top of his chest was revealed, tight with muscle. His eyes were focused on the phone in his hand, oblivious to me standing there. He stopped to type out a message before he pocketed it and lifted his gaze.

With expectant eyes, I stared at him, hopeful that he had succeeded in his mission.

With that intense stare he wore without effort, he approached until he halted in front of me. His handsome face was free of the marks of a brawl, so he'd escaped Grave's presence without so much as a scratch. He slipped his hand into his pocket then withdrew the pearl necklace that my mother had given to me. The pearls were so shiny they looked like they'd been professionally polished. The second my eyes settled on the necklace, I smelled her old perfume…heard her laugh.

I watched him hold it up between us, the breath frozen in my lungs. "I can't believe it…"

When I didn't take it, he grabbed my wrist and forced it into my hand.

My fingertips brushed over the pearls, feeling their smoothness under my touch. Through eyes murky with unshed tears, I stared at my most prized possession, the only family heirloom we'd ever had. "How did you pull this off?" My fingers closed around the necklace before I lifted my chin and looked at him.

His hands rested in his pockets as he looked at the necklace. "I walked in and took it."

"Just like that?"

His eyes lifted to mine. "Just like that." He took the necklace out of my hand, unclasped the back, and then put it around my neck. There was a tiny click when the necklace locked together. He let go, and the pearls hung past my collarbone and rested against my skin. "Beautiful."

My fingers reached for the jewelry at my neck, wanting to feel it since I couldn't see it.

He turned away. "Goodnight."

My hand grabbed on to him before he could get too far. Through the linen of his collared shirt, I felt his muscular forearm as my fingers dug deep. I gently pulled him back to me, bringing his stare back to my face.

He moved with the pull, those deep eyes locking in place.

My arms wound around his neck, and I pressed my body into his. My lips found his with a desperation that exploded from my chest. My fingers latched on to his short hair, and I rose on my tiptoes to meet his hungry mouth as it reciprocated my desire. Slowly, we backed into my bedroom, heads turning to deepen the kiss, our passionate breaths filling the silence.

I pushed his jacket off his shoulders.

He got my shirt over my head.

Piece by piece, our clothes and shoes littered the floor.

I backed up to the bed, but he clearly had other ideas when he grabbed me by the shoulders and pushed me to my knees on the rug. "Show me your gratitude." His fingers wrapped around my neck, and he tilted my head back slightly, guiding his cock to my mouth.

My lips automatically parted, and before I could flatten my tongue, he was inside me. The breath I was about to take was stolen from me as his large size pushed deep into my throat. That intensity was back in his eyes, mixed with a depth of possessiveness he'd never shown before.

I flattened my tongue and moved forward and backward, timing my breaths with the reprieve of his evacuation from my throat. Saliva already built up at the corners of my mouth and began to spill.

"Eyes."

My head tilted a little more, and my stare moved up to his face.

He thrust his hips as he kept his hold on my neck, fucking my mouth relentlessly. "Say thank you."

With a mouth full of dick, I could barely form the words. "Th–thank you."

He gave a satisfied moan as his fingers contracted into my neck. Red blotches moved into his tanned skin, and the tightness that came over his features just before release appeared. With a loud groan, he hit his trigger and released, dumping his seed across my tongue and into the back of my throat.

I wanted to gag, but I managed to get it down.

When his cock left my mouth, I could finally take my first real breath. His large dick was still in my face, pulsating and big like he hadn't just hit a climax a few seconds ago.

Next, I was on the bed, his massive body covering mine like a heavy blanket in winter. His narrow hips fit between my thighs, and he slid into my slickness like honey poured out of a jar. His shaft was so thick it throbbed inside me, just a little bigger than I was used to. My nails dug deep into his back as I moaned at the feel of him. My performance on my knees was just foreplay, an appetizer to the feast. Now, he really wanted me, had the appetite of a bear out of hibernation.

With my lithe body folded underneath him, he pounded me into the mattress, the necklace gliding back and forth across my chest with every thrust. My eyes traveled down his hard chest and tight abs, the way the lines between his muscles were more prominent when he worked his body hard.

"Eyes."

Obediently, my eyes flicked back to his.

His face immediately tightened in desire, like he was already prepared to blast off again. "Say it."

My nails dug deeper into his back as my hips rocked into his. "Thank you."

One hand slid farther into my hair, and he brought us closer together, his pelvic bone grinding against my clit. "I own you. Say it."

"You own me…" I felt the burn deep in my core, the fiery beast that wanted to come forth and explode. My knees squeezed his torso, and I writhed underneath him, so close to the edge that I could feel it before it even began.

He ground against me harder, his dick throbbing because he was just as anxious as I was.

It hit me like a freight train. Tears. Moans. Nails. I scratched his back as I writhed, moaned in his face until they became quiet screams. My hips bucked all on their own as my body went into free fall.

His hand secured around my neck and pinned me as he watched. "Eyes."

Locked in place, I finished, tears streaking across my cheeks like shooting stars.

His pumps slowed but deepened. His breaths turned irregular. It was the quiet before the crescendo. He gave a deep groan as he hit the finish line. The explosion was so intense that I could actually feel it between my legs, feel his dick thicken then soften after release. His hard body became harder. His intense eyes became wild.

Everything came to a standstill. Our breaths filled the room as our eyes continued to drink in each other. My ankles locked around his waist because I didn't want him to leave, even when I was fully satisfied, because I could never get enough of this man.

He didn't try to move away. He let my long legs tether his body to mine.

"Thank you." The emotion caught in my voice because the gratitude came forth, mixed with so many other emotions. My palm moved up his neck and cupped his handsome face. "Thank you…"

His eyes held on to mine for a while before he turned into my palm and kissed it. "You're welcome."

THIRTY-TWO

CAULDRON

"A yacht party?" It was morning, and the two of us enjoyed breakfast on the terrace. Two mugs of coffee with assorted cheese and freshly baked croissants were on the table, along with homemade jams.

"Yes."

"Whose yacht party?"

"An acquaintance."

"Acquaintances invite you to fancy yacht parties?"

"Yes. He races horses."

"He races horses and can afford a yacht?" she asked incredulously.

"Horse races are a big business."

"But that big?" She took a sip of her coffee. "I clearly got into the wrong business…"

"It's a different world for men than it is for women."

She cocked an eyebrow. "As in, a woman can't do what a man can?"

"No. As in, society makes it more difficult for a woman to do what a man can."

That cooled her steam.

"We'll leave in a few hours."

"Where is it?"

"Monaco."

"Driving or flying?"

"Yachting."

"We're going to take your yacht there?"

"Yes." I finished my coffee then got to my feet. "Your dress will be delivered within the hour. Pack enough for the weekend."

"Alright."

I walked into the house, took care of a couple things in my office, and then prepared to depart for the harbor.

Once our things were packed away, the driver took us to the port where my yacht was waiting. We walked on, our luggage was carried away, and we were greeted with flutes of champagne and caviar.

She dismissed the waiter with a slight wave. "Sorry, never been a fan of caviar." In a baby-blue dress with one shoulder and one side of her stomach revealed, she was stunning in her gold heels. The pearl necklace was around her throat, and I imagined it would be there forever.

Every time I looked at it, I felt like a king.

If this was a pissing content, I had the most pee.

Laurent came on to the ship next, bringing his date. No idea who she was, if she was an actual lover or a whore on his payroll. He greeted me with a smile as we clasped our hands together in a display of friendship. "Thanks for the ride."

"You're always welcome."

"Whoa, watch what you say. My boat is still in Positano."

"Why haven't you gotten it back?"

"Been busy with work…and women."

"And booze."

He chuckled. "You got me." A woman came up behind him, pretty and tall, wearing a dress that was classy but slutty at the same time. She introduced herself and gave me her name, but I forgot it the second I heard it. I turned to Camille, who stood at the bow of the ship so she could take in the view with the flute in her hand. "Camille."

She turned at the sound of her name, the wind catching in her hair at the first perfect time to fly behind her. Sunglasses sat on the bridge of her nose, but her eyes still twinkled through the tint. She walked over, sky-high heels loud against the deck of the ship. She came to my side.

My arm circled her waist. "This is my woman, Camille."

She flinched in my embrace. I could feel it in the way her body tightened. "Camille, this is my cousin Laurent and his date for the evening." Didn't remember her name and didn't pretend otherwise.

Laurent shook her hand before he introduced his date again.

"It's lovely to meet you," Camille said politely. "Cauldron didn't mention he had a cousin."

"On my mother's side," I explained.

"My mother and his mother were sisters," Laurent explained. "God rest their souls."

"I'm sorry that you lost your mother," she said. "I've lost mine too."

Laurent gave a nod before he accepted the champagne from the waiter. "We can be sad later. Tonight, we party."

———

The four of us sat together at the front of the ship, in the half-dome couch with the large table in front. It was laden with appetizers and bottles of booze. My arm around Camille's shoulders, Laurent and I talked shit back and forth and made a few jokes at each other's expense. Sometimes Laurent would end up with a tongue in his throat, and he could never say no to that.

Camille's hand was on my thigh, as close as she could be to my crotch without actually touching my dick. "My woman?"

I tilted my head back as I finished off the scotch in my glass. "Do you prefer to be introduced differently?" I set the empty glass on the table and relaxed back in the chair, my arm draped over her shoulders.

She didn't outright smile, but the brightness in her eyes was undeniable. "It's perfect." She snuggled closer to me before her small palm cupped my cheek. She turned me into her, giving me the kind of kiss that only happened in private. Her hand gripped my thigh tighter before roaming closer to my crotch so her palm could pet my dick. There was tongue, hot breaths, passion that you couldn't pay for.

"Mr. Beaufort, we'll reach Monaco in five minutes."

Camille pulled away and retracted her hand.

I was a bit annoyed with the interruption, but I did ask him to let me know when we were close. "Thanks, James."

She had a bit of redness in her cheeks due to her embarrassment. It was a quality I liked about her, that a woman who had sex for money could be embarrassed about anything. "I'm going to freshen up before we get there. Be right back." She walked around the couch then headed to her quarters.

What's-Her-Name did the same.

I watched Camille walk away, those sexy hips swaying in her tight dress. Her ass looked like a nectarine in that sheer material. It was going to drive Grave fucking crazy tonight.

Laurent poured himself another glass. "Got her wrapped around your finger, don't you?"

My eyes shifted to his. My only answer was a slight grin.

"She seems like a nice girl. You don't feel bad about what you're doing?"

"What am I doing?"

"Using her to fuck with Grave."

"She's the one who came to me, remember?"

"But you're the one who made her fall head over heels."

My arms relaxed over the back of the couch. "I didn't *make* her do anything. Her feelings are her own."

"And you don't feel the same way?"

"Did I say I didn't?"

"Well, do you?"

I never answered.

"I think Grave is a piece of shit too, but the girl is innocent in all this."

"She came to me and needed help. We made a deal."

"Is it really a deal if she doesn't know her end of it?"

My eyes narrowed on his face. "Why don't you get the fuck out of my business?"

He raised both hands in a gesture of surrender. "Alright, alright. Sorry."

I looked away.

"It's just… It seems like she really cares for you. Can't say that about most women, right?"

I looked back at him again.

"Just don't want you to sabotage your own happiness, you know? You tend to do that."

"Are we done here?"

"Fine. Won't say another word."

"Good."

We sat in silence, the yacht approaching the lights of Monaco.

"So, I'm guessing Grave is gonna be here?" Laurent asked.

"Yes."

"I know you guys won't kill each other because it's complicated and whatnot, but I think you'd both be better off if one of you were dead." He shook the ice in his glass before he took another drink. "That way, you could finally move on."

It was a big yacht, so it was a big party.

Five levels high and double the size of Cauldron's, it was the kind of ship that you could call home. No need to have a residence on land when you had a mansion on the water. There were hundreds of people there. Maybe even thousands. It was hard to tell when there were so many places to go.

Cauldron kept his arm around my waist and introduced me to rich people I didn't know. Grave used to do the same thing, and sometimes, I came across people I recognized. They recognized me too, but no one acknowledged the awkwardness.

"This doesn't seem like something you would like," I said when we were alone.

"How so?" He guided me to the edge of the ship, where he held me close.

"Well, you're not much of a talker."

"You have to advertise yourself without asking anyone to buy anything."

"I see. So walking around with a pretty girl accomplishes that?"

"Pretty girl?" His eyebrows furrowed, his features becoming more handsome as he focused. "You're a woman, not a girl. And not just any woman—but my woman." He pulled me close, his eyes glancing down at my lips. When I was fully scooped up in his embrace, he kissed me, kissed me in a way that made me feel weak from head to toe.

I clung to him because I didn't want it to end. I wanted to be back on his yacht, alone together in his quarters, rocking with the waves as they gently lapped at the hull of the ship. My hand found his cheek and the scruff of his jawline, and I kissed him longer than I should.

He let it go on like he didn't care who saw.

When I pulled away, I stayed close, my face practically touching his. I got lost in his eyes, lost in the way he looked at me like I was the only thing that mattered. I'd left Grave because I wanted to find this, a man who made me feel things without being paid to feel them. Cauldron wasn't exactly what I wanted in a man—he had his issues—but my heart had made its decision. I think his heart had too. "You think there's somewhere we could go…?"

That boyish smile made me melt into a puddle. "I know a place."

———————

There were five different levels to the ship, so we wandered into different hallways until we found an unoccupied room. With my dress pulled to my waist and my thong between my knees, he took me from behind at the edge of the bed. With his bottoms at his thighs and his hands on my hips, he nailed me hard enough to make the bed frame tap against the wall.

I tried to be quiet, but he took me so good I found myself clenching my jaw to suppress my screams. I wanted to shove my face into the duvet to muffle my moans, but that would ruin the makeup that took me hours to do.

I'd been on the verge of a climax from staring at him all evening, so it was a relief when I got to release it.

The second I hit my trigger and slammed my body back onto his dick as hard as I could, he released too, unable or unwilling to suppress his moan.

We came down from the high slowly, and then once it was over, we put our clothes back on as if nothing had happened.

"I'll go to the bathroom upstairs," he said. "You can take the one down here. We'll meet at the bar."

"Alright."

He gave me a kiss before he walked out.

I waited a moment to make sure no one spotted us leaving the room at the same time. I wanted to take my time anyway because my cheeks were sore from grinning at strangers for the last hour. I almost wished I had a stick of gum to chew and loosen up the muscles in my mouth.

After I smoothed out my dress, I went in search of a bathroom. I finally found one, and after waiting for three women to use it first, I got inside and saw that I looked exactly as I felt—thoroughly fucked. I fixed my hair with my fingertips then cleaned up my makeup with the folded corner of a tissue. My purse didn't have any extra supplies, so I had to make do with what I had. My lips looked chalk-white without my lipstick, but Cauldron had kissed it all off.

I left the bathroom and made my way through the throng, trying to get to the stairs so I could meet Cauldron near the bar.

A man stepped into my path.

None other than Grave.

And he looked pissed. His eyes immediately darted down to the necklace around my neck, the one he'd used to keep me in line like a treat for a dog. When his eyes flicked back to me, they were dilated like he was on cocaine. "How do you not see it?"

I should just walk away and get back to Cauldron as quickly as possible, but my curiosity was piqued. "See what?"

"That he's playing you for a goddamn fool. Maybe I'm not the best man, but at least I actually give a shit about you. He's doing all of this just to piss me off—and it's working." His eyes dilated a little more. "He only wants you because I want you. If I didn't, you would be worthless to him."

The insult stung, but I dismissed it. "Grave, you don't know anything about our relationship—"

"I know everything about it because he loves to rub it in my face. Like the video he just sent me."

"What video?"

"The video of him fucking you." His voice was louder than it should be, making people nearby turn to look.

My heart and lungs all plummeted in my stomach. "He would…he would never show that to you—"

"He sent it to me." He pulled out his phone and played it.

And I was fucking horrified.

When I'd seen enough, he pocketed the phone. "He gave me these too." He pulled out pieces of paper from his pocket, all covered in lines from where they'd been crumpled.

It took me a moment to grab the first one as I was so overwhelmed by shock. I slowly opened the pages and saw my own handwriting.

I'm not sure when it happened…but I've fallen so hard for Cauldron—

I stopped reading. It was too much. I'd tossed all these in the wastebasket, but that stupid weasel must have dug them out and given them to Cauldron. Every private moment I ever had…was violated.

Grave watched me process all of it surrounded by people and music and waiters. "He wanted to prove to me that you're in love with him, and he succeeded. I see it now even though I wish I didn't."

My eyes dropped to the floor.

"I don't know if he's told you, but we're half brothers. And he hates me for something I did a long time ago—"

"Yes, he told me."

"Then you realize you're caught in the world's biggest pissing contest."

I would never cry in front of anyone. Couldn't endure the humiliation. But fuck, it was so hard not to. I wanted to cry because I was hurt, but also because I was so thoroughly humiliated that I wanted to die.

"I realize that I'm not the best man, but I treated you a lot better than that asshole. Forget him, and come home with me. We can start over. We can make this relationship whatever you want it to be."

I stared past Grave, seeing his out-of-focus face. In that moment, I realized I didn't have a home. That Cap-Ferrat estate was never mine. Cauldron's bed was never mine. Cauldron was never mine. Now it all made sense, why he'd abruptly changed his mind about letting me stay with him. Why was I so blind? He even told me how much he hated Grave…and I never put the pieces together. "Okay."

Grave stilled in surprise.

"Yeah, let's go."

There was a ferry that whisked people to and from the yacht, so we waited for it to approach the yacht close enough for us to board. I didn't look behind me to search for Cauldron. He must have been wondering where I'd gone off to. He was too arrogant to believe that Grave would tell me everything. Or he was too arrogant to believe I would believe him.

Grave stood in front of me, studying my face like I was sick and about to hurl.

I avoided his gaze.

He continued to stare, and he actually looked sympathetic. He wasn't the fire-breathing demon that I remembered him being.

Before the boat could dock, Cauldron appeared.

His onslaught was silent. He appeared at my side, his hand reaching for my elbow. He looked his brother in the face with a warning in his eyes. An entire conversation seemed to pass between them before Cauldron yanked me away.

I twisted out of his grasp. "No."

Cauldron released me, but it wasn't from a loose grip; it was sheer shock.

"I'm going with Grave. You can fuck off, Cauldron." I moved away from him, coming to Grave's side, my allegiance set in stone.

Cauldron shifted his gaze back to his brother.

"You heard her." Now his voice was cold and deadly, exactly as I remembered. "You thought I wouldn't tell her?"

Their stare-off continued.

"This is over, Cauldron," Grave said. "You got your kicks. Now leave the girl alone."

The boat parked next to the yacht, ready to ferry people aboard.

Cauldron punched Grave so hard he toppled over the edge and splashed down into the water below.

I gasped and stepped back.

No one else seemed to notice because Grave didn't scream as he plummeted below.

Cauldron moved into me. "Let me explain—"

"You think I want to listen to you justify sending that video? I let you film me because I trusted you. You said you wouldn't show anyone—"

"I never said that."

Now I wanted to punch him off the boat. "I shouldn't even have to ask, Cauldron."

The hardness of his face flickered, like a light that briefly lost electricity. "Let me explain—"

"Explain why you took my private thoughts without permission and showed them to someone? What the fuck is wrong with you? You violated my privacy… irrevocably broke my trust… What possible justification is there?"

He had the humility to drop his gaze.

"I have more to say, but what's the point when you don't care that you hurt me? When I never meant anything to you anyway…" I wanted to slap him until his face was beet red, scream at the top of my lungs as I cried a river of tears, but it was all pointless when he didn't give a shit.

"That's not true." His eyes lifted once again. "Let's go back to my yacht so we can talk."

"Talk about what?" I asked in a monotone because I was dead inside.

"I have a lot to say, but this isn't the place to say any of it." He nodded for me to follow him to the other side of the boat. Parked right beside the yacht was his own. He must have called for it when he spotted me with Grave. We crossed over and got onto the deck, and then the yacht immediately pulled away.

I knew Grave would get back on board because the ship wasn't moving. I needed to grab my things from the house anyway. All my clothes, my entire life. The ocean air moved through my hair and loosened the curls that were so tight just a couple hours earlier. The night had been full of magic and excitement, and now it was a fucking horror movie.

He stood in front of me and yanked his tie loose because any extra moment wearing it was unbearable. He ran his fingers through his short hair too, acting distressed when I was the one who had just lost everything.

"I thought Grave was bad…but you're just evil."

His eyes met mine, shattered like broken glass.

"I feel…so fucking stupid." It was there, just beneath the surface, the heavy tears that wanted to come free. But I wouldn't look weak in front of this asshole. I couldn't let him see the hole he'd dug with his spade. "You don't want me. You don't care about me. My only value is your brother's pain. The second he stops caring, I'm out on the street. So that was your plan all along? To make me fall in love with you to torture your brother? Everything you said was just a bunch of bullshit? None of it was real? What kind of sick fuck does that? Having me wasn't enough? I had to be a victim in your revenge scheme too?"

He was quiet for a long time, as if he had no defense. "We made a deal when you came here. You do what I want, and I keep you safe from Grave. That was the only promise we made to each other. I didn't make you feel anything for me. That was all you."

"Wow. So this is all my fault? Don't fucking gaslight me. I remember what you said in the pool and at dinner. I remember everything you've said to me. Everything."

He took a step forward. "And I meant everything I said to you."

"Right."

"I did."

"How could you mean any of that and then send him something so private?"

He looked away for a second. "Because it's nothing he hasn't already seen before—"

"Fuck. Off."

"I let my obsession get the best of me, and I fully admit that—"

"Good. Otherwise, I was about to call you a psychopath."

"But that doesn't mean I didn't feel everything I said I felt. They're two separate things."

"You're saying you cared about me?" My arms crossed over my chest.

"Yes."

"So do you treat everyone you care about like complete garbage?"

He gave a quiet sigh.

The boat approached the harbor at Cap-Ferrat. The dock came closer, and the lights from the city were visible. Thank fucking god we were about to get off this goddamn boat. I would never have to set foot on it again. "I want to get my stuff and leave. And I never want to see you again."

When we were in the house, I took the stairs two at a time and entered my bedroom. My bathroom was covered with all my supplies, and the closet and dresser were full of my things. Unceremoniously, I shoved everything into suitcases just to get the hell out of there as fast as I could.

Cauldron stood in the doorway.

"Move."

He remained still.

"Move your ass."

His jacket was gone now, and he stood in just his collared shirt. His hands slid into his pockets as he leaned against the doorframe. "You're not leaving."

"Bitch, what did you say?"

He gave me a hard stare. "You heard me."

I let go of the suitcase and marched up to him. "Maybe your brother won't kill you, but I won't hesitate. Get the fuck out of my way."

He continued to stand there. "Going back to Grave isn't the answer—"

"Where I go and who I fuck is none of your concern, Cauldron. Not anymore." I shoved him hard in the chest.

He hardly moved, but his reaction was quick. Like a viper, he snatched my forearm and twisted it down so I couldn't use it. He backed me into the opposite wall and kept me there with his other arm. "Listen." He blocked my knee with his own and kept me in place. "I'm sorry that I hurt you. I admit my plan was short-sighted, and I didn't think too far ahead. I didn't think about the consequences of my actions. I didn't think how they would affect you or us. All I thought about was making that motherfucker suffer the only way I knew how. My focus was solely on Grave, when it should have been on you, and I'm sorry for that." His dark eyes shifted back and forth as they looked into mine, piercing my exterior for feelings underneath. "The video and the notes…that was fucked up. I won't apologize for it because that betrayal is beyond apology. I'm sorry you were a pawn in a game you didn't know you were playing. You came here and needed protection from him, so I thought everything was fair game."

"That might have been fine if you didn't know how I felt about you, but you did." He'd gone through with his plan, knowing full well how I felt, using it to his advantage. "You're a monster far worse than he is, and I wish I'd never left him in the first place."

His hold on me immediately weakened as if he was the one betrayed.

I pushed past him and grabbed the handle on the suitcase. "At the end of the day, you got what you want, so you don't need me anymore." I started to walk out.

He grabbed the bag and pulled it out of my hand. "I said, you aren't leaving."

"Why? You got what you wanted, Cauldron. What do you need me for?"

"I'm not letting you go back to him, not when you deserve better."

"Fine. I'll go somewhere else, then. Just let me go."

"He'll track you down and find you."

"And how is that your problem?" I snapped.

"It's my problem because we made a deal. I keep you safe from him. Nothing has changed."

"Asshole, everything changed when you stabbed me in the back. I don't trust you. I don't like you. No, I fucking hate you. Hate is the word I'm looking for."

He kept up his poker face, but his eyes changed a little bit. "Be that as it may, you aren't going anywhere."

"What the fuck did you just say?" I walked straight up to him. "This isn't about keeping me safe from Grave. This is about you having what he wants. This is all still part of your sick scheme to get back at him. What the fuck is wrong with you?" I shoved both of my palms into his chest and pushed him as hard as I could.

He stumbled back but only slightly, coming back at me instantly.

Instead of slapping him across the face, my signature move, I punched him. Punched him right in the nose.

Blood burst from the hit, but he still twisted my arm down as if nothing had happened. He didn't even react to the pain. With both of my hands now bound behind my back, he shoved me up against another wall. "It's not just about having what he wants. It's about having what I want too. And I want you."

"Well, I'll never want you. Ever. Not after what you did to me."

"I apologized—"

"And that means nothing to me. Literally nothing." I tried to wiggle from his hold, but he was too strong.

He stared at me for a long time, his hold so tight it was forever binding. "I hope that changes because I'll never let you go. You'll remain here with me at my estate. You're still my woman."

"I was *never* your woman."

His eyes shifted back and forth between mine.

"I ran from Grave because he's a monster. But you're a fucking demon."

With a dead look in his eyes, he spoke. "I'm sorry you feel that way." He finally released me and headed out the door.

"I'll fucking kill you. I'll stab you over dinner. I'll slit your throat when you sleep. I'll find one of your guns and shoot you in your study. If you don't let me go, you're a dead man. You hear me?"

He walked down the hallway and entered his bedroom.

"*You hear me?*"

Camille was wrong about Cauldron. Instead of solving her problem, he's become an even bigger one. Find out what happens next in **Better Man**.

.

Made in United States
Orlando, FL
26 April 2025

60799838R00256